FAST KILL

DEA FAST SERIES

KAYLEA CROSS

FAST KILL

Copyright © 2017
by Kaylea Cross

* * * * *

Cover Art & Formatting by
<u>Sweet 'N Spicy Designs</u>

* * * * *

ISBN: 978-1545296875

Dedication

For my husband, who I force to help me work out all the little plot kinks before, during and after the writing of my books. I'm so glad you still love me after all these years, in spite of all my little quirks. Or my big quirks. Love you!!! xo

Author's Note

Dear readers,

Here we are at book #2 in my **FAST Series**. I adore Taylor and Logan together, because they're so different. My favorite thing about them is that in spite of their differences, they don't try to change the essence of who the other is. Hope you enjoy this one.

Happy reading!

Kaylea Cross

Chapter One

Dillon leaned against a sturdy tree trunk with his phone in his hand and watched as two of his men passed by with the loaded wheelbarrow. Normally at this stage of a job he was in full vigilant mode no matter how many men he had watching the site. Right now, however, he was too preoccupied to act as sentry to their security situation.

He paid only partial attention to the men as they dumped the wheelbarrow's load on top of the pile of gasoline-soaked wood they'd built earlier for this purpose. In the sunlight, the plastic containing the body parts glinted. He didn't worry about burning them in broad daylight. Not out here.

One lit match, and whoosh, the whole pile went up in flames. The wave of added heat hit him even over where he stood fifty feet away.

Dillon wiped his sleeve over his sweaty face. Wasn't even May yet and Houston was already sweltering, the humidity clinging to his skin like a film and making it hard to breathe.

God, he hated this place. Wouldn't have come back at all except for this job…and the recent lead in the investigation he had to follow up on.

He bit back a sigh, wishing there was another way. It wasn't like him to procrastinate about something like this. When it came to business, there was no room for hesitation, and he always did what had to be done, without any twinges from his conscience.

This time was different.

While the remains of his biggest business rival burned before him in the small clearing, he stared at the prepaid phone in his hand, the stink of charred human flesh mixing with the acrid tang of smoke and gasoline. Back in the early days it would have made him puke. Not anymore.

Still, he wasn't entirely dead inside.

He couldn't be, because he dreaded what he had to do next. Had been putting it off for the better part of two days now. Since he was at a dead end, he was growing desperate. He couldn't hold off any longer, no matter how unpleasant the task he had to undertake, and this was the only possible way he could find her now.

Letting out a slow, deep breath, he pushed aside the guilt threatening to resurrect what was left of his withered conscience, and locked it away where he couldn't feel it. From memory, he dialed a number he'd learned years ago, let his mind go blissfully blank for the few moments while it rang and a plume of dark, oily smoke rose into the sticky air.

"Hello?" a familiar female voice answered, slightly raspy with age.

Thank God the old woman was still alive, because she was his best chance now. "Janet? It's Dillon."

A moment of stunned surprise filled the line. "Dillon! Oh, honey, how are you?"

Bittersweet pain arrowed through his chest. She'd always been so warm and sincere, had truly cared about him, for whatever reason. "I'm good. Sorry it's been so long since I called last." He forced his voice to be light, playing the part. It was good to talk to her again, but the purpose for the call ruined it.

He shot the shit with her for a few minutes, catching up while being vague about his activities until a natural pause happened. "So I was wondering, have you heard from Taylor at all recently?" he finally asked.

"As a matter of fact, I just talked with her about a month ago. She called me out of the blue one day, saying she'd moved out of the state."

"Where did she move to?" Last he'd heard, she was still here in Houston. That had been a year ago, though.

"Washington."

He tensed. "The state?"

"No, as in D.C. She started a new job there."

"Really?" Long way to move for a job, although it synched with the rumors he'd heard. "Is she not doing accounting anymore?" He was fishing, but hopefully not in a way that Janet picked up on.

Of all the social workers he'd dealt with in his earlier life, Janet was the only one he'd liked. She was one of only two people on this earth who had ever truly loved him. And he had no choice but to betray both of them. Not if he wanted to stay alive.

Thinking about all the ways she'd gone above and beyond for him, even to the point of taking him into her own house when he needed a safe place to go, made him feel like shit that he was using her this way now.

"I think so, but now she's working for the government or something."

His stomach clamped tight. *No.* Were the rumors true, then? He didn't want them to be.

He waited for Janet to elaborate, but when she didn't

he was forced to fill the gap to keep the conversation going. "Oh, that's great, good for her. I've been thinking about her a lot lately, thought I'd try to get in touch with her again. When I tried her old number, it wasn't in service anymore." And now he understood why his search hadn't turned up any leads here in Houston.

"I think she'd love that," Janet said, her voice full of warmth. "You two were so close, I always hoped you would stay in touch."

He squelched the twinge of guilt. He didn't have time for it. "Would you mind giving me her number?" He would have asked if she had Taylor's address, but didn't want to come on too strong and arouse her suspicion.

"Sure, I'll text it to you. Tell her I said hi."

"I will." After ending the call, he waited for the number to come through while his pulse thudded in his throat. When it popped up on the screen of his burner phone, that unfamiliar apprehension began to surface again.

This time there was no shoving it aside. Of all the evil things he'd done in his life, this was surely going to be the one that landed him in Hell.

*****

"You are worthy."

DEA Special Agent Taylor Kennedy stared into her own eyes in the bathroom mirror as she repeated the same words she'd said to herself every morning for the past three years. Somewhere between that day and now, they'd lost their impact, but she was a creature of habit who thrived on routine and refused to stop simply because the message didn't resonate with her these days as much as they once had.

"Okay. Moving on," she muttered in annoyance, giving her light brown, shoulder-length hair a final fluff before exiting the bathroom. Taylor had a busy day ahead of her, helping her friend Charlie unpack at the new apartment she'd just moved into with her boyfriend.

On the way through the kitchen she snagged her phone from where it was charging in its little station she'd set up on the counter, and paused to glance around. A sense of peace and satisfaction filled her at the sight of the spotless kitchen. No dishes in the sink, countertops gleaming, glass cooktop scrubbed clean. Everything in its place, and a place for everything. Exactly the way she liked it.

Exactly the way she *needed* it, in order to function mentally at an optimum level.

She pulled her shoes from the little basket she kept beneath the padded bench by the mudroom door and grabbed her coat and purse from the panel of mounted hooks she'd installed on the wall.

In the midst of setting her alarm, her phone rang. Not recognizing the number with the out of state area code, she didn't answer, set the house alarm and hopped into her car in the neatly-organized garage.

Charlie's place wasn't going to look like this when they were done with it, so Taylor had to make an effort to scale back her anal-retentive control freak tendencies today.

Fifteen minutes later she knocked on Charlie's new apartment door. Her friend pulled it open, gave a big smile and enveloped Taylor in a tight hug. "So glad you're here! Help me," she said, grabbing Taylor's hand and towing her inside. "I'm so overwhelmed I don't even know where to start."

A mountain of moving boxes filled the hallway, kitchen, and spilled into what looked like the living room. "Oh, wow…" Taylor didn't know what else to say. It was worse than she'd imagined.

"I know, right? Worst timing for Jamie and the team to get called out of town."

"Yeah, another day or two later would at least have let you guys get settled in." They'd just moved into the two-bedroom unit together yesterday.

Charlie turned sideways to squeeze past the boxes blocking most of the hallway, her long, dark brown hair hanging damp between her shoulder blades. "I figured I'd start in the kitchen, since I'm gonna need food sooner or later. Though we managed to get the coffee pot out this morning before he left."

"Good thinking." Taylor's phone rang in her purse. Fishing it out of its little pocket, she checked the number and put it back again when she saw the same number as before. Very few people had her number aside from her coworkers, so she assumed it must be a wrong number.

She followed Charlie into the surprisingly spacious kitchen—well, it would be once they got all this stuff unpacked and put away—and took a quick survey. "Do you care how it's organized?" Because there was a right way and a wrong way when it came to organizing things in order to make a functional space. Not that Taylor would say that aloud. She tried not to fly her OCD freak flag high in public.

"No, but I know you're the queen at that sort of thing, so have at 'er."

Oh, thank God, maybe this wouldn't be so bad after all. "Deal. Let's start over here with this pile." She gestured to the one marked "dishes and silverware".

They started with the one nearest them and tackled the mountain from there. Taylor quickly decided where everything should go to maximize functionality and convenience, and Charlie went with it. Within two hours they had the kitchen and master bedroom all squared away, and Taylor was fully invested in finishing the job.

Charlie's phone rang. She answered, chattered away for a minute from the depths of the master walk-in closet, then poked her head out. "That was Piper." Charlie's soon to be sister-in-law, engaged to the youngest of Charlie's three brothers, Easton, who was also a member of FAST Bravo. "She'll be here in twenty minutes, with pizza."

"I was so craving pizza." Taylor left the boxes in the master bathroom for Charlie to deal with, since she didn't want to invade her friend's privacy by rummaging through toiletries and other personal items. Instead she headed out to the hallway to start unpacking linens. "How did you guys get all the furniture moved in here so fast, anyway?" she called over her shoulder.

"The team guys all helped," Charlie replied from the master bedroom. "Three of them loaded the trucks, two of them drove the trucks over, and Logan and Easton helped us carry everything in."

Logan.

At the mention of that name, two distinct and opposite images of the incredibly sexy Bravo member popped into her head. One from the night of their fake "date" a few weeks ago, when they'd been doing surveillance while Jamie and Charlie were at dinner during an undercover op. He'd sat across the table from her in the swankiest restaurant in midtown Manhattan, in a dress shirt and slacks, his blue-green eyes fixed on her in a way that had made her aware of every masculine inch of him.

Too aware.

The other was of Logan the next day in full operational mode, M4 in hand as he burst from the van she and the other members of the surveillance team had occupied in Long Island. In those moments, he'd been nearly unrecognizable to the man the night before, transforming from laid-back to lethal warrior in the blink of an eye.

She couldn't decide which version was sexier, but the combination of the two, knowing he was *both* of those men, was hot as hell. Their paths had crossed a few times since then and he'd been friendly enough, but she'd maintained a careful professional distance from him, unsettled by her instinctive reaction to him.

"That was nice of them," was all she said. She didn't want Charlie to suspect she was attracted to him. When Charlie got wind of something like that, she turned into a damned bloodhound.

"Yeah, they're all great." Charlie emerged from the bedroom and stepped into the hallway with some empty, folded moving boxes.

"Any idea where they are now?" Probably out of the country.

"Somewhere down in the Caribbean, I think. Jamie couldn't give me details," she said, making a face as she set the boxes aside. "I should be used to it, after all the deployments and missions my brothers have gone on, but it's different when it's your man."

Taylor couldn't relate, but she could imagine and sympathize. "I'll bet."

Charlie stopped to fish her phone out of her pocket, smiled as she looked down at it. "Speak of the devil. Hey," she answered. "Everything good?"

Taylor mostly tuned Charlie out as she went through the next box, organizing the linen closet into four sections. One for sheets, one for extra pillows, one for quilts and the other for towels. Probably wouldn't stay all neat and tidy for long, but at least it would start out well. And what she didn't know wouldn't hurt her.

"Yeah, Taylor's here helping me, and Piper's on her way over." Charlie's brown eyes shot to her from down the hallway, and she winced before pulling the phone from her ear, turning it toward Taylor. A male voice was shouting something out of it, but Taylor couldn't make out a single word. "Logan says hi."

"Oh." He did? "Um, say hi back."

But Charlie thrust the phone at her, gave her an admonishing look when Taylor started to protest.

Feeling all kinds of awkward, Taylor took it. "Hi."

"Hey, long time no talk to," Logan said, his deep voice sliding over her like an invisible caress. "How've you been?"

She had no idea why he even wanted to talk to her right now, and her awkwardness was worse with Charlie right here. "Fine, just busy working. You?"

"Same. Any big breaks in the case yet?"

"Unfortunately, no." Not for lack of trying though. As the lead forensic accountant in her department, she'd been putting in ten to twelve hours a day since that terrifying afternoon in Long Island, and had little to show for it.

"Well, I'm sure you guys will crack it open sooner or later."

"Hope so." Seriously, why had he asked to talk to her? They weren't friends, and hardly knew each other. Was he bored? On a layover?

"We never did get a chance to talk after the op. We should grab dinner together sometime after I get back. Want to?"

What? She blinked. "Do you?" The way she remembered it, their previous dinner "date" had been forced and uncomfortable and weird, and she'd been certain he'd hated every minute of it. Had she missed something?

He laughed, a low, amused chuckle that set off a flutter deep in her abdomen. Oh yeah, the man was dangerous all right. "Wouldn't have asked if I didn't. I meant to tell you that you handled yourself damn well under pressure, getting the response team organized to back us up."

Please, she'd done jack, making a series of phone calls while he and Jamie had rushed headlong to mount a rescue on their own. "Which you didn't end up needing." By the time the help she'd called arrived, it had all been over.

"We were lucky. So? You in? No pressure."

So, *not* a date, then. Just so she was clear. She pushed

the ridiculous disappointment aside. "I…sure."

"Great. Well, duty is calling. Hang on, I'll put Jamie back on."

"Okay." It was on the tip of her tongue to urge him to be careful, but that seemed too personal. "Bye."

She handed the phone back to Charlie and whipped around before her friend could see the blush trying to work into her cheeks. He hadn't asked her on a date, it was just to catch up and talk about the Long Island op. No need to be nervous about it. Or wish it could lead to something more.

Charlie finished up her conversation with Jamie just as the doorbell rang. "Oh, I gotta go. That's Piper. Be careful, okay? Love you."

Taylor carried an empty, flattened packing box into the kitchen just as Piper stepped inside in a whirl of energy, and smiled at them both. "I brought sustenance. And wine."

"Yay for wine," Charlie exclaimed, grabbing the bottles from Piper's hands. "We're making pretty good headway already."

"I'm impressed," Piper said, her blond ponytail swishing down the middle of her back as she carried the pizzas into the kitchen.

"It's Taylor's doing. You two are like peas in a pod when it comes to organizing stuff," Charlie said, already in the process of uncorking one of the bottles. "And I just talked to Jamie. The team's just about to head out, wheels up in twenty minutes. He said he'll text me a thumbs up when the op's over, so I know he's okay, just like Easton does with you."

Piper smiled. "It helps me stay sane when he's gone, so I don't worry as much." She switched her attention to Taylor, her expression curious. "What about you? Are you seeing anyone?"

"Me? No." No time for that BS. Dating wasn't her

thing. She wasn't good at it, and the past few disastrous attempts confirmed that. Charlie had saved her during the last one a few months back by sending a fake emergency text about an hour into dinner.

Taylor grabbed some paper plates and napkins from the pantry and set them on the counter. "Thanks for the pizza," she said to Piper.

"You're welcome. Let's eat."

"How is Logan, anyway?" she asked Charlie, trying to sound casual and not overly interested.

"He's good." Charlie snagged a piece of pizza and dug in.

"How well do you know him?" He was the newest member of the team, had only been with them a couple months.

Charlie stopped mid-bite, her teeth sunk into the pizza, then hurriedly chewed and swallowed. "Not that well. Why?"

Taylor shrugged. Damn. She was at risk of overplaying her hand. "No reason." She'd spent some time with him during the op, but not enough to get to know him well. Still, she'd be lying if she didn't admit she was intrigued by him and would like to get to know him better.

And of course that had *nothing* to do with why he'd been featuring in her fantasies recently.

"He's been over a few times since Jamie and I got together. Seems like a nice enough guy. You've spent more time with him than I have. And you've been on a date with him too," Charlie added in a wry tone.

"A date?" Piper asked, looking all interested.

Taylor made a face. "Don't remind me." She'd felt like a total dork all night. "It was for work. Not my best moment."

"Oh, come on, it couldn't have been that bad. He just made a point of saying hello to you, and he asked me how you were doing yesterday during the move," Charlie said, her gaze probing.

He had? Taylor snapped her head around to stare at her. "What did you tell him?"

A slow, startled smile curved her friend's lips. "I told him you were having a wild fling with a guy you picked up at a biker bar last week."

She gasped, horrified. "You didn't."

"No, I didn't. But I should have, to see what he would have done."

Taylor scowled. "He wouldn't have done *anything*."

She and Logan were about as opposite as two people could get. He was friendly and outgoing, oozed confidence and charisma.

He also reminded her of a sexy lumberjack—he was from Maine, after all—with those broad shoulders and muscular build, the dark auburn scruff on his chiseled face. A rugged man's man, who probably had to beat away women with a stick. Hence the fantasies.

Yeah, he was her polar opposite in every way except that they both worked for the same agency—though in very different ways. She spent her days poring over spreadsheets and following money trails, and he spent them kicking in doors and arresting the most dangerous criminals in the narcotics world. She liked to play it safe, to play by the rules, and he liked to live life on the edge. Not her type at all, and yet...

The truth was, she'd been thinking of him a lot more than she should over the past couple weeks since the op, and not in a professional manner. It was just... She was so impressed with how Logan had just taken charge of everything and covered Easton while he went to pull Jamie and Charlie out of the excavation pit at the building site the cartel money launderer had taken them to.

"I'm betting it was the worst date he's ever been on, and I'm pretty sure he dates a *lot*, so that has to be saying something," she said.

"I don't know if he does or not, but it's not like he has a ton of downtime to put much energy into that kind of a social life." Charlie's brown eyes held an interested gleam as she regarded Taylor. "Want me to find out for you?"

What? "No! No. I was just asking." And now she was going to shut the hell up.

Thankfully she was saved from more embarrassment by her phone ringing once more. The same number again, but this time whoever it was left a voicemail. Since it would give her an excuse not to continue the awkward conversation she wished she'd never started, Taylor listened to the message.

"Hey, Taylor. It's Dillon."

She blinked in astonishment as shock detonated inside her. She would never in a million years have recognized that masculine voice, way deeper than she remembered it.

"I was talking to Janet and she gave me your number. It's Saturday, but knowing you, you're probably in the office. I'm in D.C. for another few days on business and wondered if you'd maybe like to get together to catch up. It's been a long time. Anyway, hope to hear back from you. Take care."

A torrent of emotions hit her, vivid memories flooding her brain like jagged, vibrant shards of stained glass.

She hadn't heard from him in years. Hadn't seen him in nearly twelve, and she'd made the decision to cut him out of her life back then because he'd been into bad shit she'd wanted no part of. Now that she was working for the DEA, she was even more reluctant to reestablish communication.

Maybe it was stupid, but knowing he'd reached out to the social worker responsible for rescuing them in order to find her tugged at her heartstrings.

When she lowered the phone into her lap a moment later, Charlie and Piper were both staring at her. "You okay?" Charlie asked with a concerned frown.

"Yeah, fine." Except she felt like she'd just seen a ghost. Or at least heard a ghost's voice.

"Who was it?"

"An old..." Not a friend.

That was too simple a term for what she and Dillon had shared, and it didn't really fit now anyway, after so many years without seeing each other. More like the closest thing she'd ever had to a brother. An older, protective one.

"...acquaintance of mine," she finished.

Taylor couldn't believe it. Incredible as it seemed, Dillon was in town, and he wanted to see her. She'd never expected this. The logical part of her was tempted to ignore the message because of her job, but the greater sense of loyalty won out.

Bottom line, she owed him. Would always owe him for what he'd done, and the truth was, she desperately wanted to see him again.

Not ready to talk to him yet, she texted back instead.

Hey! Would love to meet up.

She suggested a place they could meet for dinner the following night. Just so she didn't seem overly eager to see him. *Does that work?*

Taylor hadn't even put the phone down when he replied.

Sounds good. Looking forward to seeing you.

A part of her was conflicted about seeing him, but she shrugged it off. It was only one dinner. What harm would it do to meet up for a few hours for old times' sake?

Chapter Two

❖◇❖◇❖

*S*how time.

DEA Special Agent Logan Granger leaned forward to peer outside using his night vision goggles as the Pavehawk lowered into a hover above the drop zone. Out the open side door, the calm, dark waters of the Atlantic rippled below with the force of the rotor wash.

Since FAST never operated unilaterally on foreign soil, they were here at the request of the Bahamian government on a joint op with their special police to find and stop a submarine suspected of carrying cocaine for the *Veneno* cartel before it could leave port.

"Okay, boys, let's do this," Hamilton, the team leader said. He motioned for Freeman, the longest-standing member of FAST Bravo, to move into position in the doorway.

At the pilot's okay, the helo's crew chief released the Zodiac slung beneath the aircraft's belly. The rubber hull splashed into the water and floated aft, pushed along by the force of the rotors.

When the coast was clear the crew chief signaled to the team and Freeman jumped feet first into the water. The former SEAL surfaced, his dark skin blending in with the black water, and gave a thumbs up. Four others followed, then Hamilton and Zaid.

Logan was next out the door, arms folded across his torso, and plunged into the surprisingly warm water, surfacing a moment later. He turned on his stomach in the water to face the helo, then aimed a thumbs up at Easton, standing in the doorway. His buddy jumped, and Kai went last.

Logan watched in admiration as the big Pacific Islander plunged into the water feet first and shot up through the rippling surface like a cork under pressure. A guy his size with that kind of muscle mass should sink like a rock in the water, but not Kai, because the water was his element. No one on the team could touch him in the water, except maybe Freeman, and that was saying a whole hell of a lot since the latter was a former SEAL.

With all nine of them accounted for and safely grouped together in the water, Logan turned onto his front and began swimming for the Zodiac as the helo lifted away from them. Freeman was already on board the boat, positioned at the helm, hand on the throttle as he guided it toward them. Other than the quiet sound of the motor and the moving water, all was quiet.

Logan reached the starboard side just as Easton climbed over the port side. He levered himself up and out of the water, throwing one thigh on the inside of the rubber gunwale, soaked to the skin and glad it was spring off the coast of Nassau and not somewhere in a colder climate.

Kai was the last one to pull himself out of the water. He hauled his body over the rubber bow and crouched there at the front while everyone readied their weapons.

Freeman opened the throttle and made for land under

cover of darkness while every man kept their gaze pinned toward the shore and their target: a little cove off the southeast side of the island where their backup force waited for them to spring the trap.

The latest intel from headquarters said that the smugglers were going to launch the submarine within the next hour, once it was fully loaded. The plan called for FAST Bravo to approach the target dock and catch the men loading the sub off guard.

Logan leaned forward more to better absorb the bounces as the bow skipped over the waves, the heavy tropical air rushing over his wet uniform, forming goose bumps all over his skin.

As the team's Fucking New Guy, he'd earned the right to be here, but only because he'd been called up from the selection pool after they'd lost another member due to permanent injury during their last tour in Afghanistan. He was also the only member who hadn't come from a military background. He'd spent his entire career with the DEA, joining fresh out of college, and worked in undercover until he could apply for FAST.

It didn't matter that he and Easton had helped save Jamie and Charlie a few weeks back. This was the first time he'd been sent on a combat op with the full team. He was itching to prove himself and earn his teammates' respect.

Everyone had their game faces on as they sped toward shore. They were prepared to face several different scenarios, all depending on what they found once they reached the target.

Up front on the bow, Kai had his night vision binos in hand as he scanned the approaching shoreline. At a signal from him Freeman eased back on the throttle. The Zodiac slowed, the noise of the motor dropping to help them avoid detection.

So far, the intel seemed accurate. That was refreshing.

Through his NVGs Logan could just make out the distant dock and the dozen or so men on or around it.

Freeman cut the engine completely when they neared the beach. Four men pulled out oars and paddled the boat closer to shore.

Logan's muscles tensed as they rounded the short peninsula that hid them from view. Everyone watched Kai, poised there on the bow, his massive shoulders now blocking Logan's line of sight.

As soon as they reached the shallows Kai and Logan both jumped out and pulled the boat onto the beach, well out of sight of anyone watching from near the dock. The others leapt out and together they dragged the boat over the sand behind a cluster of palms. Freeman took point from there.

Everyone fell in line behind him, careful to stay in the shadows as they approached their target. Logan and three of his teammates would take the left flank, while Hamilton and the other four would take the right.

Logan lowered himself to his belly on the back side of a low sand dune and put his rifle to his shoulder, watching intently through the scope as five of his teammates looped around to take the dock from the right. The rules of engagement specified that FAST could only fire their weapons in self-defense, or if their local counterparts were attacked. Given the unpredictable response of their target, they had to be ready for anything.

"Hammerhead is in position. Standing by," Hamilton murmured through Logan's earpiece, alerting the Bahamian commander that their team was ready.

Sighting down the barrel of his rifle, sand sticking to his wet uniform, Logan waited, motionless. Moments later the special police burst from behind a copse of palms near the foot of the pier, yelling at the stunned suspects to freeze and put down their weapons.

The tangos on the pier all scattered and reached for

their weapons instead. Gunfire erupted in the night, shattering the stillness, the muzzle flashes lighting up his NVGs.

Logan remained in position, his muscles coiled and ready to neutralize the threat.

Then Hamilton's quiet voice came through Logan's earpiece with a single word. "Engage."

Logan was up and running toward the dock without a moment's hesitation, his boots thudding over the loose sand, Easton and Zaid right behind him.

Three tangos jumped up and headed toward them, unaware of the danger.

"Drop your weapons!" Logan yelled.

The three men whirled around and almost as one, raised their weapons. Logan fired, hitting the lead man in the chest as his teammates hit the other two. The guy barely hit the ground when another tango sprang up from inside a boat tied to the pier and swung the barrel of his weapon straight at Zaid.

Logan didn't have time to yell a warning.

He fired and launched himself at his teammate, catching Zaid around the waist in a hard tackle. They hit the sand with a thud, Zaid on top just as a hail of bullets pounded into the trees behind them, right through where Zaid had been standing a second ago.

Pain splintered through Logan's left knee as Zaid's weight came down on top of it. He sucked in a sharp breath and fought through it, immediately rolling to his stomach and bringing his weapon to his shoulder to return fire.

He sighted the shooter and fired a double tap, center mass. The man grunted and dropped to his knees before keeling over sideways and hitting the sand.

Zaid scrambled into a prone position next to him, firing at one of the narcos trying to jump off the far side of the dock. It was all over in a matter of minutes, the sudden cessation of fire bringing an eerie silence.

"Move in," Hamilton commanded in a low voice.

Logan gritted his teeth and pushed to his feet, his knee protesting each movement. Every step sent needles of fire streaking through his kneecap. Ignoring it as best he could, he forced himself forward with his teammates as they converged on the dock and the surrounding area, securing the scene.

A dozen dead tangos littered the dock and the beach. Almost as many had decided to surrender, holding their hands in the air.

"Face down and don't move," Logan snapped at the first man he reached, who was bleeding from a gunshot to the lower leg. The man glared up at him for a long moment and Logan lost his patience, the pain he was in giving his voice an added bite. "*Now*."

The guy rolled over with a grimace and laid his cheek against the wooden surface of the dock, hands laced behind his head and blood pooling out around his lower leg. Logan and Zaid stood watch while the Bahamians moved in to arrest the survivors.

Once everyone still breathing was either in cuffs or being looked at by medics, Logan limped for the sub berthed at the end of the dock. Kai was already there with some of the locals, carefully checking the hatch with the help of a tactical flashlight.

"What've we got?" Hamilton asked, stopping beside Logan with the head of the Bahamian special police.

"Don't think they had time to rig it," Kai said, shifting his knees and pushing his upper body back to give their team leader a better look. "But it never hurts to be cautious."

"True enough." Hamilton gave him a firm nod. "Do it."

Logan was closest to Kai so he edged up to the hatch, the muzzle of his weapon aimed at it just in case they encountered any surprises once Kai twisted the sucker open. The team's big man cracked it and yanked it open with one hand, a Glock in his other. Thankfully nothing exploded, and no one shot at them from inside.

Logan leaned forward with his weight on his good leg and aimed the tac light on his rifle into the vessel, favoring his left knee. It was already throbbing like a bad tooth. Something was definitely wrong with it; he just hoped it wasn't serious.

The intense beam of light sliced through the blackness of the sub's interior like a laser, revealing a hold stuffed full of plastic-wrapped bricks. Cocaine. There was no room for anyone to be in there with all that cargo, so one thorough sweep with the tac light proved more than enough to make the call.

"It's clear," Logan said, and straightened with his weight on his right leg, biting down on his back molars as his left knee protested the slight movement. The good news was, all the narcos at the dock were either dead or captured, and the amount of drugs seized was way above the arrest threshold needed.

He looked up to find Hamilton watching him closely, with narrowed eyes. "What did you do?"

"Nothing." He stepped out of the way, making sure not to limp no matter how much it hurt.

His other teammates moved back out of the way and the Bahamians swarmed in, documenting the seizure with photos and then beginning the process of unloading the drugs.

Logan mentally cursed with each step on his way down the dock, refusing to let anyone know he was in pain. The last thing he wanted was to be pulled off duty because of a stupid injury.

Zaid was waiting for him when he reached the end and stepped onto the sand. In the glare of all the floodlights mounted on the Bahamian vehicles now ringing the scene, his teammate's hazel eyes glinted with a touch of humor. He strode up and clasped Logan's left shoulder, looking him dead in the eye. "Thanks, brother."

A little uncomfortable with the recognition, Logan shrugged and looked down the beach where more emergency vehicles were arriving. Was his left pant leg tighter, or was it just his imagination? "Hey, no worries."

"No." Zaid squeezed again, waited until Logan met his eyes before continuing. "You saved my ass back there. I owe you."

"Forget it, man. You'd have done the same for any of us."

"Damn right, I would have." One side of his mouth quirked upward. "Now tell me what you did to your left leg."

Despite the pain he was in, Logan couldn't help the wry twist of his lips. The team medic was one of the most observant people Logan had ever met, so it shouldn't have surprised him that Zaid had already noticed. "You're damn spooky sometimes with that shit, you know that, right?"

"I try. Now what are we dealing with?"

"It's fine," Logan said with a shrug. "No big deal."

"We'll see about that." Zaid squatted down and immediately began rolling up Logan's left pant leg. Logan bit back a protest, knowing it would do him no good, but wished they had more privacy. The other guys were all gathering around now, watching. "When did it happen?"

"When you fell on me."

Zaid looked up at him and winced. "Sorry, man."

"No worries." But he *was* starting to worry, because it hurt like a bitch. What if it wasn't something minor that he could muscle through? What if it put him out of action for a while?

"What's this? Granger got fucked up on his first

mission?" Kai said as he walked up, watching with interest as Zaid began his exam.

"Yeah, what's with that, man?" Easton asked Logan, coming up to stand beside Kai. "You take a bullet?"

"Nah, it's nothing. You can all go on about your business," Logan told them. He didn't want an audience for this sissy shit.

"Guess I smashed his knee in while he was saving my ass," Zaid said.

Kai shot Zaid an incredulous look. "You took out Granger's knee on his first mission? That's cold, brah. So cold." He shook his head.

"Yeah, I'm a heartless bastard. This hurt?" Zaid asked Logan, probing the knee.

Logan winced, barely resisted the urge to swat Zaid's hands away. "Shit yes. Quit poking at it." The sooner everyone left him alone and he could get off his feet, the better.

Zaid stood and grabbed Logan by the upper arm. "How about we find you someplace to sit down before this swells up even more," he said, starting across the beach toward the nearest vehicle.

It was that swollen? Face hot, wishing the others would just go away already, Logan did as he was told. The pain in his knee was worse now without the numbing effect of the adrenaline that had been pumping through his veins during the firefight. He limped over to the closest truck and hopped up on the lowered tailgate, biting back a growl as he bent his knee.

Zaid stuck a penlight in his mouth and resumed his inspection. After squeezing and prodding he tried to bend the knee more and earned a warning snarl from Logan, who'd now broken into a cold sweat. Zaid pulled the penlight from his mouth. "You need an x-ray once we get back to base, and you'll need to keep your weight off it until we know what's going on."

"I can walk," Logan grumbled stubbornly, removing his helmet. No way he was pussying around on crutches or whatever in front of the guys because of a sore knee.

Zaid looked up at him, his expression bland. "I think you might've fractured your patella. Not too sure about ligament damage."

Oh, a fracture would suck huge donkey balls. He glanced down at his knee, which was throbbing in time with his heartbeat, and saw that it was already roughly the size of a grapefruit. His heart sank. "Shit. How long would something like that take to heal?"

"Depends on how bad the fracture is, and how good you are about staying off it until it can heal. Every time you put your weight on that leg, your quad tendons pull on the bone. That'll screw with the healing, if you get what I mean. Hope you didn't plan to go out dancing when you got home."

Logan scowled at his kneecap. No, he didn't plan to go dancing, although he did have dinner plans. He hadn't gone dancing much since his divorce three years ago.

Did Taylor even dance? He couldn't picture it; she seemed so serious and contained all the time, it just didn't fit. Still, he got a kick out of her rigid and sometimes snarky personality and wondered just what it would take to tear all that rigid control to shreds, get her to let go. Might be fun to drag her out to a club sometime, see what she did.

"My first mission," he muttered in disgust. He'd finally seen action with the team and didn't want to be sidelined for any amount of time. The fast operational tempo of the unit was one of the reasons he'd wanted to join in the first place. He lived for action, for a challenge. A fucked-up kneecap was not what he needed.

"Well, now it's even more memorable," Zaid said with a grin, standing to thump the side of Logan's shoulder. "Sorry about the knee, brother, but welcome to the team."

A grudging smile tugged at Logan's mouth at the official acceptance. "Good to be here."

Zaid ruffled Logan's hair with one hand, then bent and looped Logan's arm across his shoulders. "My turn to look after you now, rookie."

Logan might have argued, but the fear of worsening the injury stopped him cold. He hopped along using Zaid as a human crutch, until they reached Hamilton and the others near one of the command trucks.

While Zaid relayed what had happened, Logan surveyed the action going on at the dock. His eye caught on a female figure standing over at the foot of the pier, and everything inside him stilled. She was facing away from him, her shoulder-length brown hair tied back into a ponytail, and she was the same height and build as Taylor...

A burst of excitement swept through him, taking his mind off the pain in his knee. What the hell was she doing down here? Had she been called down to investigate the money trail? "Hey, is that—"

Zaid and Easton turned their heads to look. "Who?" Zaid asked.

The woman pivoted. In the glare of the floodlights, Logan saw her face, and a surprising jolt of disappointment hit him, taking him off guard with its force.

He'd thought about Taylor a lot since the New York op, but until that moment he hadn't realized just how much he'd wanted to see her. She was so different than any woman he'd met before. He wanted to get to know her more, see if the tug of attraction was as strong as he remembered it. And find out whether it was mutual.

"Nothing. Forget it," he murmured, feeling stupid. Of course it wasn't her. There was no reason for her to be here on an op like this.

Easton looked at him, a sly, knowing smile spreading

across his face as he realized who Logan had thought it was. "Got a certain someone on the brain, huh?"

Logan scowled. "No." Except he did, and a vision of SA Taylor Kennedy's pretty face was now stuck in his head.

That was almost as bad as the news about his knee, since recent experience over the past few weeks had taught him that the picture of her wasn't going away any time soon.

Chapter Three

Most people she knew hated paperwork. Not Taylor. She thrived on it.

Here in her cramped but tidy cubicle in the Organized Crime and Drug Enforcement Task Force area, surrounded by her spreadsheets and data, she was in her happy place. Here, she was in her safe zone, comforted by the knowledge that her work was valued and making a difference in the war on drugs.

Because at the end of the day, money really did make the world go around, especially for drug cartels.

Her computer screen showed various financial statements and offshore bank account transactions for several shell corporations thought to belong to members of the *Venenos* cartel. Unlike many of the previous cases she'd worked on, this time they ranged from banks in Dubai, the UAE, Caymans and of course Switzerland. A lot of ground to cover, but she was making steady progress along with the two other analysts working under her.

Movement in her peripheral vision had her glancing

across the office floor. A big grin split her face when she saw Charlie coming toward her. "Hey, what brings you to this side of the compound?" Normally Charlie was busy in the next building over with her Computer Forensic Examiner colleagues.

Charlie walked through the center aisle and stopped at Taylor's cubicle. "Wanted to thank you again for all your help yesterday. Couldn't have done it without you, even with Piper there."

"No problem." She cast a glance around to make sure no one was listening in and lowered her voice just in case. "Everything all right with Jamie?"

"Yes, he texted me just after midnight to say he and the others were on their way back. Well, to Florida. They're due home early tonight."

"Glad to hear it." She reached for the bottle of water on her desk.

"Apparently Logan was injured though."

Taylor's hand froze around the bottle, her gaze shooting to Charlie's. "Is he okay?" He hadn't been shot, had he?

"Hurt his knee pretty bad."

"Oh no…" If the injury was serious enough to put him on disability, it would kill him to lose his place on the team. He'd only been on it a short time. "Did Jamie say what happened?"

"No, but I'll find out tonight. I'm sure he'll be fine. And anyway, I came over to bring you this in person." She held out a thick file marked Top Secret.

"What is it?" Taylor asked as she took it, intrigued.

"What you've been waiting for. Just came back from the cryptologists."

She blinked at her in surprise. "They cracked it?"

"Apparently."

Not wasting any time, Taylor set it down and flipped it open. Sure enough, there were the files Charlie had managed to transmit to her during the op to expose *Veneno* cartel money launderer Dean Baker in The Hamptons.

Charlie's team only had a few files to work with. Except instead of gibberish, the pages now contained what appeared to be bank names, account numbers, fund transfers and names. Odd names.

"Yesss," she murmured under her breath. This was the biggest break she'd had in the case yet.

Charlie chuckled. "Thought you'd like that."

"Oh, I really do." The strange names listed were likely either code or aliases—cartels had a thing for using weird monikers—and probably set up using fake IDs. Still, at least it was something substantial for her to dig her teeth into, compared to what she'd been working with up to this point. "I'll get started on this right away."

"I'd expect nothing less of you," Charlie said, her voice teasing.

Taylor couldn't help but grin. Charlie was one of the few people she'd met since moving to D.C. who really seemed to get her, and didn't mind her idiosyncrasies. It was probably why they'd bonded so quickly, because Taylor didn't have many friends—never had—and none of them as close as Charlie. Relationships were complicated, and given the chaos she'd come from, she liked all aspects of her life to be orderly and safe.

Okay, she liked it boring. But she had her reasons.

"We're going to have a low key dinner at our place tonight, if the guys get home at a decent hour. You wanna come?" Charlie asked.

It was so early on in Charlie and Jamie's relationship, Taylor would feel like a fifth wheel. "Nah, y'all should have the place to yourselves for the night. It's technically your first full night in your new place together."

Charlie sighed. "That's not gonna happen. Easton will be over for sure, and probably my middle brother. Maybe

Logan too, if he's feeling up to it."

The possibility of Logan being there only made Taylor not want to go more. She'd be seeing him soon enough anyway—assuming he actually did want to meet up for dinner after he got back. "No. Thanks for the invite, but I'll probably be working late tonight anyway."

Charlie set her hand on her hip and frowned at Taylor. "Oh, come on. If Easton comes then Piper will too, and if my middle brother comes then he might bring his girlfriend—and she's even more of an introvert than you, even around us still. We drag her out of her shell as much as we can, so she's slowly getting used to us all."

Yes, the Colebrooks were a force to be reckoned with when they were all together. Overwhelming, actually, especially for someone as introverted as her. Taylor liked them all, but not enough to sit through an evening with a bunch of people she didn't know, feeling totally out of place and wishing she was home with a cup of tea and her cat. "We'll see."

Her friend's eyes narrowed. "When you say that, it always means no."

"Well, I've got a lot of work to do now that you've given me the files."

"Uh huh, and you not coming over has nothing to do with Logan possibly being there." Charlie gave her a bland look that dared her to deny it.

The knowing tone was really damn annoying, even if she was dead on. There was something about Logan that pulled at her. Attraction, yes, but more than that. He was strong. Dedicated. Dependable. All the things she'd never found in a man. And he was terrifyingly masculine, in a way that every cell in her body responded to without her permission.

Yeah, and that probably means he's too good to be true.

Well, there was that. "Actually, I've got plans. I'm

supposed to meet up with someone tonight."

Charlie's eyebrows lifted. "Someone as in, a guy?"

"Yes, a guy."

"What? Like a date? Who is he?"

"Just an old friend who called me out of the blue. He's in town and wanted to meet up." She was still a little nervous about it, to be honest. It had been so long since they'd seen each other, she dreaded sitting through an awkward dinner if things didn't go well.

Charlie studied her for a long moment. "So...not a date," she said, seeking clarification.

"No."

"And you're not going to tell me who it is?"

"No." It was too complicated an explanation, and Dillon wasn't the type of guy she wanted to introduce to anyone in her current life. He'd done things she didn't want to talk about, let alone have anyone involved with the agency know.

Mostly, she didn't want to open up that window to the past she was so ashamed of. Not even for Charlie.

"Well, damn. Can you come over for a bit after, then?"

Taylor chuckled. Charlie just wanted her to come over and spill all the details, which wasn't going to happen. When it came to keeping secrets, Taylor was a human vault. "We'll see."

Charlie sighed in exasperation. "Fine. I'll text you once I hear from Jamie. If they're not coming home tonight, will you come over *then*? Spend some time with me after your dinner?"

She couldn't say no to that. "Sure."

Charlie shook her head, one side of her mouth quirking up in a half-smile. "Was it the idea of a group gathering that turned you off, or the possibility of Logan being there?"

"Neither." *Both.* Although it was exhausting to constantly feel like she had to defend herself for being introverted.

She didn't expect an extrovert like Charlie to understand it, but she wanted her friend to at least try to respect that for Taylor, being around a group of people for more than half an hour was tantamount to having the life force sucked right out of her.

So she preferred peace and quiet and her own company most of the time. Why couldn't people accept that? Live and let live.

"Chicken," Charlie accused softly, humor warming her eyes.

No, more like cautious. Hypothetically speaking, even if Logan was interested in her either in a physical or romantic way, that didn't mean Taylor would reciprocate. She wasn't sure she wanted to make room for a relationship in her life with any man—and she'd learned at a young age that men couldn't be trusted anyway.

Still, there was something about Logan that told her she could trust him. Maybe because she'd seen him in action.

Thankfully Charlie let it go and squeezed her shoulder. "Good luck with the files. I'll text you as soon as I know what's going on tonight."

"Sounds good."

She'd only been working on the new file for a few minutes when her boss called her into his office. She closed the door behind her, gave him a polite smile. "Charlie Colebrook just dropped off the files from the cryptologists."

Chris was at his computer and didn't look up at her. "Oh, great. Have a seat, Taylor."

A tingle of unease threaded its way up her spine at the seriousness in his tone, and how distracted he seemed. "Everything okay?" she asked as she sank into the chair opposite his desk.

"Yes. Headquarters sent over some security footage

from Baker's party. I need you to look at it and see if you can match any faces here to the IDs you pulled from the bank account info."

The unease faded away. "Sure." She scooted her chair closer to his desk and he turned the monitor to face her.

"I've reviewed the files you compiled from the IDs, but it's always good to have a second set of eyes to look with me. There are rumors of some of the higher-up *Veneno* members being present."

Taylor didn't say anything as he loaded the video. The feed began from a camera overlooking a pool/patio area at Baker's luxurious summer house in Sagaponack. Since Baker was dead, shot by his pilot, his property had been seized by the government, along with all his other assets.

The entire patio was filled with men in suits and tuxes, and women in classy cocktail dresses. Taylor spotted Baker right away, wearing a white tux so he stood out in the crowd, his dark blond hair carefully styled. On the outside, he looked like the rich, successful businessman he'd presented to the world. How many people at the party knew what he really was?

"There." Chris stopped the video and touched a fingertip to a man standing off to the left side of the patio, near what looked like a bar area. "Does he look familiar?"

He opened a folder on his desk and began flipping through it, then pulled out a piece of paper and turned it toward her. "Headquarters lists this guy's real name as Javier Quinta. Better known in the narco world as *El Jaguar*, enforcer for one of the *Veneno* bosses, and known for his sadistic methods when he kills."

"Yeah, that's him. I've got him listed on a different ID though, under another name. I'll trace his accounts as soon as I get back to my desk." She grabbed a pen and paper from his desk and jotted down notes. "And what about this guy right here?" She pointed to someone standing a few yards behind Quinta. "He looks familiar too."

Chris flipped through more pages, then smirked. "Good eye. It's him." He held up another sheet, listing a lawyer suspected to work for the cartel.

Taylor made more notes, a wave of excitement racing through her. Her job wasn't normally this exhilarating. Usually she just chased down money trails and talked to a lot of bankers while working on the case. This was way better and made for a nice change of pace. Who'd have ever thought that she would enjoy a break from normal routine?

They reviewed all the footage from that camera, then the feed switched to another one, capturing a view of some kind of garden courtyard just off the patio.

"There's Charlie," she said, pointing as her friend walked through the camera's field of vision in the cocktail dress she had helped Charlie pick out that morning. Little had they known that Charlie and Jamie would both be fighting for their lives a few short hours later.

"This guy. He look familiar? He's a *sicario* for one of the *Veneno* lieutenants."

She looked up, her heart seeming to freeze when she spotted the man beside the one her boss indicated. Even without having seen him for so many years, she recognized him instantly.

Dressed in a black tux with a drink in his hand, he appeared to be surveying everything going on in front of him. His sandy-brown hair was a little longer in front than the back than how he used to wear it, his jaw more angular. But the rest of him was all power and hard edges now and he radiated an authority that was impossible to miss.

She couldn't answer, her gaze locked on him, stomach sinking. *It doesn't prove he's involved with the cartel. Just because he's there doesn't automatically make him guilty.*

She desperately wanted him to be innocent.

"Taylor?"

She glanced up at Chris, who was watching her intently. She was still in shock, hardly able to believe what she'd just seen.

"Are you okay?"

"Yes, fine." She put on a smile and forced her attention back to the man he'd pointed out, but her mind was now racing, the blood rushing in her ears.

Chris was way too perceptive, however. "Do you know him?"

"No." Not the man he meant, and she wasn't going to volunteer anything more about the other. Not yet.

You just lied to a DEA agent. Your boss.

She shoved aside the guilt and worry about what future repercussions might come from this, refusing to say anything. The reaction to shield the man on screen was instinctive and automatic, something she couldn't control. She didn't understand it, she only knew that her immediate reaction was to protect him, out of an ingrained sense of loyalty.

Dillon Wainright. The boy she'd always thought of as her knight in shining armor...before he'd allowed himself to be poisoned by the darkness surrounding him. Now here she was, faced with irrefutable proof that he was at least socially linked to Dean Baker, and a *Veneno* enforcer.

Her stomach gathered into a tight ball of dread at the possible implications. Because she'd promised to meet him in only a few hours from now.

Chapter Four

This was a fucking disaster.

Dillon had been up all night dealing with the aftermath from the disaster in the Bahamas and hadn't gone to bed yet, so he deserved a damn drink. Or five.

With agitated strides he walked to the bar in his hotel suite and poured himself a much-needed highball, his hand tight around the bottle of single malt scotch.

An entire shipment seized. Christ. They'd lost several smaller ones over the past few weeks, which wasn't uncommon in the business. This was different. He'd planned everything so carefully, from hiring the subcontractors to build the sub, to hand-picking the men to load and sail it to the U.S. mainland.

The liquor burned down his throat, igniting a warm glow in his stomach. There was no way anyone would have just randomly come across the sub or the loading dock, because he'd ensured there was good security on site. All he knew was, the Bahamian special police had done a joint raid with an American force. The sub was gone, many of his men killed, others taken prisoner.

His best trafficker was dead, along with more than a dozen others. Dammit, he'd liked Eduardo. Hell, he was godfather to Eduardo's two kids.

Annoyance burned through him, stronger than the alcohol. Everyone in this line of work knew the risks, and that they could wind up ripped apart in a hail of bullets just as easily as they could get rich. But the promise of that kind of money made the risk worthwhile.

Now he had to build a new crew, from scratch. A pain in the ass he couldn't afford right now.

He'd have to find someone to replace Eduardo as soon as possible, and it was so hard to know who to trust these days. Competition among rival cartels was fierce, and the head of the *Veneno* cartel was anxious to expand their power base throughout all of the U.S. rather than the several corridors it had established already.

His heavily encrypted cell phone rang. Franco, one of his best men. "Give me good news, man."

"Wish I could, boss," he said in Spanish.

Hell. "How many were captured?" That was the real concern here. The dead couldn't talk. The living might.

"We still don't know yet."

He tamped down the irritation pushing his blood pressure to unhealthy levels. Some of the captured men would be tempted to talk under interrogation, to try and get themselves protection or a better deal from the Bahamians, or the U.S. if the Americans had enough on them to extradite.

Little good it would do them to try and save their skins now. The cartel was powerful and had tentacles everywhere. It could get to them easily enough inside prison walls, no matter where they were being held. They had people on their payroll in almost all divisions of the prison system throughout Mexico and were making serious forays into the U.S. system as well.

"Find out who they are. I want everything you have on them. If they talk, they know what will happen to them and their families." He was good at compartmentalizing to get the job done, however dirty. He didn't care if innocents died—he'd stopped caring about that kind of shit a long time ago. Maintaining power was the most important thing.

In the ruthless world of the cartel, that required absolute control over those beneath him. Which meant pretty much everyone but a handful of people in the cartel. And past experience had taught him the only way to do that was through fear and intimidation.

The more brutal, the more effective it was.

"I need the intel by noon."

"*Sí, señor*." Franco hung up.

Dillon downed the remainder of the scotch in one quick swallow, barely noticing the burn as it slid down his throat. He dreaded this coming conversation, but there was no way around it. Carlos was his direct boss, a lieutenant of *El Escorpion*, the mysterious and elusive head of the *Veneno* cartel. He needed to hear it straight from Dillon, and no one else, even though the boss didn't like to be disturbed or talk business before eight in the morning.

Dillon rolled his eyes. This couldn't wait any longer.

His pulse accelerated as the ringing droned in his ear. Carlos was notoriously unpredictable. Dillon had known and worked for the man for five years, and even he couldn't predict his boss's capricious moods. Carlos was one obnoxious bastard.

"Yeah, D. Why you calling so early?" Carlos answered, sounding annoyed.

Since there was no point in dancing around it, he bit the bullet. "Last night's shipment was seized. Bahamian special police on a joint op with Americans."

"Americans?" A cold silence filled the line. "DEA?"

"Don't know yet." Could be, though. The bastards had been all over them lately, ever since the Baker incident. Another thing in a long list of problems that he had to deal with. The pressure would only increase from here.

"*Hijos de putas*," Carlos spat.

Yep. "I just wanted to tell you I'm on top of it. I'll let you know as soon as I get more details."

Carlos grunted. "What else?"

"Eduardo's dead, along with several others. No word yet on how many were captured."

Carlos swore under his breath. "You think he was behind it?"

"No." And given that Eduardo had died last night rather than surrender seemed good enough reason to believe he was innocent.

Carlos gave a long-suffering sigh. "I'll send his wife flowers." A pause. "So. Who sold us out?"

His hand tightened around the empty tumbler. "I don't know. But I'm gonna find out." And when he did, they would pay dearly.

"Fucking rats," Carlos said in disgust, then his tone hardened with a steel Dillon recognized. "You will find out who was behind this betrayal and deal with it, do you understand me?"

Yeah, he understood perfectly, as well as the implied threat buried in the command. "Yes, *patrón*."

"I mean it. This is bullshit, and I want it to end. These fuckers are costing me too much money. The boss is gonna be pissed."

"I know. I'll handle this personally." He had to, if he wanted to live.

"What about the other thing you were looking into, with the girl?"

"I'm meeting with her tonight."

"Cancel it. Find out who turned on us and deal with that first. That's your biggest priority right now."

He bit down on his back molars. "All right."

"I'm late for my massage. Call me when you know something."

"I w—" The line went dead in his ear. He released a heavy breath and put the phone into his pocket. He'd wait to shoot Taylor a text later on to reschedule.

He turned to stare out the suite's window overlooking the harbor, seeing nothing. None of this felt right. If the American commandos last night had been DEA, it was just another link to pull him toward Taylor. She'd been seen near the location where Baker had died a couple weeks back, along with a few other people from the DEA.

What had she been doing there? So far he hadn't been able to confirm whether she worked for the agency or not, but the pieces were all lining up in a way that made it impossible to think she wasn't involved somehow.

If she was, how much did she know? Was she on to him? Could he persuade her to take bribes and be a source for him?

The meeting tonight was supposed to be a way for him to feel her out, and now he'd have to wait at least a day or two before he could. It made him damn uneasy. Still, there was a chance it was all just coincidence. Maybe she didn't know anything.

For her sake, he hoped she didn't.

If she did... Because she knew him and could risk exposing all the work he'd put into the cartel, he'd have no choice but to make that problem disappear.

****

Balancing the cake box in one hand, Taylor knocked on Charlie's door with the other, a low-grade nervous buzz in her stomach. She could hear the rumble of male voices inside the apartment, and one of them was Logan.

Charlie pulled the door open and a huge smile lit her

face. "You came!"

She shrugged. "My friend had to cancel, so I thought I'd drop by on my way home from work. For a bit," she added, making it clear off the bat that she didn't plan on staying long.

In truth, she was relieved that she didn't have to see Dillon. It had been so long, she didn't know what they'd even talk about now, especially after she'd seen him in that video clip in her boss's office.

Charlie laughed. "We had bets on whether you would show or not at all tonight. You'll be happy to know I had your back on that one," she said, slinging an arm around Taylor's shoulders to draw her inside. "And you brought us something delicious and fattening?"

"Tuxedo layer cake." She wasn't much of a baker, so she'd picked it up at her favorite pastry shop on the way over.

"This is partly why I love you. Come on in." Charlie took the box from her and headed for the living room where the guys were.

Taylor could all but smell the scent of testosterone in the air growing stronger as she followed Charlie. She saw Jamie first, who grinned and got up to give her a hug.

Easton and Piper were on one couch, and her heart thudded a little harder at the sight of Logan seated in a recliner with his left leg up, a tensor bandage wrapped around it. A pair of crutches rested against the wall behind him.

His knee must be pretty bad, if he was actually resorting to crutches.

He smiled at her, those sharp blue-green eyes and neat, reddish-brown beard making him every bit as ruggedly sexy as she remembered. Her heart did an annoying fluttery thing against her ribcage.

When she'd first met him, being near him had unsettled her because of his size and sheer masculinity.

Now he put her on edge for a different reason. One that stirred a swirl of hot tingles low in her belly. That was annoying too. She had no time or patience for tingling when it never led anywhere.

"Hey, you made it," he said to her.

"I did. How's the knee?"

He made a face. "It's okay. Just supposed to stay off it mostly for a little while."

"What happened?"

"Little christening gift from a teammate, to commemorate his first mission," Jamie said, grinning as he raised his beer bottle to his mouth.

Taylor looked back at Logan in surprise. "Your teammate did that to you?"

"Was an accident," he said with a shrug. "So, how've you been?"

"Good." She had to admit, it was far less awkward talking to him with the others around. Although the room did seem tiny all of a sudden with three men that size in it.

Since there was nowhere else for her to sit than the chair beside Logan, she took that one. Thankfully that old, ingrained and instinctive fear of big men never surfaced, but this close to him a different sort of nervousness took hold, every one of her senses heightened with female awareness.

"Taylor brought us cake," Charlie announced, carrying in a pile of plates and forks. "I say we dig in."

While everyone sat around talking, joking and eating cake, Taylor mostly observed. The camaraderie between the men was comfortable and obvious, and Piper and Charlie gave as good as they got in the teasing department.

As always, Taylor was the odd man out, staying quiet and pretty much only speaking when spoken to. She was far better at one-on-one than she was with a group, though that wasn't saying much.

She made herself stay for an hour, sneaking glances at Logan when she thought no one else would notice, before finally making her excuses to go. Long day, had to be up early, lots of new data and intel for her to sift through, blah blah.

When she got up, Logan surprised her by reaching for his crutches as he started to rise. "I'll walk you down to your car."

That was ridiculous. She was a trained agent able to defend herself against any would-be muggers, and he was on freaking crutches. "I think I should be walking you to yours."

He cracked a laugh. She liked that about him, that he could dish it out as well as take it. "Okay, then I'll leave too, and we'll walk each other out. How's that?"

"Sure." She put on her coat and waited while he hobbled behind her to the door, trying not to stare at the way the muscles in his arms flexed every time he moved the crutches. The T-shirt's sleeves gave her a great view of his biceps, triceps and forearms muscles.

Mmm, yeah. Sexy lumberjack and then some. Not that she should be thinking about him that way, but come on, she'd have to be dead for her endocrine system not to react around him. Or for her brain to conjure up erotic images of him when she was in bed.

Holding the elevator doors open for him a minute later, she stepped aside to give him room to enter, unprepared for the effect of being trapped inside an enclosed space with him. He was over six feet tall and powerfully built, but his presence was even larger, all male confidence and charisma.

With him standing so close it was impossible not to notice his spicy, masculine scent, or feel the warmth radiating from his big body. It heated something low in her abdomen that she hadn't felt in a long damn time, and sent tingles racing over her skin.

Realizing she'd been staring a second too long, she jerked her head around to face front, kept her eyes locked on the display at the front of the elevator as they rode down to the lobby.

"So, Taylor." His deep voice seemed to reverberate in the enclosed space, wrapping around her like an invisible embrace.

Invisible embrace? Are you drunk?

"Yeah?" she said.

"What do you like to do for fun?"

Taken off guard, she glanced over at him. "What do you mean?"

His eyes twinkled at her answer. "You know, fun? Stuff you do that makes you happy."

Staying home with Sudoku puzzles and a cup of tea in front of a crackling fire. Peace and quiet with which to recharge.

No way she was admitting any of that to him. He probably already saw her as uptight and socially awkward, no need to prove him right. "I don't know, a lot of things."

He raised a dark auburn eyebrow. "Such as?"

The elevator dinged as they reached the lobby. Come on, hurry up, she urged the elevator doors, wanting to get out of there. "I like spending time with my friends." One or two at a time, for a few hours at a time. Not usually a problem, because she only had a few friends anyhow, although she mostly hung out with Charlie.

"Doing what?" He followed her out of the elevator.

She didn't know why he was even interested in this, but since it would be rude to rush ahead when he was still trying to talk to her, she stayed only a step in front of him as they walked to the building's front doors.

Deciding it was easiest just to go with it, she rattled off a few things that wouldn't make her seem like the antisocial hermit she was. "Going out to eat, working on a project together, relaxing in front of a movie. A bit of shopping."

Emphasis on a bit, because some days it was just too damn people-y out there at the stores. And it was high time to shift the focus off her and onto him. "What about you?"

"Outdoor stuff. Hiking, skiing, snowshoeing, canoeing, kayaking. Stuff like that." He caught up to her at the front door, reached past her with one long arm to push it open.

All things that didn't appeal to her in the slightest. "Thank you," she murmured, anxious to get going.

This conversation only proved how impossibly opposite they were, and that he would find the real her completely boring. Most people didn't understand her innate need for solitude, but it made her happy and she was sick of defending herself, so she didn't bring it up.

"Ever gone white water rafting?" he asked, hurrying to come up next to her.

She slowed a little, feeling bad. "No."

"It's fun. A total rush. I bet you'd like it."

It sounded awful to her. Stuck in a rubber boat bouncing down some river, drenched and cold for hours until it was finally over? No thanks.

She wrinkled her nose. "I doubt it."

"How do you know if you've never tried it? You could try a really tame river to start. It's not like you have to take on class five rapids right out of the gate, you know."

Whatever. "Maybe one day. We'll see." *No way in hell.*

"Okay, then tell me one thing you love. Something you couldn't live without."

She paused at her vehicle and made herself face him. Big mistake.

Looking up into that rugged, masculine face, the

bottom of her stomach fell out. In a good way. A really good way.

He kept watching her, waiting for an answer. He seemed truly interested in getting to know her better, though she couldn't imagine why.

You are worthy. Worthy, dammit. "Ice cream," she blurted.

He blinked. "Ice cream?"

She nodded. "Yeah."

The slow grin he gave her made her insides flutter, even as she got the sense he was amused by her. For some reason, that didn't irritate her as much as it normally would have. "Huh, okay. What flavor?"

"Most flavors. Except pistachio. I hate pistachio." When he kept staring at her, she flushed and started babbling to fill the gap in conversation. "I didn't get ice cream very often as a kid. I guess I've always seen it as a luxury item, so now that I can afford it, I get a small carton pretty much every time I do a big grocery shop."

As soon as she said it she felt like a giant dork, but rather than the dreaded pity she braced for on his face, his grin only widened.

"So you're an ice cream hoarder," he murmured, and she couldn't help but smile because it was such a weird thing to hoard. "I knew there was something about you."

"Yes." And she had a chest freezer full of ice cream in her garage to prove it. "You?"

"I like ice cream, but apparently not as much as you. I'm more of a peanut butter guy. Any shape or form, I don't care, love it all."

"Huh, good to know." This was the oddest conversation she'd ever had with a man. And given the awful dating history she boasted, that was saying something.

"So, you still up for having dinner sometime?" he asked as she opened the driver's side door.

The question threw her for a second. He still wanted to go to dinner with her after this?

She might be socially awkward, but even she knew asking him flat out whether this was as friends or a date was kind of rude. "Yes, for sure."

"Since I'm laid up for the moment, my evening schedule's kind of wide open for the next while. I know you're busy with the investigation though."

"I'd make time for dinner with you."

A startled smile flashed across his face. "You would?"

Why did he seem so surprised? "Yeah, I would." She liked him. He had depth, probably more than even she suspected. It was just that her growing attraction to him was scary.

"Okay, then. What about tomorrow night?"

She thought about it for a second. "Sure, tomorrow night. Are we having peanut butter sandwiches and ice cream?"

He chuckled. "No, I thought I'd take you to an actual restaurant. Unless you *want* peanut butter sandwiches and ice cream," he teased.

This sure didn't feel like a coworker dinner he was asking her to. No. She refused to dwell on it. "I'd be perfectly fine with those, but sure. Restaurant it is." She eyed his crutches. "Want me to drive you to your car?"

"Truck. And nah, I'm parked just a few spaces down. So, tomorrow night. Want me to pick you up?"

She wasn't comfortable needing anyone, and if he viewed this as an actual date, she didn't want to feel like she owed him anything. "No, I'll just head from work and meet you there. You pick the place." And they'd be splitting the tab.

"Okay, I'll text you the address."

"Perfect. Have a good night. Go home and put your leg up."

Another of those slow, sexy smiles, and the damn

tingles went lower this time. Low enough to make her want to squirm in her seat. "Will do." He shut her door for her, stood there watching as she drove away.

When Taylor turned out of the lot and onto the street, she couldn't stop the smile from forming. She might be rusty with the whole romance thing, but this definitely felt like it had the makings of an actual date.

Chapter Five

After parking her car in the garage, Taylor hit the remote on her sun visor to close the garage door. As it lowered behind her she grabbed her purse, climbed out and headed for the door that led into her mud/laundry room.

"Hello?"

She barely swallowed the scream as she whirled around, heart in her throat. A man was ducking under the closing garage door, his wide shoulders blocking the light cast from the streetlamps outside as he nimbly stepped over the sensor that would have made the door go back up.

Automatically she reached for the can of pepper spray in her purse, at the same time as he straightened and faced her. Dillon Wainright stood there, watching her. "Hey, Taylor."

"Jesus, Dillon." Her heart leaped at the sight of him.

She put a hand to the center of her chest and sucked in a deep breath, her other hand still holding the pepper spray. What the hell was he doing here? And how had he gotten her address? Her driveway was empty and she hadn't seen a car parked along the curb near her house. "You scared the shit out of me."

"Sorry." He'd stopped halfway to her and now put his hands in his pockets, giving her a chance to compose herself. After a moment, that familiar lopsided smile spread across his face, and her throat constricted at the sight of him. It had been so damn long. "I was waiting on the front porch when you got here. I waved when you pulled into the driveway, but I guess you didn't see me."

Wow, she really needed to make more of an effort to be aware of her surroundings. She hadn't realized how complacent and sloppy she'd become since moving here. "No."

"So." He rocked back on his heels. "It's been a long time, huh?"

"Yeah." He looked so much the way she remembered him, and yet so different. More mature. Harder. "How did you find me?" And *why* had he, after he'd been the one to cancel earlier?

"I called Janet earlier and she gave me your address." He cocked his head, watching her with a slight frown. "Is that…okay?"

If she hadn't seen him on the Baker video, she wouldn't have thought twice about him showing up here, and she hated that part of her was now questioning his motives. Last time they'd spoken a few years back, he'd told her he'd given up his criminal ways and turned legit.

"I guess so." But no, she'd make sure to tell Janet not to give out her address to anyone ever again, even to an old friend like Dillon. Her heart was still recovering from the shock. "You should have called me."

"I felt really bad about cancelling tonight. I wound up finishing my work thing early, and thought I'd come by to surprise you." He gave her another crooked grin, his sandy-brown eyebrows rising in question. "Surprise."

Then he opened his arms and waited, that goofy smile still in place.

Even though his methods felt invasive, she had never been able to resist that smile and couldn't now. She'd missed him so damn much, and mentally reprimanded herself for being so stiff and standoffish with him. This was Dillon, and even if she still had some reservations about him being here, he'd gone to the trouble of coming here because he wanted to see her so badly.

As though pulled by some magnetic force, she closed the distance between them and stepped into the hug, wrapping her arms around his ribs. "It's one hell of a surprise, all right."

Dillon squeezed her tight, and the size and power of him was startling. He'd been big for his age as a teenager, but he'd filled out a lot since then and obviously worked hard at keeping in shape. "A good one, right?"

"Yes."

God, he still smelled the same. Like home—the only one she'd ever known as a kid. She closed her eyes a moment and leaned her forehead against his solid chest, a huge lump forming in her throat at the feel of the familiar embrace and the rush of emotions and memories it unleashed.

There had never been anything remotely romantic between them, although she'd had a bit of a crush on him at one point when she'd first arrived at the foster home where he was living. During that unstable, frightening period of her life he'd become like a protective big brother, representing comfort, safety and security, the first she'd ever known with a man. For the better part of three years he'd been her safe haven, and then he'd gone.

"I'm really glad I came," he murmured against her hair, his arms holding her close. "I've needed this more than you can imagine."

Taylor sucked in a deep breath and fought the tide of

emotion clogging her chest. He'd meant so damn much to her and then he'd just up and left. She understood why he'd done it, even agreed that he'd had to do it, but it had still hurt like hell. Losing him had ripped a giant black hole in her world and left her reeling and feeling abandoned for a long time.

Except now she was torn. She couldn't stop thinking about the video.

He couldn't be part of the *Veneno* cartel. Not her Dillon, who'd been so brave and selfless and risked so much for her. Who'd stepped in and protected her when no one else would, even though it had cost him.

She swallowed hard, battling the rise of tears.

"Hey." He nuzzled his nose against the top of her head. "Don't cry."

She shook her head, her throat too tight to speak. When she'd agreed to meet up with him, she'd never expected this kind of reaction at seeing him. But then, she'd long ago become an expert at burying her emotions deep down inside where they couldn't interfere with the controlled façade she'd worked so hard to project to the rest of the world.

When the threat of tears finally passed, she lifted her head and gave him a wobbly smile. "It's good to see you."

The past arced between them, reflected back at her in the almost wistful expression in his chocolate-brown eyes. "You too."

"Come on inside," she said, stepping away and heading to the door. "Have you eaten?" She disarmed the security system on the way in, careful to make sure he couldn't see her doing it. Even though she trusted him because of their past, she wouldn't let her guard down completely until she knew why he had been at Baker's house.

"Yeah, on the way here." He followed her into the mudroom and through to the kitchen, then stopped to look around. "Nice place you got here. It's a craftsman?"

She nodded. "1920s, I think. The people I bought it from did a good job with the restorations. I barely had to do anything when I moved in." It had one main floor and a loft, her favorite spot in the house, and as soon as she'd seen it, she'd known this was home. "Want something to drink?"

"Sure. A beer, if you've got one."

She got two from the fridge, excited and a little nervous to be seeing him in person again after all this time. After they talked a bit, maybe she could ask him about his work and find an innocent reason as to why he'd been at Baker's party that night. Maybe he was a real-estate developer or businessman of some kind now. It would certainly take a load off her mind.

But she didn't want to think about any of that right now. "Let's go sit in the loft."

"The loft?"

"Best spot in the house."

She led the way up the wooden staircase, a cozy, comforting feeling surrounding her like an invisible hug at the sight of her private little haven. The dark hardwood floors gleamed in the glow of the table lamp set on a side table next to one of the couches, and a stone fireplace was nestled in the corner.

Her smoke-gray cat, Nimbus, lifted his head from the ottoman he was curled up on and eyed them with half-closed green eyes. Taylor paused to scratch him under the chin before sinking into the corner of the cream-colored couch and tucking a knit throw blanket around her legs.

Dillon paused a moment to look around, then sat on the couch opposite her. "This place really suits you."

"Thanks. I love it here." She stroked a hand over the length of Nimbus's back as he climbed into her lap and began purring.

"Still a neat freak, I see."

"You can't be surprised by that."

"No. You always liked everything organized and uncluttered." He looked so at home there on her couch, one ankle resting on the opposite knee, one big arm thrown along the back of the cushion.

"Keeps my mind calm." Guilt wrestled with joy at having him here, but a part of her wondered if she'd crossed a line by letting him in, given that he was likely about to be on the DEA's radar because of the video footage. She was still holding out hope that they could dismiss him as a suspect soon.

"So Janet said you moved here for a job?" he said, twisting off the cap on his beer.

She looked down at her own beer to avoid his eyes. "Yes."

He laughed. "Just yes? No other details?"

She shrugged, hoping he'd let the matter drop because she didn't want to tell him she was with the DEA, just in case. "Boring government job. But the benefit package and pension plan was too good to pass up."

"Must've been, to bring you all the way to D.C. I thought you loved Houston."

"Nah, I was over it a long time ago, and it's been a good change. Even in August the humidity here is nothing compared to there." He'd been her closest friend and companion. Had they seriously fallen into talking about the weather? "What about you? What've you been up to since we last talked?"

He broke eye contact as he set the bottle cap on the table and reached for a coaster, because he knew better than to set the bottle down on the wood without one. "Work. All work, all the time."

She quirked a brow at him. "No other details?"

The smile he gave her was a tiny bit strained. "Not much to tell. I got into business with a few other guys, distributing pharmaceuticals all over the country."

Pharmaceuticals. Legal drugs. She prayed that really was the case, although the mention of him selling any kind of drugs touched off a zap of unease in the pit of her stomach.

"And what else? You're not wearing a ring, so I'm guessing you're not married or engaged. You seeing anyone?"

"No. I'm a self-professed workaholic, I'm afraid."

"Why does that not surprise me," he said with a smirk, then sobered. "So you're not seeing anybody at all?"

She wrinkled her nose. "Not at the moment, no. I've tried the online dating thing, but it never worked out."

He frowned. "That sounds...lonely."

"I guess it can be sometimes, but honestly with the guys I've met, I prefer being on my own. You?"

He swallowed a mouthful of beer. "Nothing serious at the moment. I was with one girl for about four years." He looked down and fiddled with his bottle.

Taylor shifted and leaned forward, something giving her the sense that it bothered him. "What happened?"

His smile was tight. "Irreconcilable differences, I guess you could say. I came home one night from a business trip and she was gone. She'd packed up all her stuff and left without a word."

"Oh, I'm so sorry." Given that his addict parents had ditched him at a mall when he was five, that would have cut him to the quick.

He nodded once. "Thanks." He took another swig of beer.

"Sometimes I think it's better, being alone. Less painful that way."

He met her gaze, and she caught a flash of empathy there. "I know it's been hard for you to trust men. But I don't think you're meant to spend the rest of your life alone, Taylor. You're not built that way, even if you wish you were. One day someone's gonna come along and throw your safe, controlled world off kilter, in the best way possible. And when that happens, don't be afraid to let him in. You'll regret it if you do."

She stared at him, his words setting off a painful ache beneath her ribs, because they hit far too close to home. She *didn't* trust men. It was surreal, how well Dillon still knew her, even after so many years spent apart. He knew every one of her dark, shameful secrets and had never judged her for them.

The truth hurt, didn't it? All her life she'd kept men at a distance, in a bid to protect herself from being hurt and abandoned. And it was damn lonely sometimes, living alone on her side of the wall she'd erected.

An image of Logan flashed into her head, reminding her of the way butterflies danced in her stomach whenever she was around him. He was the opposite of safe and controlled, a true adrenaline junkie who seemed determined to milk every ounce of excitement and action possible out of life.

So different from the rigid, sterile existence she'd made for herself. Could she ever open herself up to a man like him? After what had happened to her, she wasn't sure she was even capable of it at this point.

Headlights swung across the window at the far end of the loft as a vehicle pulled into her driveway. She glanced toward it, expected whoever it was to simply turn around, but instead the sound of an engine became clear as it neared the garage door.

"Expecting company?" Dillon asked, a slight tension in his voice.

"No." She got up and went to the window. A white pickup she didn't recognize was parking in front of her garage. The driver switched the headlights off.

"Recognize it?"

"No. Be right back." It was weird. She rarely had visitors, and never two in the same night.

She hurried down the stairs and back through the kitchen to the front door, where she checked the peephole. The driver's side door opened and someone began climbing out. A crutch emerged from the vehicle and planted itself on the concrete driveway.

Logan.

Her heart skipped a beat and warmth radiated through her body. Everything female inside her sighed as he emerged from the truck, tall and powerful and sexy.

"Who is it?"

At Dillon's terse whisper behind her she jumped and glanced back at him. He stood a few feet away in the shadows, his back to the wall, a strange tension about him as he stared at her front door.

It put her on high alert and she rushed to reassure him, not understanding his reaction. "It's okay, it's just a friend from work. I don't know why he's here."

Dillon's dark gaze cut to hers, and the cold, steely look in his eyes sent a sudden chill through her. "Open the door, find out what he wants, and then make him go away."

A prickle of unease rippled through her.

She opened her mouth to ask what was wrong, but the words died in her throat when he reached behind him and pulled a matte black pistol from the back of his pants.

Chapter Six

———◇◇◇◇◇———

Logan swore under his breath as his right hand slipped on the grip of the crutch, barely catching it before it hit the ground. If he weren't so desperate to keep weight off his knee so it could heal enough to get him back in action as soon as possible, he'd throw the fuckers away and just suck up the pain.

He hobbled up to Taylor's front door, a cute little bungalow-style place in a quiet residential neighborhood. No easy feat while juggling the crutches and the bakery box carefully cradled between his upper arm and ribcage.

The front porch was dark except for the small amount of light coming through the tall, thin windows on either side of the door. He tramped up the wooden steps and balanced his weight on his right foot to reach for the doorbell but the door swung open before he could press it. Taylor stood there backlit by the soft glow of the hall light behind her, wearing glasses, still in the same skirt suit she'd had on at Jamie's.

Rather than seeming pleased or even surprised to see him, her greeting smile was as stiff as her posture. Forced.

As though she was annoyed. "Hey," she said, her terse tone all but eliminating her south Texas drawl.

For a moment, Logan faltered. Okay, he hadn't expected her to throw the door wide open and invite him in, but he had expected a bit warmer of a welcome after the way they'd left things tonight. Unless he'd just imagined that they'd gained some ground back at the apartment parking lot? And the female interest he thought he'd seen in her eyes?

"Hey. Did I catch you at a bad time?"

"Sort of."

Something about her stance, about the way she watched him, didn't feel right. A couple of times now he'd gotten the sense that he made her uncomfortable when he got too close. She'd hidden it well, but he'd still noticed, especially at dinner that night back in New York City.

Maybe him showing up here alone and unannounced made her nervous. If that was the case, then he felt bad. If her past was as rough as he suspected, then fuck him, he'd screwed up. She was such a contradiction: quiet and competent, strong, and yet there was an underlying vulnerability about her that tugged at him. Her almost wary reaction to him now threw him off.

Since she didn't seem interested in making an effort at polite conversation, he got right to the point. "Jamie came running out and caught me just as I was getting into my truck. Charlie wanted you to take the leftover cake, so she wouldn't eat it. Jamie gave me your address," he explained, hoping to put her more at ease and stop her from wondering whether he was a stalker, if that was what she was thinking.

Again with the stiff smile. "Oh, okay. Thanks for bringing it by." She took the box from him and immediately retreated back inside, standing half-hidden by the door as if she didn't trust him not to barge in and couldn't wait for him to leave.

Well, hell, wasn't that a kick in the ass. And the ego. Did she have a guy over or something and he'd interrupted? Charlie had told him tonight that she wasn't seeing anyone.

He cocked his head, wondering what the hell had happened between their conversation in the parking lot and now. Taylor seemed almost…worried. "You okay?"

She straightened, frowned as she pulled the bakery box closer to her chest, the door still partially concealing her like a shield. "Yes, fine. Thanks again. You going home to put your leg up now?" At least her drawl was back. He liked it.

That was the nicest go-away-and-leave-me-alone he'd ever heard, but that's still what it was. *Okay then.* "Yeah. See you tomorrow."

"Sure. Bye."

She shut the door in his face. And the immediate sound of the deadbolt turning was like a slap in the face.

Baffled and a little frustrated by her cold reaction since he'd never done anything but be nice to her, he turned around and made his way back to his truck, shaking his head at himself. Clearly he was way off his game, because he must have only imagined the interested signals he thought he'd picked up from her earlier tonight.

****

Taylor's heart thudded in her ears as she waited behind the locked door, all her muscles pulled tight while Logan's crutches thudded lightly on the driveway. A few moments later his truck door opened and shut and the engine fired up.

Only when he reversed out of the driveway and drove away down her street did she allow herself to release the breath she'd been holding and turn around and face

Dillon.

He'd stepped out of the shadows now to peer through the window to the left of the front door, pistol held loosely at his side.

She swallowed, her gaze jumping from the weapon to his face. Her training kicked in, heightened by her protective instincts.

There was no telling how he'd react if she kicked him out now, and her service weapon was tucked away in her bedroom at the far end of the hall. A hand-to-hand struggle with him was out of the question, if he got violent. Even with her minimal agency training she didn't have a chance against him physically. He was too close, too on guard, and far too big.

"Dillon. What the hell?" Would he actually have shot Logan if he'd come inside? Jesus. What was going on?

Fear pricked at her skin like hot needles while her mind raced. The weapon. The Baker video. She'd been hoping there was another explanation for it all. Now she knew there wasn't and it made her heart drop into her stomach.

Dillon quickly tucked the weapon into the back of his waistband and relaxed his posture. "Sorry about that."

Sorry? *Sorry*? Not about to be cowed, she faced him head on while clutching the bakery box, refusing to let him know she was afraid of him now. The trials of her childhood had made her an expert at hiding fear. "What the hell is going on?"

With a sigh, he tucked his hands beneath his armpits and regarded her. "Nothing. I was just being careful."

The *it's-no-big-deal* tone wasn't fooling her. "I told you he was a *friend*."

Now that the immediate danger was over she was more pissed than scared, because there had to be a reason Dillon had come here armed in the first place. How dare he knowingly bring trouble to her doorstep?

"Is someone after you?" There was no other explanation.

He gazed back at her, his brown eyes haunted. "Like I said, I was just being careful."

She shook her head slowly, dread sweeping through her in a cold wave. "What have you done?" she whispered, stricken.

He'd sworn to her last time they'd talked, back when she still lived in Houston, that he'd gone straight and given up criminal life completely. She'd been such a fucking idiot to believe him—to let him fool her—and for letting him into her house tonight. Obviously he'd brought trouble with him.

"I can't believe you'd come here if you're in that kind of trouble. If I ever meant anything to you at all, why would you put me in danger?"

"Hey, don't worry." He gave her what he probably considered a charming smile, though it didn't quite reach his eyes. "Everything's fine, I promise. I would never do anything to put my best girl in danger."

Even despite what he'd just done, the familiar endearment set off a searing ache in the center of her chest. Dammit, she'd loved him like a brother once, and a part of her always would, no matter what he'd done. She owed him too much not to care what happened to him.

"Well, he's gone now, and won't be coming back." Not after the way she'd treated him.

God, she'd hated doing it, but she'd been focused on trying to protect him by making him go away as soon as possible. Logan was no doubt wondering why she'd turned into an icy bitch in the space of twenty minutes since he'd last seen her.

At least she'd played the part well enough to hide what was really going on and made him leave. At this point she didn't know whether Dillon would have threatened Logan if he'd tried to come inside.

She drew a deep breath. "Tell me what the hell's going on. Right now."

Dillon lowered his arms to his sides. "Okay, I didn't mean to scare you." He searched her eyes. "Taylor. Tell me you're not afraid of me."

She'd never imagined being afraid of Dillon. But he was like a stranger now and she didn't know if she could trust him anymore. "You pulled a gun in my house because someone showed up at my front door." A trickle of fear hit her. Why would he do that unless he was prepared to use it?

"I know, and I'm sorry for scaring you."

That he carried a weapon didn't bother her as much as that he'd felt the need to draw it because someone had shown up at her door. If Dillon was that on edge, whoever was after him had to be close. "Are we both in danger right now?"

He frowned as though that was a crazy question. "No, of course not."

She didn't believe him. "You need to tell me the truth, Dillon."

"Okay. Let's go back upstairs and finish our beers, and we'll talk."

She should kick him out, but part of her was afraid it might enrage him. For all their shared history, she didn't know him at all anymore. It chilled her to think what he might be capable of now. She also wanted to know the truth and find out what he was involved in. And it wasn't pharmaceuticals. So if he was willing to talk, she would hear what he had to say.

"Fine. But you have to be honest with me."

He looked away. "Come on," he murmured, gesturing for her to follow him as he headed down the hall to the stairs that led to the loft.

Her mind raced as she followed him. She was pretty sure he wasn't going to hurt her. If he'd wanted to, he would already have done it when her guard wasn't up.

In the loft Dillon sank onto the couch opposite her while she lowered herself stiffly into the corner of the other. "So, what do you want to know?" he asked with a wry grin.

There was no way she could fake it and pretend she wasn't upset, and he'd never buy it anyway. She'd always been completely honest with him, even when the truth hurt.

For her, his behavior downstairs had changed everything, and now she wished he'd never contacted her at all. She had to tread carefully here though. If he found out what she did for a living and that she'd seen him on the Baker video…

What if that's why he's here? "You're not selling pharmaceuticals."

His eyes locked with hers, and a grudging smile tugged at his mouth. "Wow, straight for the throat. Still telling it like it is, huh?"

"It's a personality flaw. Now tell me what you're doing." *Other than being a wanted man.* God, she'd invited a wanted freaking criminal into her home.

He reached for his half-finished beer, not looking at her. "I think you already know the answer to that."

Taylor clamped her back teeth together. Drugs. It was always drugs. He didn't do them, only sold and distributed them. Unless that had changed too. And she guessed whatever he was into now was a hell of a lot more sophisticated than what he'd done when he'd been a teenager.

"You swore to me you'd given all that up."

"Yeah, well, it's kinda hard to get out once you're in as deep as I am."

She held back asking him flat out if he was working with the *Venenos* and thought about the turn his life had taken at age sixteen.

All he'd wanted back then was quick money, to improve their lives. Put food on the table when their foster father couldn't be bothered to feed them. New shoes to replace the ones she'd repaired with duct tape to keep the soles from falling off, so the kids at school would stop bullying her. A warm coat to keep her from freezing in the winter, because the only one she had was three sizes too small and she couldn't do up the zipper.

Little things at first. Then more expensive and extravagant ones. A TV for her room so she didn't have to be around their foster dad when Dillon wasn't there. A pre-paid calling card so she always had a way of contacting him, even when he disappeared for days at a time.

God, she'd been such a hypocrite. Taking the cash and all the things he bought with his dirty money because she'd been so desperate for a better life.

But it hadn't been enough for Dillon. He'd wanted more, no matter the cost to the rest of his life or the people he cared about. It was why he'd had to run in the first place, because the choices he'd made had inevitably caught up with him, along with rivals and the police.

Why were you at Baker's house that day?

She was dying to ask him, and couldn't for fear of exposing herself. "You could have broken away from all that years ago and started over. You told me that's what you wanted, that you hated having to look over your shoulder all the time." Hence him carrying a weapon wherever he went.

His lips twisted into a bitter smile. "Sorry to see I'm still such a disappointment to you after all these years."

His tone was dry, but his eyes were flat and it made her feel like her chest was full of concrete. "You *swore* to me last time we talked that you'd gone straight. Was that a lie too?" She was angrier about that than everything else. Angry that he'd lied to her and fallen back into that lifestyle when he could have done so much with his life.

"I did. For a while." His gaze lingered on hers, almost as if he were gauging her reaction.

That look sent a warning shiver down her spine. Fuck. *Fuck.* She was beginning to worry that his visit had nothing to do with catching up at all, and everything to do with her job. Did he know who she worked for? "God, Dillon…"

"Okay, so I told you the truth. Now it's your turn."

She blinked at him. "My turn for what?"

"I heard a rumor that you're working for the DEA now."

Her lungs seized. She stared at him, the blood draining from her face. He was here because of her *job*.

The clock on the mantel downstairs struck the hour, sounding as loud as a gong. Dillon had a dark, dangerous vibe to him now. How could the man before her now be the same boy she'd had up on a pedestal all these years? She was such an idiot.

Somehow she kept her face blank and found her voice. "Did you?"

"That true?" he asked, his quiet words slicing through the suffocating silence like a blade. She didn't know whether he meant to imply a threat or not, but she felt it all the same.

"And if it is?" she flung back, neither confirming nor denying it.

He pressed his lips together in a sad sort of smile and shook his head once. "It would make things complicated, wouldn't it?"

"Complicated how?" she asked, raising her chin as she held his gaze. God, she didn't have the guts to flat-out ask whether he was working with the *Venenos*. The probability that he was, was just too damn terrifying.

"Would put us both in a hell of an awkward position. Testing our loyalties and all that."

Taylor stared back at him, his words hitting hard. He was testing to see whether she'd turn him in or not, and hinting that he could do the same to her. Trying to figure out if their bond was strong enough for her to protect him now that she knew he was breaking the law. It made her as angry as it made her want to cry.

She thought fast. "What the hell are you talking about? Test what loyalties?"

Dillon sighed and dragged a hand through his hair, then settled his elbows on his knees as he regarded her, his expression earnest. "Shit, this isn't the way I wanted things to turn out between us. I really have missed you, Taylor."

In spite of herself, tears pricked her eyes. He'd been her hero. She would always be grateful for that, and some part of her would always feel obligated to repay the favor. But not now, with them on opposite sides.

Her voice broke. "I can't believe you'd do this to me." If he'd known or at least suspected that she worked for the agency, then he'd come here tonight knowing it would put her in the worst position imaginable. Did he know that she was involved with the Baker investigation too?

His expression softened. "I had to see you. Even if the rumors about your job were true, I still had to come."

"Why?" She blinked furiously to keep the tears at bay. Tears were weak. Useless. And she was neither of those things. Not anymore. "To drag me into whatever you've done? Cover for you or something? Because I'm a paper pusher, Dillon. Even if you wanted me to do something for you, I only work low profile cases. I wouldn't be much help to you anyway."

"No. Because even all these years later, you're still the only person I can really trust."

His words sent invisible fingers reaching through her ribcage to crush her heart until it bled. There it was again, that damn instinctive urge to protect him. Save him, even if it was from himself. Jesus, she hated this.

"So what do you want from me? A favor?" She couldn't keep the bitterness out of her voice.

"No." He stood, drained the last of his beer and placed it back on the coaster. The soft thunk of the glass hitting the wood seemed to echo in the stillness.

Without another word, he headed down the stairs. On wooden legs, Taylor got up and followed him down to the kitchen. He snagged his leather jacket from the island and headed for the front door.

Wait.

The word lodged in her throat, nearly choking her. She wanted him to leave, yet part of her wanted him to stay, so she could convince him to turn his life around. This wasn't a game. His actions would probably cost him his life one day.

It was too late to help him, let alone save him.

He didn't look back at her as he opened the door. But then he paused, his hand on the door. Taylor swallowed, ordering herself to stay put.

When he looked back at her, his dark eyes were somber, and something twisted inside her. She ached to save him, drag him out of the danger he'd immersed himself in. But how? He would never listen. He never had.

"I'm sorry. I wish things were different. Just...don't tell anyone I was here, okay? That's the only favor I'll ask you for. It was good to see you. Take care of yourself." He walked out and shut the door firmly behind him, leaving her standing alone in her kitchen while her heart ripped in two.

He was going to die. She knew it with utter certainty.

Without thinking she raced over and grabbed the doorknob, intending to rip the door open and go after him. At the last second, she stopped and took a steadying breath.

No. Chasing after him and demanding answers would

get her nowhere. Even at the closest stage of their relationship she had never been able to pry something out of Dillon if he didn't want to disclose it.

At that moment, she'd never felt more alone. She thought of Logan, and the ache inside her intensified. The urge to call him right now was so strong it was a live thing inside her. He would keep her safe. But it wasn't fair to ask that of him, or to drag him into this nightmare of a drama. So as usual, she was on her own once again.

Numb inside and out, heart thudding against her ribs, she turned the deadbolt and stood there for a long moment, considering her options. She only had two, and no matter which one she chose, each would eat at her insides like acid.

Either she betrayed the closest thing she'd ever had to a brother, or she jeopardized everything she'd worked for to help protect him.

Chapter Seven

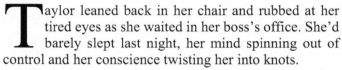

Taylor leaned back in her chair and rubbed at her tired eyes as she waited in her boss's office. She'd barely slept last night, her mind spinning out of control and her conscience twisting her into knots.

All night long she'd wrestled with her dilemma, trying to decide what to do about Dillon, and thinking of Logan. She'd been so cold to him last night, though not by choice. Did he think she was a bitch now? Had she ruined any chance of something happening between them?

By morning the cold, hard truth had settled heavy in her chest. She couldn't sit back and do nothing, or hide her association with Dillon any longer. He may have been the most important person in her life at one point, but not anymore. He'd made so many bad choices. She couldn't help him now, and shouldn't have to suffer the consequences for his poor life decisions.

And Logan… She'd think about him once this meeting was over. How long was her boss going to be? She was on pins and needles waiting for him.

Pushing out a deep breath, she shifted in the chair and

closed her eyes, letting herself go back in time. In an instant, she was twelve years old all over again, back in that stark, brick bungalow that had been more of a prison than a home, and yet ten times better than the home she'd been taken from.

She was in the kitchen, looking for something to eat. She and Dillon had routinely done without lunch at school, eating whatever the school offered in its breakfast program. The weekends were harder, because it often meant they went without even that. The only ingredients to be found in the fridge were a slice of bologna and stale white bread, along with some mayonnaise and mustard—and the pizza box.

The pizza was off limits for her and Dillon. They both knew it, just as they knew what the consequences would be if they dared touch it. That day, however, she was too hungry to care.

Her heart beat faster as she reached in and opened the lid of the box. Four pieces of deluxe pizza lay there, tempting her beyond bearing, making her mouth water.

Just one little piece.

Since it was Friday and their foster dad usually stopped by the bar on the way home, he'd likely be too drunk to notice if she took the smallest one. It wasn't much, but enough to stop the awful grinding in her stomach.

Hunger got the better of her. Before she'd thought it through she was already shoving the pizza into her mouth. She barely tasted it as she devoured the first half of it in two bites, focused on eating it as fast as she could.

Footsteps behind her made her whip around. Dillon stood there in the kitchen doorway, his rangy frame filling the jambs even at fifteen. His hair was matted to his head, his T-shirt damp with sweat. Oh God, she'd missed his football game.

Those brown eyes seemed to pin her in place for a

moment while she stood frozen with a mouthful of pizza she could no longer chew. Her pulse thudded in her ears as she waited for him to give her hell.

Instead, he sighed, his eyes full of an unbearable sadness. "Don't do that again. I'll get you pizza if you want some that bad."

Somehow she forced the cold mouthful of cheese and dough down her tight throat. "Sorry I missed your game."

"Don't worry about it." He walked past her to the sink and filled a glass with water. As he did, headlights cut across the window above the sink and the sound of a familiar engine reached them.

Dillon set his glass down, his entire back going rigid as he turned away from her. "Get to your room and stay there."

A wave of gut-churning fear rolled over her. "No, I—"

"Go, Taylor," he snapped.

She turned and ran for her bedroom with the pizza still in hand, shut the door and jammed her desk chair beneath the knob to help barricade it. In the dark, she whipped the covers on her bed back and climbed in, pulling them over her head.

And there in the dark silence, she wolfed down what was left of the pizza. It seemed to churn in her stomach, the rising dread threatening to make it come right back up again.

The front door to the house opened. Her foster father's footsteps echoed along the hallway. His rough, deep voice growled something, and Dillon answered quietly. Too low for her to hear the words.

Beneath the covers, she shut her eyes tightly and held her breath, waiting. Hoping the storm would pass.

It was not to be.

Moments later she heard that angry voice reverberate down the hall. "God dammit, who the hell ate my pizza?"

Taylor bit her lip and curled her hands into fists beneath her chin, fear locking every muscle. Dillon could defuse it. Sometimes he could find a way to avoid the explosion. But she never could. It was why she always tried to make herself invisible.

"There were four pieces, and now there are only three. You think I can't fucking *count*?"

He was drunk again. He was so much meaner when he was drunk.

Dillon said something in reply, his voice calm.

"You know the rules. So who the fuck did it? Her?" Angry footfalls headed down the hall, coming her way.

The breath halted in her lungs, a wave of cold breaking over her.

"It was me. I was hungry after the game, okay?" Dillon said.

"You? You little fucker, I'll teach you to steal food from my own damn fridge." Something heavy hit the wall a second later. She cringed, prayed.

And then the beating began.

Hot, acidic tears of guilt rolled down her face, dripped into her pillow as Dillon took the punishment meant for her. This was her fault. All her fault. She wished she'd never touched the stupid pizza.

Dillon was so strong, much stronger than her, and took it in absolute silence. But she felt each blow as if those cruel fists were hitting her own flesh. Once again, she thought of calling the police, then dismissed it. She'd already been warned what would happen if she did.

When it was over a minute later she was trembling so hard her teeth chattered. She lay in absolute terror as those heavy footfalls approached her door and paused just outside it.

A meaty fist thudded on the wooden door. "I know it was you, bitch. Don't think I don't know any better." Then he belched and continued down the hall, slamming his door behind him.

A wave of relief sluiced over her. She sagged against the mattress, waited a solid five minutes to ensure he'd passed out in a drunken stupor before getting up and sneaking back to the kitchen.

Dillon wasn't there, but there was a new dent in the drywall next to the doorframe. She swallowed and went into the living room. He wasn't there either.

She finally found him outside on the front porch, sitting there in the dark, curled up on a rickety lawn chair facing the street. He didn't look at her as she approached, his profile to her, the already angular jaw tight. "Dillon?"

He turned his head and she bit her lip at the sight of the blood seeping from his lips, the fresh bruise forming around his eye. "Go to bed, Tay."

"I'm sorry," she choked out.

He nodded once and went back to staring at the street. "I know. It's okay. Go to bed now. He won't bother you tonight."

Stricken, not knowing how to fix what she'd done, she crossed to him and stroked a hand over his damp hair. "I'm so sorry…"

He reached up one hand to capture hers, tipped his head to give her a brave half-grin that broke her heart, then squeezed her hand and released it. "It's all right. Just go to bed now."

Taylor had wandered back to her room in a guilt-stricken haze and shut the door behind her. Then she'd rushed straight to the trash bin next to her desk and thrown up the pizza she'd eaten.

The door opening behind her yanked her from the past and made her eyes fly open. She jerked upright and swiveled in her seat to find her boss entering the office.

"Taylor." He offered her a polite smile as he crossed to his desk. "Sorry to keep you waiting."

"No, it's fine," she managed, her throat aching and raw

with regret.

"You said you had something urgent to tell me?"

"Yes." She drew up straight in the chair, reaching deep for the courage to come clean.

"I've got something important to talk to you about too." He gathered some paperwork from a drawer in his desk and typed in something to his computer. "The footage we reviewed yesterday. It turned up some more leads, and I just got out of a briefing that gives us more evidence." He turned the monitor so she could see it and brought up an image. The one of Dillon and the *Veneno* enforcer.

Her stomach tensed as she waited for the dreaded words to come.

"This man." He pointed straight at Dillon and her heart sank. "Not only was he present at Baker's party that day, but according to some of the men captured during the Bahamian sub operation, he was responsible for organizing the shipment. He's the right-hand man of one of the *Veneno* lieutenants. Name's—"

"Dillon Wainright." Her voice was hollow, wooden.

If the agency was already investigating him and suspected he was linked to a *Veneno* lieutenant, the decision about what to do had already been taken out of her hands anyhow. If she wanted to keep her job and avoid being investigated herself, she had no choice but to come clean immediately.

Chris blinked at her in surprise. "That's right. How did you—"

"I know him."

His eyebrows rose. "You *know* him? How?"

"We were in foster care together from when I was twelve to fifteen." For three hellish years Dillon had stuck it out with her in that house, enduring too little food and frequent beatings, all because he hadn't wanted to leave her there alone.

Chris sat back slowly, staring at her. "Wow. Okay." He seemed to regroup for a moment. "Have you had any contact with him since then?"

She nodded, already decided on giving just enough information to help the agency proceed with the investigation, without volunteering every detail about their relationship, or last night. She'd already betrayed Dillon by asking for this meeting. She didn't want to be the one to bring him down as well, even if he deserved to face justice for whatever crimes he'd committed.

"A few phone calls over the years, an occasional email." Pausing, she drew a deep breath. "And I saw him last night."

Those keen blue eyes locked on her like lasers, making her want to squirm as much as her conscience already was. "So you recognized him on the footage yesterday and didn't say anything."

Heat burned in her cheeks, but the rest of her felt icy cold. "Yes."

"Jesus, Taylor." He got up, rubbed a hand over the back of his neck as he paced behind his desk for a moment. "Why the hell didn't you say anything?" he asked, voice full of frustration.

There was no excuse. None that the agency would accept. "It was a shock to see him after so many years. And I kept hoping it was just a coincidence, him being at the party."

He stopped and pinned her with furious blue eyes. "Well, it's not. He's working for one of their damn lieutenants, Taylor."

She bit the inside of her cheek and dug her fingernails into her palms, feeling queasy. It was even worse than she'd imagined. All she could do was nod.

He pushed out an impatient sigh. "What did he want? Last night?"

"Just to see me."

"At your house?"

"Yes. He got my address from a former social worker we used to be close to, and was there waiting when I got home." She left out the part about him pulling a gun when Logan showed up, because she already felt stupid enough for being duped into letting Dillon into her house.

"Christ. Does he know you work for the agency?"

Prickles of cold raced down her neck, traveling along her arms to her fingertips. "He suspected. I didn't confirm it." But he'd known. He'd known before ever showing up at her door. Whatever it meant, it couldn't be good.

He swore under his breath. "All right. Look. I'm gonna need your phone and access to your laptop and desktop." He held out a hand.

She pulled her phone from her purse and handed it over without a word. Inside, she was shaking. Were they going to fire her for this?

"Do you know where he is right now?"

"No." Hopefully somewhere far away where she'd never have to lay eyes on him again.

"Is he still in D.C.?"

"I don't know." It wouldn't surprise her if he'd left town last night, after their conversation. Or even left the country.

Now Chris looked truly worried. "Is he going to make contact with you again?"

"I doubt it." She'd made her feelings clear enough last night.

Taylor gave him a rundown of most of what had happened, and didn't dare move while her boss sat back down at his desk and made a series of terse phone calls. Ten minutes later he escorted her to the boardroom where she faced an inquiry from no less than five department heads.

By the time she'd explained to them in detail everything they wanted to know, she felt empty inside and beyond exhausted. She felt…betrayed.

And scared.

Anxiety burned in her stomach. "So does this mean I'm on probation?" she asked Chris when everyone else had left the room.

He flicked a glance at her, his expression stern. "Not officially, no. But you should have come clean yesterday, the moment you recognized him. Your actions have made me question your honesty and loyalty to the agency. I can't pretend I'm not hugely disappointed in you, Taylor."

She lowered her eyes and nodded, the words hitting her hard. But she deserved them. "I understand."

He stopped in the act of gathering his papers and straightened to study her a moment. "You've been a hard-working, invaluable member of my department since you got here. I understand why you initially withheld the information from me, and I even empathize about your situation, but that doesn't make it right."

"No." The urge to fidget was so strong she had to lock her muscles to stay still.

Standing, he gathered up his papers and motioned for her to follow him. "Come on. We've all been putting in long hours these past few weeks. Get out of here, go home and do something relaxing." He handed her back her cell phone.

Surprised, she took it. "Thank you."

His blue eyes bored into hers. "If he contacts you again, tell us immediately. You may be our best hope of catching him."

They'd likely have someone monitoring her phone anyway. "I will."

At her desk she tidied everything up then sat there for a long moment. It had been a monumentally shitty day, made even worse because she'd not only been reprimanded by her boss, she'd also turned up the law enforcement heat on Dillon. It's his own fault, she reminded herself, annoyed that she still cared.

She glanced at her watch. It was only a few minutes after four. The whole evening and night stretched ahead of her, long and lonely.

The thought of going home to an empty house made it seem like a weight pressed on the center of her chest. Normally she liked to be by herself, especially when she was stressed, but right now she'd kill for some company. She didn't want to burden Charlie with all this, and Jamie had only gotten home last night. They needed alone time.

Logan.

At the very least, she owed him an apology for last night. The mere thought of seeing him made her feel better. Not that she'd unload all this on him either. That wasn't how she operated, and it wasn't fair to dump this on him, no matter how badly she wanted to.

Nerves tickled the pit of her stomach as she texted him.

I'm really sorry about last night. Can I drop by for a few minutes? I want to explain myself.

She didn't even know if he'd answer her after the way she'd treated him last night.

She puttered around with some files on her desk for a while, waiting for his reply. After fifteen minutes she guessed he wasn't going to respond, and she really didn't blame him considering the way she'd acted—even if it had been to protect him.

And yet…an overwhelming sadness filled her that she'd crushed the fragile spark between them.

The parking lot was still mostly full when she made it to her car, the leaden gray sky overhead matching the heaviness in her chest. She'd just shifted into drive when her phone chimed with a text message.

She grabbed it from her purse, pure relief spearing through her when she saw Logan's reply, along with his address.

Sure. I'm at home. Come by whenever.

Chapter Eight

Funny how people took their health for granted until something went wrong.

Seated in his favorite leather recliner with his sore knee elevated in front of him to reduce the swelling, Logan flipped back and forth between the two ballgames on TV and absently reached for the bottle of sparkling water beside him.

He'd kill for a beer instead, but with him sitting on his ass most of his waking hours these days, he couldn't afford to put on weight that would slow his recovery down even more. The bag of frozen corn he'd used as an ice pack after he'd come home from his physio appointment lay limp in a puddle of water on the side table next to him.

The doorbell rang just as the batter hit the ball into a gap between center and right field. As he stood up he tempered the burst of anticipation at seeing Taylor. The mixed messages she'd given him yesterday were a major red flag. She was smart and hot and he was definitely attracted to her, but he had no interest in pursuing anything with her if she was a head case.

Drama wasn't his thing. She hadn't ever been like that to him before, so last night had really surprised him.

Crutches in hand, he gingerly walked to the front door of his townhouse, putting a fraction of weight on his bad leg with each step. Since the latest x-rays had shown only a partial hairline fracture in the patella, his doc and physio had both told him to start weight bearing a little at a time, more each day, and see how it went.

He pulled open the front door to find Taylor standing on his welcome mat in another of the fitted skirt suits she seemed to favor—this one a pale gray that hugged every feminine curve.

He loved them on her for two reasons. One, the sexy, sophisticated look of them. And two, because on her those form-fitting power suits radiated a professional self-assurance he found sexy as hell. Today she wore her light brown hair loose around her shoulders, and she held a white square box in one hand, the same kind she'd brought to Charlie and Jamie's last night.

The smile she gave him was hesitant, and behind the lenses of her tortoise shell-framed glasses he noticed faint shadows beneath her eyes that suggested she hadn't been sleeping well lately. "Hi," she said, that soft, feminine voice a stark contrast to the steely persona she presented to the world.

"Hi," he answered, keeping his tone neutral.

"Thanks for letting me come over."

Oh yeah, he loved her drawl. "Sure. Come on in." He turned sideways, balanced his weight on his good leg while he held the door open so she could pass by.

She waited until he'd locked up and crutched his way back toward the kitchen before holding up the box, a hopeful, slightly sheepish smile on her lips. Her pink, soft-looking lips. "I brought you something."

She'd frozen him out and shut the door in his face last night, and now she'd come over with a gift. What the hell did that even mean? "You didn't have to do that."

She shrugged. "Go ahead, open it." After setting it on the counter she stepped back and clasped her hands in front of her.

He opened it, aware of her hovering there, watching his reaction. It was some kind of pie with a graham cracker crust and a topping of smooth, melted dark chocolate.

Oh yeah. "You're an angel," he said, inhaling the delicious scent of peanut butter. His mouth started watering.

She let out a quiet laugh. "It's a peanut butter mousse pie topped with bittersweet chocolate. I saw it and thought of you."

He looked up at her, her thoughtfulness making him smile. "You remembered."

"I did." Her eyes twinkled behind her glasses.

Before now he'd thought her eyes were brown, but this close with the late afternoon light streaming in through the kitchen window, he could see they had a lot of green in them. Pretty eyes, with long, thick lashes surrounding them. Together with that skirt suit and glasses, she had a definite sexy librarian vibe going on.

He found it hot as hell. A total surprise, because he'd never been into that kind of look before.

Until now. Taylor had him redefining his entire definition of sexy without even trying.

He decided that her going to the trouble of bringing him pie was a good sign. "I'm totally diving into this bad boy. Want some? I'll share."

"I do, actually. It's been a bitch of a day."

"Yeah?" He eyed her as he reached behind him for the cupboard where he kept his dishes. She did look tired, and a little pale. Overworking herself, no doubt. Charlie had told him a few times now what a workaholic Taylor was. He understood that, because he was the same way with his job. "The investigation not going well?"

In the space of a heartbeat, her entire expression closed up. "You could say that."

He waited a beat for her to continue, but she didn't, so he got busy cutting two generous slices of pie. The chocolate topping gave way to the pressure of the knife, then slid easily through the smooth peanut butter layer before crunching into the graham crust. Heaven on a plate.

"You're trying to make me fat," she accused as she took her plate from him. "This is like, two helpings worth."

"Nah, it's protein-rich because of the peanut butter. And it sounds like you're in need of some comfort food." If she really was worried about her caloric intake, he could think of a few ideas of how she could burn the excess off. With him. Naked.

"That's true."

"Come on, let's go sit and eat these things."

"Let me take that." She scooped up his plate and followed him into the living room.

He dropped back into his chair, took his plate with a grin and waited until she was seated on the sofa beside him and looking around. Decorating wasn't his forte, and it showed.

The living room was sparse but functional, just the sofa, chair, coffee and end tables, and of course his big flat screen mounted on the wall. The walls were the same neutral beige they'd been when he'd bought the place, because what the hell did he care what color they were? He wasn't home all that much, and when he was in this room all he cared about was the TV anyway.

Taylor crossed her shapely legs at the ankle and started to lift her fork, but paused, her gaze on the short stack of books he had on the coffee table. They were crooked. She seemed to wrestle with herself a moment, then darted a hand out to straighten the books with a fingertip before easing back into the sofa and cutting a bite of pie with her fork. He hid a smile. She was so cute with her little neat nick tendencies.

Her eyes swung toward him. "So? How is it?"

"Mmmmhmmmm," he groaned around a mouthful. The chocolate ganache was just stiff enough to give a bit of a snap when he bit into it, then immediately melted in his mouth. The peanut butter mousse was smooth and creamy, heavy on the peanut butter, and the graham crust gave a crunch to the mouthful.

Taylor smiled a little as she took her first bite. "Oh yeah." She closed her eyes, her profile to him, and a sexy moan of pleasure came from the back of her throat. "Oh, that's good."

Logan's mouth suddenly went dry, the peanut butter sticking to his tongue. His hand froze around his fork, mid-way through carving off another chunk of pie. That sound she made was so damn sexy, and made him wonder if she'd make that exact same sound when he found one of her sweet spots with his hands or mouth.

He swallowed the bite and washed it down with a sip of sparkling water. She kept herself so tightly contained all the time, so guarded, but there was an innate sensuality about her that he wasn't sure even she recognized. If a mouthful of pie put that look on her face and got that kind of sound out of her, he could only imagine how she'd react to the things he would do to her in bed.

As if sensing his stare, she opened her eyes and met his gaze. He hurriedly shoved another bite of pie into his mouth and got busy chewing, not wanting to make her uneasy. If his size or nearness tended to make her stiffen up, ogling her like a sex-starved maniac definitely wasn't going to help his cause.

And that cause was to get past Special Agent Kennedy's defenses. If she'd ever let him.

Taylor shifted and lowered her gaze, took her time

cutting her next bite. "So I'm um, I'm really sorry about last night. I must have seemed like a bitch after the talk we had at Jamie and Charlie's place."

Yeah, her coldness had confused the hell out of him. He'd chalked it up to her being uncomfortable with him showing up at her door uninvited, and wouldn't hold it against her. "It's okay, don't worry about it."

"No, it's..." She sighed, set her plate in her lap and seemed to consider her words carefully before continuing. "It wasn't anything personal. I was just caught off guard by you showing up at my place like that."

Her explanation confirmed his theory, but she didn't look at him as she said it. It was driving him nuts, trying to figure out why she was so closed-up around him, and why he made her nervous. It wasn't a good or exciting butterflies-in-the-stomach kind of nervousness, either.

Something bad had happened to her in the past, he just knew it. He wanted to know what it was, and then he wanted to beat the asshole who had hurt her.

"I get it. No big deal." If he found out some dude had either threatened or physically hurt her, he'd be so pissed.

She glanced at him, opened her mouth as though she was about to say more, then stopped. Nodded. "Okay. Thanks."

What had she been about to say?

"Wow, you polished that off pretty quick," she said in a brighter voice, nodding at his empty plate. "Want another piece?"

"Do I want one? Yes. Should I have one considering I'm off duty and sitting around on my keister all day? No."

She laughed at that, and the sound made him smile. He'd noticed that Taylor didn't laugh easily. She was always so serious. He wanted her to have more things to laugh about in her life. "Please, look at you. You probably burn off a piece of pie just sitting there, with all that muscle mass. Unlike me, who would have to do I don't even want to think about how many miles on the treadmill to level out the caloric balance sheet."

This time it sounded like she was noticing his size in a non-threatening, and maybe even appreciative way. That was progress, and he'd take it. "Maybe you're just not doing the right kind of exercise." His words dripped with innuendo, and she caught it. She looked away, her cheeks turning pink. It was charming as hell.

"Maybe not."

Okay, he needed to tone it down a little before he made her really uncomfortable. "You ever been married? I never even asked you." She didn't wear a ring, though he knew plenty of married agents who didn't.

Surprise flashed in her eyes. "No. You?" She forked up another neat bite, those big hazel eyes watching him.

"Divorced. Three years ago."

"Oh, I'm sorry."

He shook his head. "No, believe me, it's for the best. We're both happier now, and we're better people apart."

She only nodded, still watching him. It wasn't like him to sit and blab about himself or his personal life, but Taylor wasn't going to divulge anything about herself and if he wanted to gain her trust then he felt like he had to keep going.

"We met in college, then I went straight into a job with the agency. I worked undercover as soon as I became an agent, long hours and lots of secrets, and that didn't help matters. We'd been together long enough by then that our families were pressuring us both to get married. I was dumb and naïve, felt like I owed it to her, and part of me stupidly thought that maybe once we tied the knot, it would prove to her that I was committed and she wouldn't be insecure anymore."

"But that didn't happen."

"No. Turned out, all our problems were still there, only

then they were bigger because we were talking about bigger stakes. A family, the rest of our lives together. So yeah, things didn't get better. I was addicted to my work, and she felt abandoned. It was a no-win situation and I wasn't willing to give up the job I loved. She was the one who finally asked for the divorce. Pretty sure she was just as relieved as me when it was all over."

"Do you have any contact with her now?"

"Not really. Every once in a while she'll call me about something, usually advice on a decision she has to make or whatever. It's not like we hate each other or anything. We both realize we made a giant mistake in getting married, that we were trying to force something that was never going to work. She's moved on and so have I. And her brother and I usually go hunting together once a year if our schedules allow it." He put his empty plate on the coffee table. "What about you? What's your family like?"

Again she looked away and forked up more pie. "I don't really have a family."

Oh, shit. No family? Why not? Had they died? "Sorry."

"It's okay." But she'd closed back up again, and quickly finished the last of her pie. "Well thanks for having me over. I'd better get going. Lots of work to be done."

"No need to rush out on my account. I'm just gonna be sitting here getting fat from the pie I won't be burning off. Want to stay and watch a movie or something? I won't make you watch the ballgame, promise."

She flashed him a smile but shook her head. "Thanks though. I'd better get some more work done. No, stay where you are, I'll get these," she told him when he grabbed his plate and started to stand.

He let her take his plate, but followed her to the kitchen on his crutches and ordered her to leave them in the sink. Of course she ignored him, rinsed them and put them neatly in the dishwasher. He was pretty sure she wrinkled her nose at how crowded and dirty everything inside it was.

She glanced at the cupboard beneath the sink, then looked at him. "Where do you keep your detergent?"

Logan fought a smile. "Under the sink." He started toward it but she bent and took out a packet of detergent, popped it in the dishwasher then turned it on.

It was so hard to keep from grinning when she straightened. "Thanks for the pie. It was great."

"You're welcome. But mostly I wanted to come and apologize for last night in person. I...felt badly."

"I'm over it." He should have called to warn her he was on the way over, and her coming here to apologize made it all a non-issue. Plus, peanut butter pie. The woman could turn him into putty in her hands so easily. And for some reason, that didn't worry him in the least. But was she into him or not? She had him second-guessing his instincts now.

Her smile was full of relief. "I'm glad. And now I'll let you get back to your game." Purse in hand, she headed for the door.

He went with her, stopped a step further away from her than he would have anyone else, because he didn't want her to feel crowded. "I still want to take you to dinner. If that's okay."

Another smile, this one sweeter than all the others. He wanted to hug her so bad. "Yes, I'd really like that."

He didn't want her to go. Not yet. He wanted to touch her. Kiss her. "Drive safe."

With her hand on the knob she paused and turned back to him slightly, her gaze on the mat inside the door. She seemed to wrestle with herself before speaking. "In your job back when you were undercover. Did you ever have to do something that made you feel like you'd been torn in two?"

More than the words themselves, the way she said it—in that lifeless tone—and the haunted look on her face when she finally looked up at him, hit Logan in the chest like a punch.

His gut tightened, instinct screaming at him that something was wrong. Big time wrong. She was an agent. Something minor wouldn't rattle someone like her, and she sure as hell wouldn't have mentioned anything to him if it wasn't huge. That alone worried him.

"Are you in some kind of trouble?" She'd told him she'd had a shitty day, but he'd never guessed she'd been dealing with anything this serious. Add to that the way she'd acted when he'd gone to her house last night....

Something was definitely wrong. She could have just apologized by text, but she'd not only made a point of coming over to do so in person, she'd brought him a pie she had known he would love.

Because she was dreading going home, he realized with sudden clarity. Why? Was it that she didn't want to be alone with her thoughts and whatever problem she was facing? Or was there something more to it?

He opened his mouth to offer to follow her there, just to make sure she was okay, but then she shook her head.

And her careless shrug was less than convincing. "No, I'll be fine. It's just been...a really hard twenty-four hours, that's all."

Logan clamped his fingers tighter around the grips on the crutches to keep from reaching for her. After so many years in undercover work, he had the street equivalent of a PhD in reading people.

Strong as Taylor was, closed-off as she tried to be, right now she looked like she needed a hug in the worst way, and he'd love to be the one who gave it to her. But he wasn't sure if she'd push him away if he did, and didn't want to risk her shutting down.

"Once," he said, and those green-flecked eyes lifted to

his. "Once I had to do something that made me feel that way." A drug trafficker he'd come to admire—even cared deeply about, in a twisted sort of way. Logan had been forced to turn on him at the end of a two-year-long op.

There'd been no way around it. But to make it in undercover work meant you had to get close to the target. Real close. Earn his trust, his loyalty. And it sucked when the target you had to bring down was more like a brother to you than your own flesh and blood.

The look of anguish and betrayal on his friend's face when the bust happened had haunted Logan for a long time afterward. Even now he got an occasional twinge when he thought of Santos rotting away in a federal prison in Colorado.

Taylor searched his eyes for a long moment. "And did you... Eventually did you learn to live with your decision?"

That glimpse of vulnerability from her shredded his heart. He wished he could dive into her head and see what the hell was going on in there. But he wouldn't lie to her.

"Mostly." That op had been his last in undercover. He'd applied for FAST the following week and hadn't looked back since. Except for in his guilt-riddled dreams.

Her long lashes lowered and she gave a slow nod. He'd never seen her this defenseless, this sad. He ached to hold her, make it better somehow, but he couldn't help if she wouldn't let him in and he didn't want to scare her away by moving too fast.

"You know, not to brag, but I'm pretty decent with advice about stuff like that. I mean, if my ex-wife still calls me up to ask my advice, then I must be, right?"

She smiled a little, but it didn't reach her eyes. It was like someone had hit a dimmer switch and turned down the light inside her. It bothered him and roused his protectiveness all at once. He wanted to make sure she was okay.

"I guess you must." She reached for the knob. "Well, thanks again."

"Hey." Before he could overthink it or question his actions, he set one crutch against the wall and reached out to cup the side of her face.

Taylor froze, her gaze jerking to his, no fear there, thank God, only surprise and maybe a little wariness. He'd been wanting to touch her for a while now, and was only sorry it had taken this to give him the opportunity.

He held her like that for a moment, stroking his thumb over the softness of her cheek as he searched her eyes, wishing he knew what had put those shadows there. And whose ass he could kick to make them disappear. "I'm here, okay? If you ever need someone to talk to, you can talk to me."

For a moment she stared back at him in stunned silence, whether because of the intimate touch or the offer, he didn't know. He took advantage of it and shifted his hand around to cradle the back of her head, his fingers moving gently in her soft, shiny hair.

She was tough to read but he caught a glimpse of something in her eyes as they stared at each other that made his heart turn over. A deep, empty sadness that made him ache inside.

"Thank you," she murmured.

She wasn't going to tell him. Disappointed but not all that surprised, Logan dropped his hand and straightened, giving her back the space that seemed to make her feel safe. "Anytime."

He shut the door behind her, the light scent of her still hanging in the air. For more than a minute he stood there, fighting with himself. His instinct told him to get in his truck and drive to her place, at least do a perimeter check to make sure she was safe.

God dammit. What was wrong?

He hobbled back to his recliner, but his mind wouldn't

shut off. Something really bad was going on with her, he knew it in his gut. And he'd go fucking crazy sitting here on his ass without making sure she was okay.

He made it a full ten minutes before he got up, grabbed his keys and headed out the door.

Chapter Nine

❯❯❯◇❮◇❮◇❮◇❮❮

Taylor barely remembered the drive home from Logan's place, too preoccupied by that unexpected show of tenderness from such a big, tough man.

His touch and the way he'd cupped her face, then the back of her head had been protective, yet loaded with the possibility of so much more. Her scalp still tingled where his fingers had caressed her, the ghostly reminder of his hold stirring something deep inside her that had been asleep for a long time.

If you ever need someone to talk to, you can talk to me.

It had been the last thing she'd ever expected him to say. They didn't know each other well, and she hadn't thought he was the kind of guy who would care about her problems.

More shocking even than his concern, she'd actually *wanted* to tell him what was going on. He just had this way about him that made her want to confide in him. Which was totally unlike her. But hell, the man's ex-wife still called to talk to him about stuff. That told her a lot about his character. Whatever faults he might have, at his core he was a good guy.

She hit the button on her sun visor to close the garage door and slid out of the car, looking forward to a hot bath and binge watching a few recorded episodes of her favorite mystery drama.

When she opened the door to the mudroom, two things registered at once. The smell of something rich and garlicky hung in the air, and the light on the alarm system keypad was glowing green instead of red.

She jerked around to face the kitchen, her gaze sliding past it to the adjoining living room. A jolt of panic shot through her and she barely stifled a yelp when she saw Dillon sitting there on her couch.

He draped an arm casually over the back of the couch as he stared back at her. "Hey, where you been?"

Jesus.

Willing her heart back down her esophagus, she uncurled her fingers from around the doorknob, staying the urge to rush back to her car and escape. What was he doing here? Why the hell had he broken into her house? And…cooked, apparently? What the hell was going on?

"Dillon, God. How did you get in here?" She'd set the alarm. She never left the house without setting the alarm. How had he disabled it? What other skills did he have in his bag of criminal tricks now?

He shrugged like it was no big deal, his dark gaze fixed on her. "You didn't return my calls, so I decided to come over and wait for you. I just wanted to make sure we're okay."

They weren't okay. They were the furthest thing from okay. And she hadn't taken his calls because the number had come up as unknown. One of the techs at the agency had tried to trace the number, to no avail. Cartel members were notoriously vigilant about ensuring no one could trace them.

Her pulse drummed in her ears as she stood there in

indecision. He must know that she'd reported his visit to the agency. So why would he risk coming here now, and breaking into her place? It made no sense. Was he that confident of her loyalty to him? Did he think she wouldn't report him now? Because he would lose that bet. She was pissed.

He was sitting there on her couch so calmly, fucking with her head, and she hated it, hated how off-balance he made her feel. Like she was being paranoid and making too much of this. He seemed so relaxed and non-threatening, having made himself at home while she'd been at work, as though he didn't have a care in the world and wasn't worried in the slightest about being a wanted cartel member. God, she was so confused.

He stood and strode into the kitchen like he owned the place, gestured to the island. "Figured you hadn't gotten around to eating yet, so I brought some dinner over. Nothing fancy."

Pizza. He'd brought her pizza.

She stared at the box, her mind flashing back to that night so long ago when her selfish actions had cost him a beating. Was the reminder deliberate? Something to play up her guilt and the sense that she owed him?

She didn't know what the hell to think right now.

"And I got us a bottle of wine, too." He held it up with a little smile then waved her into the kitchen. "Come on, come put your feet up and relax for a while."

She didn't move, trying to figure out what his game was. "You broke into my house."

"I did." Another trademark, charming grin as he took two wineglasses down from her cabinet.

"How did you disable my alarm?" She'd made sure he couldn't see the keypad when she'd input the code last night.

"I have my ways."

The sinister edge to his words set her nerves jangling.

"You need to leave."

At that he paused, those brown eyes locking with hers. And something about the look in them sent a shiver of warning down her spine. "Not yet."

"Yes. Now."

He lowered the hand holding the stems of the wineglasses and tilted his head a fraction, watching her with an almost disappointed expression. "Taylor. Seriously?"

Her fingers twitched at her side, her stomach in knots. She hated hurting him if he was truly here for the right reasons, but what the hell did he expect her to do? He'd broken into her freaking house and she had no doubt he was embedded with the wrong people.

He was a criminal. She had to call her boss and tell him about this, then assist in trying to arrest Dillon. It was either that, or lose her job and the stellar reputation she'd worked so hard to build at the agency.

When she still didn't move, Dillon sighed, turned his back on her and headed back toward the couch, leaving her there staring after him in confusion. "Come on, sit down. I need to talk to you about something. It's important."

Something about that sigh—the resigned quality to it—and his leaden tone made the back of her nape prickle. Whatever he had to tell her, it wasn't good. And he wouldn't have shown up here again tonight, let alone have broken into her damn house and risk her reporting him unless it was for a really good reason.

Dread slithered in the pit of her stomach as she considered what could possibly be that important. The urge to run for her vehicle was strong, but he'd likely catch her before she could get her car out of the garage. Darting out the back door and hopping her fence might be her best chance of escape.

When Dillon looked back from the living room and

saw her still standing in the mudroom instead of following his bidding, his nonthreatening mask slipped, signaling his patience had come to an abrupt end.

His deep brown eyes chilled as he stared back at her from across the length of the room. "Get in here and sit down, Taylor," he snapped, his voice cold enough to send a wave of goose bumps over her arms. "*Now.*"

Dillon didn't take his eyes off her as she moved hesitantly toward him, her gait and posture rigid, expression full of mistrust. That hurt him more than it should have, considering he deserved it.

At least she was doing as he'd said. For a moment there he'd thought he might have to actually grab her and force her to sit down here with him.

"You normally work such long hours?" he asked as she sat on the couch opposite him, trying to put things back on a friendlier footing.

Her body was motionless, but he could tell she was coiled and ready to bolt if he made a wrong move. It wouldn't matter if she did, because he'd catch her. "Yes, when I'm working on a case." Her tone was so icy he was surprised her breath didn't fog as she spoke.

He poured her a glass of wine. "Working on a big one now?"

She crossed her arms over her chest rather than take it. "Yes."

With a mental shrug at her rebuff, he took a sip for himself and settled back against the couch. There were things he had to know before he made his next decision. "Hear anything about me?"

"Several things, actually."

This wasn't going at all according to plan. He'd intended to charm her, redirect her out of this stiff and wary attitude, but he could already tell that wasn't going to work. Hell, he should have known better. Taylor had always been too smart for her own good.

He'd been looking for proof about her involvement with the Baker case, and her reaction to him tonight was it. Although breaking into her house had been heavy-handed and he'd known it would set off alarm bells for her.

She definitely knew what he'd done, must have reported him, and might even be investigating him. That put him in a hell of a predicament, one that even their shared past couldn't erase.

As of today, they were enemies in this war, and his path was already clear. Everything else was out of his hands at this point. Still, his boss had wanted him to ask her, so he would. Even though he was already certain what her answer would be.

"So I'm guessing this means you did a little digging about me today," he said, and sipped more wine, barely even tasting it as he awaited her answer.

She didn't deny it, just kept staring at him with that set, accusing look on her face.

He summoned up a wry smile and watched her for a moment. "Guess it wouldn't do me any good to try to bribe you, huh?"

Taylor didn't smile back, her expression as guarded as her body language. "You're joking."

Not at all. "Of course I'm joking." Although it would have made things a hell of a lot easier if she'd been open to the idea. At least hear him out and consider taking money or some other kind of favor in exchange for information about what the DEA had on him and the other cartel members.

An informant in her position would have been invaluable to him and the cartel itself—maybe even more so because she was an analyst instead of a field agent. She had access to the inner financial workings of the investigation. Information he and the cartel needed, to figure out how to protect themselves and their investments going forward.

If she'd agreed to his proposition then he could have granted her protection. Now… His hands were tied where she was concerned.

"Is that what you came here to ask me?"

"I came to say goodbye, actually." That much was true. He'd taken a calculated but necessary risk in coming here tonight when he'd been almost certain she'd reported him to the DEA either last night or today. "And…to warn you."

She lifted her chin, her stony gaze pinned on him. "About what?"

"You need to be careful."

"Of what? You?" She meant the words to be angry, but he heard the hurt behind them and a painful twinge needled his conscience.

This time his smile was sad. And as genuine as his next words. "I don't want to see you get hurt."

"And why would I get hurt? I haven't done anything wrong, and I'm careful about protecting myself." She aimed another hard look at him. "Except with you, apparently."

In a way, she was right. She hadn't done anything wrong. It was a shit situation, plain and simple. But she hadn't been nearly careful enough.

He gave her a slow nod and put on a grin, though his heart felt like it was being crushed in a vise. He'd have given anything for this to end differently. "Well. Sorry to disturb your evening."

Tipping the glass up, he drained the rest of the wine with one swallow, wishing it was a quadruple shot of vodka or whiskey instead. He wanted to get drunk out of his fucking mind just to escape this mess for a little while.

He stood and carried his empty glass to the kitchen, where he rinsed it out in the sink and put it in the dishwasher so she wouldn't have to, uncaring that he'd left both fingerprints and traces of DNA on the glass. His prints had been entered into the federal database a long time ago now.

If a forensics team came in to gather physical evidence of him being here, it still wouldn't help them find him. He had too many contacts, too many people who owed him favors, and there were so many places he could go to ground.

Taylor's quiet footfalls on the wood floor behind him stopped at the edge of the kitchen. "So what now?" she asked.

He turned to face her and shrugged. "You tell me."

She didn't answer.

"You gonna call it in as soon as I leave?" Even if she did, he had plenty of time to get away. He'd go to one of his underground connections and lie low for a day or two until some decisions had been made.

"I have to tell them. You coming here tonight forced my hand. It's my job and my reputation on the line otherwise, and I already lied once to protect you."

Fondness and pride filled him at the news. She'd still been loyal to him, tried to protect him even after all this time. "I'm touched."

"Well don't be. It almost got me put on probation, and I won't do it again."

"Not even if it saved my life?"

A tiny frown appeared in the center of her forehead, and he could see the worry she was trying to hide. Concern for him, even after everything he'd done. He didn't deserve to have her in his life. Never had.

"Dillon, what..." She stopped and drew in a deep breath, regret clear on her face. "I can't help you now. I just can't."

Out of nowhere, loneliness arrowed him straight in the chest. "I know."

Her gaze was steady on his, full of regret. "You can't come back here."

"I know. But I couldn't leave without at least saying goodbye properly." He gave a humorless chuckle.

Last time he'd left her, he hadn't had time to say goodbye. That had bothered him for a long time, almost as much as the feeling that he'd deserted her in that house with that bastard before Janet had stepped in and pulled her out of there.

"Even in the old days when things were shitty and we had nothing, we still had each other, didn't we?"

Her smile was as sad as her eyes. "Yes."

"And we always stood up for each other. No matter what, we were loyal to each other right until the end."

She lowered her gaze. "Yeah." Now her voice was barely above a murmur.

Despite what she may think of him and his choices, he still cared about her. Hell, he still loved her in his own way. She'd been the sister he'd never had, and the only person in the world he'd trusted. None of that mattered any more, though.

A painful stab of grief ripped through him, so intense it stole his breath for a moment. He should be used to loss by now. But Taylor was the only glimmer of light in his dark past. Losing her meant losing the only remaining link to his humanity.

He cleared his throat. "Well. I'd better get a head start before you call the cops."

They stood there facing each other across the space of the silent kitchen, and even from where he stood he saw the sheen of tears behind the lenses of her glasses. "Can I get a hug goodbye?" he asked softly, letting his gaze rove over every part of her face, so he could memorize every last detail of it.

She pressed her lips together and pulled in a deep breath, then nodded. He met her halfway and pulled her into a tight hug. To his surprise, she clung to him, face pressed into his chest just as she'd done when things had been really bad in their foster home. The second one for her, and one of many for him.

"Will you promise me something?"

She stiffened. "What?" she asked, a note of suspicion creeping into her voice.

He pressed a kiss to the top of her head. Did she sense how final this was? "Promise me you'll remember me the way I was back then. Before I left." It had killed him to leave her in that house alone, but he'd had to go. The people after him would have hurt her to punish him.

Her hair rubbed against his lips as she nodded. "Okay."

One more kiss to the top of her head, then he released her and walked out the front door without looking back. She didn't follow him. But he knew her well enough to trust that she'd give him at least a small head start. If he had to guess, he had maybe five minutes, tops, before she made the call that would launch a manhunt to capture him.

As he walked down the front steps, a painful constriction in his ribcage made it hard to breathe. Some part of him wanted to stop there on the front walkway. Wanted to run back inside and beg for her forgiveness, whisk her out of the country to make sure she was safe and somehow make things right again.

You can't. It's too late now. For both of you.

Sick to his stomach, he forced himself to keep walking.

After slipping around the side of the house and melting into the shadows, he hugged the fence line between Taylor's house and the neighbor on the corner, and jogged the two blocks to the rental car he'd left. He drove around the block once to make sure no one was following him, then doubled back through her neighborhood.

Just as he neared her street, a white pickup turned the

corner, heading toward him. Dillon squinted in the glare of the headlights, his jaw clenching as he read the license plate. The same one that had pulled into Taylor's driveway last night.

He caught a glimpse of the driver, confirming it was the same guy. A coworker, she'd said. Dillon's instincts said otherwise. What was he to her?

Though part of him wanted to hide out and watch the house to see whether the man went inside or not, he couldn't afford the risk. Time was ticking and his window for escape was closing fast. He had to get out of the area.

And he had to deliver the report to his boss. With a heavy heart, he pulled out his phone and dialed him.

Carlos answered in his usual brusque way. "Well? Will she do it?"

"No." And Dillon admired her for that more than she'd ever know. She'd always had such stringent morals, more so than anyone else he'd ever known.

How she'd held on to that internal compass throughout all the shit life had dealt her, he'd never know. Somehow she'd pulled free of the muck and done okay for herself, had stayed on the straight and narrow while he'd fallen into the darkest cracks of society and thrived there. God, he'd pay all the money he had to change things.

"Then deal with her."

Even though he'd expected it, hearing the command to put out a hit on her made his gut clench. "There's another way."

"No, there isn't. The order comes directly from *El Escorpion*. We need the heat turned down on us. She has to be dealt with immediately, and it needs to look like the *Guerreros* did it. She's the senior forensic accountant working the case. *El Escorpion* wants her dead to slow down the investigation and make them look at the *Guerreros*." There was no give in Carlos's voice.

Fuck. When an order like that came from the top, there

was no disobeying or ignoring it.

"You know what to do."

Yeah, carry out a hit bearing the signature of the rival *Guerrero* cartel. Burn her body, cut out her tongue and leave her severed head behind as testament to what happened to those who spoke out about the *Guerreros*.

He took a deep breath, the queasy sensation in his stomach worsening. "I'll handle it."

"No. You're too personally involved. Have one of the boys do it."

"I can't do that." A moment of surprised silence filled the line. Dillon never defied his lieutenant. But he wasn't willing to give in on this one. "I'll do it myself." There was no way he'd let anyone else handle it.

His men and the other *sicarios* he worked with were ruthless, vicious killers. Sending them after Taylor made him want to puke up the wine currently gurgling in his stomach.

He didn't trust any of them to simply put a bullet in her head, kill her quick and clean without fear or pain, and then walk away. He'd seen their handiwork firsthand too many times to have any illusions about what they'd do to her before they finally killed her.

There was no fucking way he would ever allow that to happen to her. Not after how much she'd meant to him.

"All right," Carlos finally said, sounding pissed off. "You have two days, and if it's not taken care of yet, I'll order the hit myself. That's the best I can do."

Dillon's fingers were numb around the phone. "Understood."

The line went dead.

He dropped the phone into his lap, his chest and stomach full of lead as he took the onramp to the highway and headed south, speeding away in the darkness.

The only kindness he could give Taylor now, the only way to protect her from the suffering one of the cartel hit men would inflict, was a humane, unexpected death. Delivered by his own, merciful hand.

Chapter Ten

There was no car in the driveway and Taylor's garage door was shut when Logan parked his truck out front, but her kitchen light was on. It had taken him longer to get here than he would have liked because of road construction, so she'd probably beat him here by a good fifteen minutes or more.

With the help of his crutches he walked to the front door, putting as much weight on his left knee as his pain tolerance would allow. The swim this afternoon had been great for non-weight bearing exercise and range of motion but the PT session afterward had been tough.

He rang the doorbell, anxious to see Taylor. A full minute ticked past without any sound from inside, and he was reaching for the bell again when he heard her footsteps. Her silhouette moved past one of the transom windows beside the front door and she pulled it open a second later.

The friendly greeting he'd been ready with died on his tongue when he saw the look on her face. Pinched and worried. "Hey." What was wrong?

"Hi." She darted a glance past him toward the street, and he could feel the waves of anxiety coming off her.

His hackles went up and he automatically half-turned to face the street, scanning for any threats. There was nothing but an empty sidewalk and a few cars parked along the curb in front of the other houses on this part of the street.

He turned back to her. "Sorry to show up again unannounced, but I just thought you… Are you okay?" *Of course she's not okay. Look at her.*

"I'm…" She let out a frustrated sigh and opened the door wider. "You want to come in for a bit?"

"Yeah, sure." He noted how she quickly locked the door behind him. Something had her spooked, and he wanted to find out what the hell it was.

"Come on in." She headed for the kitchen, her spine stiff beneath the cream-colored top tucked into that snug pencil skirt that hugged her hips and ass to perfection.

Stop staring at her ass. She's upset about something.

Logan took off his boots and followed her. The first thing that hit him was how clean everything was.

No, not just clean. Immaculate. Not a single dish on the counter or in the sink. As he glanced around, he saw the rest of the place was the same. Neat and devoid of clutter to the point of painful.

Taylor grabbed a cloth from the edge of the sink and began wiping down the already gleaming countertops. "You hungry?"

"No, I'm good. Thanks." He wasn't sure how to ask her what was going on.

She hurriedly wiped down the last counter and set the cloth on the divider between the double sink. "Sorry. Go have a seat and rest your leg."

He glanced over at the pristine white couches in the living room, a little hesitant because he might muss them up, but he did as she said. She followed him in, paused to straighten the already straight pile of books she had stacked on the coffee table. Sudoku books, which he guessed was an accountant's idea of fun.

Taylor sat on the couch opposite him, curling her bare legs up under her and tucking her hands in her lap. Even the way she sat was neat and tidy.

She gave him a small frown. "So...why did you come over?"

"You seemed upset at my place, so I wanted to make sure you were okay. I didn't call, because I figured you just wouldn't answer."

The hint of a smile played around the corners of her mouth. "You're not wrong."

"You also seemed worried when I got here. So what's going on?"

She looked down at her lap and began picking at an invisible piece of lint on her skirt. "An old friend showed up uninvited and unannounced, and it stirred up a lot of things best left in the past."

His hackles went up. "He was just here?"

She nodded. "Left a few minutes before you got here."

"You were worried he'd come back." Maybe Logan should take a look around the neighborhood, just to be sure the dude had left.

Another nod.

"Who is he?"

She pushed to her feet and began moving around the room, fiddling with a stack of books in the bookshelf, repositioning things she'd placed on the shelves. And she didn't look at him once while she did it. "Dillon. He was my foster brother."

Foster brother? "How long ago was this?"

"I was thirteen when he left. We'd lived together for just under three years."

"And he just showed up tonight out of the blue?"

"No." She stopped, seemed to struggle with herself

before continuing, still avoiding looking his way. "We've kept in touch off and on through the years, mostly through a social worker we were both close to."

So she'd been a foster kid too? He didn't dare ask about it, afraid she'd stop talking.

"It's been years since we last spoke, but apparently he called the social worker and asked for my number, because he was in town, heard I moved here, and wanted to get together. I agreed to meet him for dinner. He cancelled on me last night, which was why I went over to Jamie and Charlie's for a while. When I got home, he was here waiting for me."

She didn't sound happy about it, and Logan didn't like where this was heading. Way fucking creepy.

Taylor paused, let out a deep breath. "Wait, I have to back up. Okay." She turned to face him finally, fidgeting with a book in her hands. Her agitation made it clear how much this was bothering her. "Yesterday at work, my boss called me into his office to review some security footage from the Baker party. I spotted Dillon in it, talking with a *Veneno* enforcer."

Holy shit. His expression must have shown his shock, because she nodded.

"Yeah, but it gets worse." She kept turning the book over in her hands. "I didn't speak up. I saw him, and told myself it didn't necessarily mean he was involved in any criminal activity. I didn't want him to be working with them. Even though deep down I knew better."

Logan winced. "So he's involved with the cartel?"

"Yes." She slid the book back into its place on the shelf and returned to the couch, once again tucking her feet beneath her. "Have you guys been getting status updates about the Baker investigation?"

Only when the intel pertained directly with their operations. "Sometimes." He couldn't divulge any details.

She chewed her bottom lip for a moment, then seemed to come to a decision. "I went to my boss today, to tell him about Dillon. Chris had just come from a meeting. Turns out, Dillon isn't just involved with the *Venenos*, he was the one who organized the sub shipment you guys took down the other night in the Bahamas."

No fucking way. His mouth fell open. "Are you serious?"

"Wish I wasn't, believe me."

He dragged a hand over his beard. No goddamn wonder she was upset. "Shit, Taylor... And he just showed up here last night?"

She nodded miserably. "Then again tonight. Except tonight, he didn't wait outside for me. He broke into the house and disabled my alarm system. Was sitting on my couch when I walked in."

Hell. "Did you call the agency?"

"My boss. I'm just waiting to hear back from him."

Not good enough. He reached for his crutches and shoved to his feet. "Show me where your security system is."

She led the way to the mudroom and gestured to the keypad on the wall. "There's a panel in my bedroom too."

He took a look at it, didn't notice any signs of tampering. "He didn't cut any wires."

"No, he knew my password."

Logan cranked his head around to stare at her. "What?"

She flushed, shifted her weight from foot to foot. "I don't even know how he saw it, I was careful to make sure he couldn't see it when I entered it last night."

Well this Dillon had obviously figured out a way around that. Logan's skin was freaking crawling with fear for her. "Did you check the rest of the house after he left?"

"Yes. I didn't notice anything out of place."

That didn't mean a hell of a lot, considering Dillon was

one of the main traffickers for the *Veneno* cartel. He shook his head. The guy could have bugged her place. Or worse. "No wonder you're scared."

Her face fell, and the bad feeling inside him expanded. There was more? "What?" he asked.

"He knows I work for the DEA."

Logan couldn't believe his ears. "You told him?"

"No, of course not," she said, looking annoyed. "But he either suspected it or knew it already before he got here. I think he was testing the waters, so to speak, to see if I knew anything."

"So then it means the cartel is watching you."

"I know. And then tonight Dillon said something that set off alarm bells. In an off-hand way he asked if I'd be open to accepting a bribe. He was trying to make light of it, but I think there was something to it. Like maybe he was hoping my loyalty to him would win out and I'd turn spy for him and the cartel."

His insides were buzzing. Did Dillon or someone else in the cartel plan to make an example of her if she didn't cooperate? "Okay, I've heard enough. Go pack a bag, and I'll get you out of here. You can stay at my place until we figure out what the hell is going on here."

"I can't just—" She stopped when a ringtone split the air, and pulled out her phone. "It's my boss," she said, hurriedly striding back to the living room as she answered. Logan grabbed his other crutch and followed her while she updated her boss about what had happened, and about the bribe Dillon had mentioned.

He stopped dead when she halted and gasped. She was facing away from him, her body completely still as she listened, one hand pressed to her chest.

"You're sure? Oh my God, I… Yes, of course. Yes. I understand. I'll be here." She ended the call and spun to face him. Her face was white as paper, her eyes haunted.

"What?" he demanded, on alert, barely resisting the

urge to rush to her.

"The team found out something else. From two of the suspects who were arrested the night of the sub bust." She hesitated.

Frustration pulsed through him. "My security clearance is higher than yours. Just tell me."

"They each gave a sworn statement saying that Dillon is the one who ordered Baker's pilot to kill him."

Logan had been there when the murder happened, but not as close as Jamie and Charlie when the helo pilot who was supposed to pick up Baker shot him down instead. Jamie had returned fire, killing the pilot, and the bird had crashed moments later, erupting into a ball of fire and incinerating any evidence they might have found useful.

Until now.

"So then Dillon isn't just your average trafficker for them," he finished.

Taylor shook her head, looking devastated. And afraid. That fear ripped at his insides, demanded he *do* something.

"He's the right-hand man of one of the cartel lieutenants," she said softly.

This was so fucking bad. Logan couldn't handle that lost, bewildered look on her face a moment longer, couldn't stand there and watch her suffer without doing something. He leaned his crutches against the kitchen counter, limped the few yards to her and pulled her straight into his arms.

She didn't resist, didn't utter a single protest as he gathered her against his chest and wrapped his arms around her. Instead she leaned into him and let out the most heartbroken little sigh he'd ever heard.

He'd already been fired up, all his protective instincts brought to the surface, but that sigh made him want to pick her up and carry her home, keep her at his place while guarding the door with his own weapon. Just so nothing and no one could ever dare threaten her again.

"They're sending a forensics team over to collect evidence," she mumbled into his shirt, the warmth of her breath and the feel of her softness pressed to him spiking his pulse rate. He was only human. He'd been thinking about her for weeks now. "I'm supposed to stay put for now."

"I'll stay with you." Before she could protest he urged her back to the living room, sat on the couch and pulled her straight into his lap.

To his surprise, she didn't resist or even argue. She simply took off her glasses, shifted closer and leaned into his chest, laying her head on his shoulder. Then she curled her body into a ball. Seeking comfort he was only too willing to give.

Savoring her unspoken trust in him and thankful for the chance to be there for her, Logan gently rubbed a hand over her back and just held her without saying anything. He might not be able to make this better for her, but he could damn well ensure she was protected and didn't feel alone right now.

"I can't believe it," she murmured, resting her cheek on him once more. "It's like a bad dream."

Yeah, a total nightmare. He was glad she wanted more comfort because he didn't want to stop holding her. She smelled good too, something light and sweet like vanilla. "Hell of a thing to find out about an old friend."

Her cheek rubbed his shoulder as she nodded. "It probably sounds stupid or naïve now, but I never would have believed he'd put me in this position."

"I'm sorry." He tipped his head forward and brushed a kiss to the top of her head. Damn, she felt good cuddled into him like this, that wall she usually had up to protect herself down for the moment.

They stayed like that for a few minutes until she shifted her weight in his lap. He hadn't been looking for anything when he met her, but his attraction to her was growing every minute, and the feel of her ass sliding against his groin had predictable results. She stiffened and raised her head to stare at him when she felt how hard he'd gotten, but didn't shove away as expected.

She searched his eyes, and he couldn't help but smile at her expression of uncertainty. As though she wasn't sure if she believed he was actually attracted to her. "Can you still see me without those things on?" he asked, to take away any awkwardness she might feel. Her glasses were in her lap.

A startled grin split her face and she let out a short laugh. "Yes."

Reaching one hand up to cup the side of her face, he gave into the need and traced his thumb along her soft cheek. "Good. But not wearing them kind of takes away from the whole sexy librarian vibe you've got going on there."

She scoffed. "Sexy librarian?"

"*So* sexy," he assured her.

Her smile faded away, and something shifted between them, the air taking on an almost electrical charge. She searched his eyes for a long moment, then put a hand on his shoulder and her gaze dipped to his mouth.

He wanted to kiss her so bad he couldn't stand it.

Without giving either of them time to overthink it, Logan leaned in, his fingers sliding around the back of her neck, and sought her lips with his. He kissed her slow and soft at first, but when she curled her fingers into his shoulders and came up onto her knees for more, straddling him in that tight skirt, lust shot through him in a white-hot stream.

Cradling the back of her head with one hand, he wrapped his free arm around her hips and hauled her tight up against his body. She gasped into his mouth, a tiny tremor running through her. Her hands went to his face, framing it between her palms as she almost shyly touched her tongue to his. The silky caress went straight to his head—and his dick, currently straining the front of his fly.

He firmed his grip on her head and took over, barely reining in the hunger roaring through his bloodstream. He'd sensed from the outset that there was fire beneath her cool, professional façade, and he'd been right.

With slow, erotic strokes of his tongue he told her how much he wanted her, how gorgeous and sexy she was. How much he was dying to push her onto her back and undo every one of those buttons on her shirt so he could see what she had on underneath. Cup the breasts he'd been fantasizing about and suck on her nipples until she was writhing and desperate for more.

Too much too fast.

He settled for sucking at her lower lip instead, then the top one, giving her little caresses with his tongue before pressing inside to taste her fully.

With a little moan, Taylor pushed at his shoulders and leaned back to stare at him, breathing hard. Her lips were shiny and swollen, her face flushed, those pretty green-and-brown eyes smoldering with hunger. And surprise.

Breathing a little faster himself, he smoothed her hair back from her face and gave her a slow smile. "Didn't know accountants could kiss like that."

"But I'm a special agent accountant, so that makes me special." Smiling, she bent and pressed her lips to his in a gentle kiss loaded with the promise of so much more.

This time when she eased back he took her face between his hands and looked her dead in the eye. The forensics team would be here soon, but he wasn't going anywhere.

Just as he thought it, headlights cut through the windows flanking the front door. She started to slide off him but he stayed her with both hands on her hips. He squeezed to get her full attention. "I'm staying here with you until I know you'll be safe."

She opened her mouth to argue but he cut her off with a swift, possessive kiss. There was no way he would let her stay here alone after what had happened. And the agency better damn well assign her some protection.

"Okay," she murmured, and let her lips linger against his for another few heartbeats before getting up to answer the door.

He stopped her. "You stay put. I'll get it." He grabbed his crutches and headed for the door.

Chapter Eleven

———◇◇◇◇◇———

There had been a few low points in the past five months since moving to D.C. to work for the DEA, but without a doubt, this day had been the suckiest one of them all.

Taylor was sick at heart as she drove home from the office after a long, miserable day of meetings and interviews with investigators, all about Dillon's connections to the Baker case and *Veneno* cartel.

She'd barely slept last night after the forensics team had finally left, and only because Logan had stayed down the hall in her guest room. He'd waited until she left for work before leaving, and just having him under the same roof had made her feel safer.

The agency had assigned someone to watch her house 24/7 until authorities could find and arrest Dillon. The agent taking the night shift was behind her now, following her home through the dreary April rainstorm. And her stupid conscience kept needling her about Dillon.

All day long she'd obsessed about the entire situation, torn between anger toward Dillon and guilt, even though the logical part of her knew she had nothing to feel guilty about. *He'd* put her in this position. He'd brought this on himself, and he'd basically threatened her. Anger felt a hell of a lot better than the guilt had.

She pressed a hand to her stomach as she turned onto her street, the windshield wipers slapping back and forth. At lunch she'd grabbed a sandwich from the cafeteria, but it hadn't settled well.

Once again, the highlight of her day had been Logan. Even though he'd been busy with medical appointments and team-related business he'd checked in with her by text a couple of times throughout the day.

The intensity of that kiss last night had stunned her. There'd been no awkwardness, no fumbling. He'd taken complete control, and now she was hungry to see how that translated into more than just kissing. It made her stomach flutter just to think of it. But she wasn't interested in casual sex. She needed far more than attraction before she was willing to sleep with a guy, needed emotional intimacy to go with it. Which was why she hadn't had many partners.

Since she wasn't sure what he wanted from her and he was otherwise occupied for the evening, she was looking forward to curling up in front of a warm fire with a hot cup of soup and one of her Sudoku puzzles for a while.

Once she'd parked in her garage, she waited for the agent to park across the street and jog up to meet her. In his early thirties with medium brown hair, he held his black jacket over his head to shield him from the rain.

After disarming the security system, she stepped back and waited for him to sweep the house. The agent in charge of watching it had reported no incidents, but they weren't taking any chances.

"All's clear," he told her a few minutes later, slipping his weapon back into the holster at his hip. "I'll keep watch tonight from across the street. You've got my number?"

The agency wanted him posted close enough to her house for him to keep watch, but not in her driveway in case Dillon or anyone else was planning to come back. If anyone did, they'd be arrested. "Yes. Thanks."

"No problem. Have a good night."

Ha. Not likely, but at least she was home now and could at least try to unwind and find something to take her mind off everything for a bit.

In the kitchen she opened a can of vegetable soup with noodles and poured it into her favorite mug to nuke it, then popped a couple pieces of frozen cheese bread into her toaster oven to bake. While it cooked, she carried the soup up to the loft and started the fire she kept laid in the grate.

The crackle and flicker of the flames instantly eased her anxiety level. Curled up on the couch with a throw blanket over her legs and Nimbus purring away in her lap, she ate the soup and set the cup on the coffee table with a relieved sigh. A bubble bath was definitely in order later, but right now she'd just rest her eyes for a few minutes.

Laying her head back on the cushion she wedged against the arm of the couch, she closed her eyes. Nimbus settled deeper into her lap and curled up with his fluffy tail over his nose.

When her eyes snapped open sometime later, the fire had died down to a mere flicker. A grayish haze hung in the air, and the acrid smell of smoke stung her nose.

The cheese toast. "Shit."

She threw the blanket off her lap. Nimbus leaped down, his ears flattened against his head. Taylor ran past him, down the steps to the main level, and rushed into the kitchen. The smoke hung in a thick layer near the ceiling.

The moment she came in sight of the toaster oven, she saw the flames. "Dammit…"

Yanking the electrical cord out of the socket, she grabbed a pair of tongs from the utensil drawer and gingerly opened the toaster oven door. Two hunks of charred, smoldering toast met her gaze, little flames licking around the edges. She coughed as she hauled the pieces out and dumped the cremated remains in the sink.

God, who knew two little pieces of bread could make so much smoke?

Eyes watering, she pushed open the sliding window above the sink and grabbed a tea towel to flap it around in an attempt to clear the air. Wait, her smoke detector hadn't gone off as she opened the window? And just how freaking much smoke did there have to be before it registered a problem?

Even more annoyed, she marched into the hallway to stare up at it on the ceiling, then noticed the little green light wasn't on. Muttering to herself, she first crossed the room to open a few more windows, then grabbed the step ladder from the hall closet and carted it over to the smoke detector.

Flapping her hands around to create a clean pocket of air to work in, she pulled the plastic cover off. And froze.

No batteries.

That just wasn't possible, because she'd replaced them just after Christmas, something she did every year as a precaution. She lowered the cover to her side and stared up at the unit, thinking fast.

She'd had an electrician in a few weeks ago to fix a faulty breaker and he'd done an inspection for her. Would he have removed the batteries to test it and forgotten to put them back in? Or...

Dillon.

Even as she thought it, she felt terrible. And ridiculous. What, he'd known she would come home tonight and start a fire by burning dinner? If he'd wanted to kill her, smoke inhalation from a freak incident in the kitchen wasn't probably a top five choice. Unless she was missing something? She had to be missing something.

"God, you're a hot mess," she muttered to herself. Her nerves were more shot than she'd realized.

Climbing down, she got some fresh batteries from her kitchen "junk drawer"—a misnomer in her house, because as with everything else, it was neatly organized—and put them in the smoke detector.

The alarm went off within seconds, screeching in her ear.

Problem solved.

It took another twenty minutes for her to create enough human-powered wind with both arms flapping tea towels around to push the smoke out the windows she'd opened. When it was finally safe to breathe, she closed everything back up and cleaned the kitchen.

Since there was no more cheese bread to be had and she wasn't all that hungry anymore, she poured herself a bubble bath. Soaking in the vanilla-scented water in the dimly-lit bathroom was heaven, and soon she was yawning. Changed into her favorite, ultra soft sleep shirt, she crawled between her cozy, cotton flannel sheets and read for a while.

She checked her phone first, saw Logan had messaged her while she'd been dealing with the smoke, and smiled. She wasn't sure what was going to happen between them moving forward, but she had no regrets about kissing him last night. In fact, she wanted a whole lot more than just kissing with him. And it touched her that he'd volunteered to stay the night to make sure she was safe.

Hey, hot stuff. You home safe yet?

From anyone else the hot stuff comment would probably have irritated the shit out of her, but from him she didn't mind. She liked knowing he found her hot. *Yes.*

Nearly started my kitchen on fire by burning dinner, but all is well now.

Ouch! I guess I should never ask you to cook for me then?

She laughed. *Probably safer not to. You still at work?*

Yes. Just finished a team meeting. Want me to come over when I'm done here?

She hesitated. She had to admit she felt safer with him in the house, but she didn't want to rush things between them and if he stayed she wasn't sure if either one of them would be able to put the brakes on. *It's okay. Long day and I've got a babysitter watching the house from outside.*

You sure?

Yes, but thanks. Her thumb paused on the electronic keys. She didn't want to seem like she was blowing him off.

Dinner tomorrow? If you have time.

Getting out of the house, especially with him, seemed like the best idea she'd had in a long time. *I'd love that.*

It's a date. Sleep tight.

A date she would actually look forward to. She bit her lip, couldn't help but smile. *You too.*

She was still smiling as she picked up her e-reader and opened to the book she was partway through. After an hour, she finished the chapter she was on, turned out the light, and fell asleep in minutes.

Only to jolt awake in complete darkness sometime later to the bleating of a loud, shrill alarm. Confused, heart thudding, she threw back the covers and surged to her feet. She didn't smell any more smoke than there had been before bedtime.

Hurrying to her bedroom door, she put the back of her hand against it to check for heat, just in case. It wasn't hot. She cracked the door open and stuck her head out into the hallway. Only a tiny haze of smoke near the ceiling. So what was with the alarm?

And then it dawned on her that this alarm was different from the one she'd heard earlier. And that the smoke detector also had a carbon monoxide sensor in it.

Unease trickled down her spine as she stood there for another moment in indecision. Maybe the smoke from earlier had built up enough to lower the oxygen level.

Deciding it was smarter to err on the side of caution rather than assume it was a false alarm, she hastily threw on her robe, grabbed her phone and headed for the front door, dialing the agent watching her house from across the street. It rang three times before she got to the door, and he didn't answer.

His voicemail picked up as she stepped outside into the darkness and looked around, her bare feet cold on the wet cement of her walkway. Hunching under the robe while the light rain pattered down on her, she darted across the street and headed for the gray sedan at the opposite curb.

A few strides from the driver's side, her gaze landed on the small, round hole in the window, the glass spider-webbing outward.

The agent was slumped in his seat, his head lolling to the side.

No.

She grabbed the door handle and jerked it, but it was locked. "Corey, can you hear me? Corey!" She banged on the window.

He didn't move, and as she leaned closer to squint through the rain-streaked window she saw the blood spattering the passenger side of the car.

"Jesus!"

Panic punched through her. Her fingers were stiff as she dialed 911. With the phone to her ear and her back to the car, she scanned up and down the street for a threat. Had whoever had shot Corey taken off? A crawling sensation at the base of her spine told her otherwise.

Dillon or someone from the *Veneno* cartel had done this. And they were still watching.

She ran back across the street and pounded on her neighbor's door just as the operator answered.

Chapter Twelve

T he *Veneno* cartel's days were numbered. Its founders just didn't realize it yet.

En route. Be there in about twenty minutes or so.

In the back of the cab taking her to the Virginia headquarters of the DEA's FAST units, Special Agent Jaliya Rabani sent the text message then set her phone down in her lap and rubbed at her dry, burning eyes.

The last leg of her trip from Kabul had been delayed at Heathrow due to mechanical problems, adding another four hours to her already grueling journey. She'd have killed for a two-hour nap before this upcoming meeting, but FAST's Commander, Taggart, had already waited long enough for her arrival, and he'd also called in his entire team for this.

Okay. Meet us in the briefing room, Taggart responded.

Will do.

With a sigh, she leaned her head back against the seat as the lights of Alexandria rushed by in a blur outside her window. She'd been called here for high-level meetings to do with the *Venenos*, based on intel she'd recently uncovered back in Afghanistan.

Strange, to think of that struggling country more as home than the States now, but after living over there so much over the past few years—far more time than she'd spent back home in Michigan in the same period—it made sense. There was a lot about the country of her father's birth that she disliked, hated even, but it was also familiar and dear to her. That was another reason why she was doing this job, to stem the tide of opium flowing through the porous, mountainous borders. She was convinced that drugs were the scourge of humanity.

Every shipment of opium in Afghanistan meant money in the hands of terrorist organizations. Money to buy weapons and power so they could wage war and subjugate the helpless. Now their poisonous reach was having real consequences here in the U.S. and Mexico, and she was going to help put an end to it.

The cab pulled into the parking lot of FAST headquarters and stopped in front of the main building. She paid the driver, grabbed her suitcase and backpack, and headed up the concrete walkway to the front door.

The lobby lights were on, but no one was at reception because it was so late. She let herself in using the key code she'd been given, and looked around for directions to the briefing room. Lights down the hallway to her right seemed to indicate someone must be down there, so she went that way, rolling her suitcase behind her. Within moments, it was clear she'd taken a wrong turn. Nothing but empty offices met her eyes, and she didn't hear any voices or other signs of life.

After trailing back to her starting point, she tried another hallway, this one not as well lit. A few steps in, she stopped again, unconvinced she was in the right area.

Frustrated and beyond tired, she started to pull out her

phone but a man stepped out of a doorway in front of her about halfway up the hall. A well-built man with short, dark hair and a pair of shoulders that stretched the fabric of the dark T-shirt he wore above dark jeans that hugged a tight, shapely backside.

"Excuse me," she said.

No response. He had his phone out, his head bent as he stared intently at the screen and kept walking away from her.

"Excuse me," she called out, a little louder.

Still nothing.

What the hell, was he deaf?

To hell with this bullshit. She was a special agent with critical intel to deliver. Taggart and his team were waiting for her somewhere in this damn building, and she needed to get to the briefing room ASAP, not continue wandering aimlessly along the corridors like a rat caught in a maze.

Jaliya released the handle of her suitcase and planted her hands on her hips, fresh out of patience as she stared after the stranger with the wide shoulders and fine ass she shouldn't be noticing. "*Excuse* me. Little help over here?"

****

Since it was past midnight, Special Agent Zaid Khan hadn't expected to receive the text message. As he read it, he was more annoyed than anything else. He'd been chatting with this girl he'd met online for a month now, had finally worked up the nerve to ask her out last week because they seemed to click, and she'd just bailed on him.

Fine. He wouldn't let it bother him. Maybe she wasn't even real. Since he'd never met her in person, for all he knew she could actually be a sixty-year-old grandmother in real life. He shook his head at himself. The whole online dating thing was like navigating a frickin' minefield.

Sliding his phone back into his pocket, he headed down the hallway at FAST headquarters and rolled his shoulders to ease the tension. Probably better this way. He was tired. After the team's constant activity of the past ten days he was beat, and now he was free to go home and sleep in, instead of having to get up and go on a breakfast date in the morning. First dates were always so damn awkward anyway.

An extra few hours' sleep seemed like a better and better alternative all the time. The team had the next two days off, unless something else came up, and he intended to make the most of them. Mountain biking, or vegging on the couch? He had two speeds, stop and go, so it could go either way.

"*Excuse* me. Little help over here?"

Huh? He stopped mid-stride and swung around at the lightly-accented, irritated feminine voice behind him.

A woman maybe in her late twenties or early thirties with long, dark hair stood at the end of the hallway, watching him with an exasperated look on her face. Had she been calling after him? There was something familiar about her, too.

He raised his eyebrows, confused. "Sorry?"

She let out an impatient sigh, her hands planted on her cargo-pant-clad hips. Her nicely curved hips. "I asked if you could point me to Commander Taggart." Her voice held the hint of a British accent.

He'd been so deep in his head, he hadn't heard her. "Sure. Sorry, didn't hear you the first time. His office is at the end of the hall. Is he expecting you?"

"Yes."

"Okay, follow me." He pointed in the direction he'd been headed. "I'll show you."

"Thank you." Her strides were quick and confident as she approached him, the strap of a backpack hitched over one shoulder.

Zaid held out his hand when she got close. "Zaid."
Yep, he'd seen her before somewhere, but couldn't place
her. It was driving him nuts. Normally he was awesome
at remembering faces and names.

She shook his hand, surprising him with the firmness
of her grip. "Jaliya." Those dark chocolate eyes did a
quick assessment of him in his fatigues, her long, thick
lashes casting shadows over the tops of her high
cheekbones. "You one of his men?"

"Yes."

"Brilliant, then you can show me to the briefing room
instead."

Zaid blinked. She was going into a team briefing with
them? "Uh, sure."

The hint of a smile quirked the corner of her mouth as
she fell in step with him, dragging a rolling suitcase with
her. "It's okay. I'm your intel officer for the briefing."

"Oh." Wasn't too often they got a female IO, and to
his recollection never one as good-looking as her. "You
work here in D.C.?"

"No. Kabul, mostly."

Then it hit him. He snapped his fingers, his expression
brightening. "Knew it. I saw you there this past March."
She'd been working intel at headquarters there, but they'd
never been formally introduced.

She eyed him for a moment before looking back down
the hallway. "Sorry, I don't remember you."

That shouldn't have dinged his already bruised ego,
but it did. "You still stationed there, or did you transfer
here?"

"Still there. I'm just here to help with a special case."
Her cell rang. She pulled it from her pocket, answered,
and began a conversation in rapid Pashto.

Zaid caught every word, and noted that she spoke it
like a native, without any trace of an accent. He didn't

have one either, because both his parents had been born and raised in Afghanistan and had taught him both Pashto and English growing up here in the States, in addition to some Urdu.

He listened as they walked the rest of the way to the team briefing room. Information about various warlords and traffickers in and around central and southern Afghanistan. Heavy shit requiring a hefty security clearance.

When they reached the door, Zaid held out a hand to indicate the room. She nodded in acknowledgment and ended her conversation. She slipped her phone back into the front pocket of her cargo pants as they stepped inside.

The rest of the guys were already seated inside, and Taggart stood up front, the lights glinting off his dark blond hair. Behind him the big screen showed pictures of some of the *Veneno* cartel members they were currently interested in. The team commander gave Jaliya a small smile and beckoned her up front with him.

Zaid grabbed a seat next to Logan and watched her.

"Who's she?" Logan whispered, his knee wrapped up with a compression bandage. Zaid still felt bad for causing the injury.

"Apparently she's an IO on this case."

Logan's reddish-brown eyebrows went up and he settled back into his chair, his left leg straightened out in front of him. Zaid had looked at the knee earlier today. The swelling was going down but it was a long way from being healed. Logan was chomping at the bit to get back to training full time with the rest of them, but if he pushed too hard too fast, it would set him back to the recovery start line and delay his return even longer.

"Boys, meet SA Jaliya Rabani, Foreign Cooperative Investigations agent working out of Kabul," Taggart announced in his booming voice, his light turquoise eyes sweeping the room. "The agency asked her here to assist with their investigation of the *Veneno* cartel, and she's been briefed about our operation in the Bahamas. She's got intel pertinent to our latest targets." He nodded at her. "Take it away."

"Thank you." Jaliya took center stage and got right to the point, mentioning names while another agent in the back of the room handled the power point presentation. Zaid paid close attention to her body language. Poised, confident. No nonsense.

Hot.

He shook off the unprofessional thought and focused on what she was saying. Wasn't hard, because he liked the sound of her voice.

"There's been a sharp increase in recent activity linking the Taliban and other terrorist organizations in Afghanistan and the surrounding region to the *Veneno* cartel."

Zaid didn't bother hiding his surprise. *Venenos* working with the Taliban?

She paused to wait for the agent working the power point presentation to bring up an image of a map detailing smuggling routes in and out of southern and eastern Afghanistan. "The latest intel we have points to the *Veneno* cartel exporting opium from the region in exchange for equipment and arms to various groups, in addition to large amounts of cash. Our agents in Kandahar intercepted a payment of US greenbacks being smuggled across the border in a small convoy of trucks carrying drums of oil. The traffickers empty the barrels, fill the bottom of each drum with opium, and cover it with whatever they think will conceal the drugs."

Turning slightly, she watched the screen as various images of the recent seizure flicked past. "Once the traffickers get the opium through the Afghan border, they send it to Karachi or another big port city. From there the shipments are sent to labs in Mexico, where it's cut and added to cocaine and heroin, along with fentanyl."

Zaid crossed his arms over his chest and took in the big picture. During FAST Bravo's most recent rotation over in A-stan, they'd spent the entire four months running around after Taliban leaders smuggling opium into Pakistan through the Khyber Pass. There'd been nothing to suggest any links to the *Venenos*. This was a whole new level of globalization in the drug trade.

"One name that's come up at various points over the past few weeks is a code name, *Víbora*. Viper," she translated, scanning the room with those dark, fathomless eyes.

Their gazes connected for a moment, and in that instant Zaid recognized the timeworn look in them he hadn't noticed before. Jaliya came off as cool and professional, yet he knew without a doubt that she had seen far more violence and death than anyone should ever have to.

It only made him more curious about her and her background.

"Your analysts here in D.C. have been working on finding out this man's identity, and now have reason to believe he's Dillon Wainright."

Zaid stiffened at the same time as Logan sat straight up in his chair beside him. Zaid rubbed a hand over his jaw, a bad feeling expanding in his gut. Wainright was the son of a bitch who'd arranged the sub shipment in the Bahamas. He smuggled opium out of A-stan too?

"Of course your team is now well aware of who he is. And as of last night, we have sworn statements given by prisoners from the Bahamas raid that he was the one responsible for ordering Dean Baker's pilot to kill him a few weeks ago in Long Island."

Wainright was also personally linked to SA Kennedy, the cute forensic accountant Logan had shown an interest in recently. He'd spent the night at her place last night because Wainright had broken into her house and tried bribing her to act as an informant for the cartel.

Zaid could feel the tension coming off Logan. Without looking at him, Zaid set a hand on the guy's shoulder and squeezed once in a show of support. The agency would find Wainright, and nail his ass to the wall for everything he'd done.

Up front, Jaliya continued with the briefing, laying out Wainright's suspected ties to the cartel, his suspected whereabouts, and how he was involved with trafficking in A-stan.

When she finished, she took questions, and it was all over within fifteen minutes. Zaid filed out into the hallway after her with everyone else. Ahead of him, Rodriguez was already on his phone, grinning, no doubt talking to Charlie.

"Anyone up for a beer?" Hamilton asked behind them.

"I'm up for a steak," Kai said from up front.

"Course you are," Freeman piped up in front of Zaid.

"I'll go with you," Zaid said, though not for a beer. He wasn't strict about the way he practiced his religion, at least not compared to a lot of people, but he never touched alcohol. "I'll be DD if anyone wants a ride." He glanced at Logan, who was limping along beside him, apparently determined not to use his crutches. "You in?" he asked, mainly to be polite because Zaid was pretty sure Logan would want to head straight over to Taylor's now.

"No. I'm gonna—" He stopped in mid-sentence when Rodriguez came to a dead halt in the middle of the hallway and looked back at him sharply.

Uh oh... Zaid didn't like that look on his teammate's face. Not at all.

Zaid came to a halt as the rest of the guys ground to a sudden stop and looked at Rodriguez questioningly. The hallway went dead silent. Even Taggart and Jaliya stopped and looked back to see what was going on.

"Yeah, okay. I'll tell him," Rodriguez finished. He lowered the phone and spoke directly to Logan, his expression grim. "Taylor's in trouble. She just found the agent guarding her place with a bullet through his head."

Oh, shit...

Logan stiffened and inhaled sharply. "What?"

The rest of the guys exchanged loaded glances.

Rodriguez nodded at Logan. "The cops are taking her to our place right now. You coming?"

"Yeah. I'll meet you there."

With a nod, Rodriguez turned and jogged for the exit. Logan picked up his pace, but he was a long way from jogging yet.

Partway down the hallway he twisted his head around and shot a look at Zaid. "Can I swap vehicles with you? If anyone's casing her place, they might try to follow the cops. I was at her place last night, and someone could recognize my truck."

"Sure." Zaid fished the keys from his pocket and exchanged with Logan. "I'll follow you out."

Together they hurried for the exit and out into the brightly lit parking lot.

Chapter Thirteen

L ogan parked Zaid's truck in a visitor spot out front
   of Jamie and Charlie's building and jumped out
   just as his teammate called Logan's cell phone.

"You there yet?" Zaid asked.

"Yeah, just pulled up. Thanks for lending me your
truck."

"No problem. Holler if you need anything. I'm gonna
go by the bar in case any of the guys need a ride home
after."

That was why Zaid was so well-liked by everyone on
the team. He looked after them all like they were family.
"Sounds good. See ya."

Without pause he jumped out and rushed for the condo
complex's front door. Charlie buzzed him in. Urgency
beat at him as he took the elevator to their floor. Normally
the stairs would be faster but there was no way his knee
was up to it, and getting to Taylor as fast as possible was
all that mattered.

God, Taylor had to be scared out of her mind, special
agent or not. Another agent shot through the head just in

front of her house. Why hadn't she called him instead of Charlie?

When he finally made it down the hallway, Jamie was waiting at the door for him. "She okay?" Logan demanded.

"Yeah, she's in the living room." Jamie stepped back to let him in.

Logan limped through the kitchen, and his heart did a painful little squeeze when he caught sight of Taylor. She was on the couch next to Charlie, wearing a T-shirt and lounge pants. He'd never seen her in anything but work attire before, and with her glasses on and her hair up in a ponytail she looked impossibly young and vulnerable.

She smiled when she saw him, but it was sad. "You didn't have to come. I'm okay."

Not come? There was no way he wouldn't have come. He needed to make it clear that he cared about her. "You should have called me."

Charlie got up and muttered something about getting drinks for them as she strode for the kitchen, giving them some privacy.

"I didn't want to drag you farther into this mess," Taylor said.

With a frustrated sigh, he closed the distance between them, sank down beside her and immediately pulled her into a hug. "Are you okay?" he murmured against her hair. It smelled faintly of smoke.

She wound her arms around his neck and rested her cheek on the top of his shoulder, making his heart squeeze. "Yes."

"What happened?"

She ran through the night's sequence of events, and at the mention of the disabled smoke/carbon monoxide detector, something hard settled in the pit of his stomach.

"The agent watching my house wasn't answering his phone, so I went out to tell him in person and that's when

I found him."

The idea that the killer might have had his sights on Taylor while she'd stood there in the rain made his blood run cold. He ran a hand up and down her back, relieved that she was okay. "Did the cops find anything wrong with a fireplace or the furnace?" Those were the first two places he'd check.

"The fire department was there when Chris showed up to bring me here. Someone will call me when they figure out what happened." She let out a shaky breath. "The agent who died had a wife and a six-month old daughter."

Logan hugged her tighter. "It wasn't your fault."

"I feel responsible. If I hadn't stayed at my house, this never would have happened."

"You don't know that. It could've happened somewhere else, too. Whoever it was could have followed you wherever you went." Might have even followed her here, which was why he was glad the agency had more eyes watching the place.

He was quiet a moment, debating how to ask the question he needed to. Since there was no gentle way to ask, he just put it out there. "Do you think it was Dillon?"

"I don't know. Maybe. Or maybe someone working with or for him. God, I can't believe he's even capable of something like this, but I guess I can't rule it out."

"I'm just glad you're okay." It didn't matter whether she thought Dillon was behind it or not. The agency would be gunning for him now. Logan didn't believe in coincidences. It had to be Dillon.

She nodded. "I came here because I had to make a decision fast about where to go, and I couldn't think of anywhere else that might be safe. But I'm not staying here. I won't put Charlie and Jamie and everyone else in the building at risk for my sake. Chris is working with the agency to find me somewhere to stay temporarily."

"You could stay with me."

She lifted her head and looked into his eyes, their faces just inches apart. "I appreciate that, thank you. But I don't want to put anyone else in danger."

He could appreciate that, but he was fully prepared to face danger to keep her safe. "Stay with me. I'll take you to my place right now and you can stay there for however long this takes."

"Thanks. But I can't."

Pushing aside his frustration, he let it go. "The offer's there if you change your mind."

The smile she gave him pierced his heart. "Thank you."

He stroked his fingertips over her cheek, savoring the softness of her skin. "What can I do to help?"

"You already have." Taking his face between her hands, she leaned in and pressed a gentle kiss to his lips.

His protective instincts were on full overdrive. Every cell in his body demanded that he plunge his hand into her hair and take her mouth, claim her even in that way, but he wasn't going to risk embarrassing her that way when they were on Jamie and Charlie's couch in full view from the kitchen.

He eased back and stroked her face again. "Does your security system have a video camera?"

"No." She was quiet a moment. "Dillon's nothing like the person I used to know," she murmured against his shoulder. "If it was him, I don't know what I'll do."

Finding out someone had tried to kill you was bad enough. Wondering whether it was a trusted friend was a hundred times worse. Logan had so many questions, about Dillon, about her early life and her time in foster care. Now wasn't the time to bring all that up though. Not when she was this upset and reeling from what had happened.

"We'll all help you. Me, Jamie, Charlie, the agency. We'll make sure you're safe, and that whoever was behind this is caught."

She let out a deep breath. "I hate relying on anyone."

"Really? I hadn't noticed."

She huffed out a laugh. "Guess I don't have much choice at this point though."

"Nope." He rubbed her back again.

Charlie called out to them from the kitchen. "Taylor, your boss is on his way up."

"Okay." She sat up and gave the hem of her T-shirt a tug for good measure, then reached up to fuss with her hair.

A minute later her boss walked in and headed straight over. If he was surprised to see Logan sitting with her, he hid it well. "Hey. How you holding up?"

"Fine." She crossed her arms over her chest and stayed next to Logan. "Anything to report yet?"

He nodded. "Fire inspector agrees with our forensics team. Initial findings are that someone plugged up all the filters in your furnace, and redirected the exhaust up through the vent that leads to your master bedroom. Definitely a professional. No prints, no signs of forced entry. Given the timeframe you gave us, and because that amount of carbon monoxide would take hours to accumulate in your room, it seems likely that it was done while Wainright was in your house last night."

Taylor was completely still as she absorbed that. Logan slid an arm around her shoulders and drew her into him. The biggest tell about her level of shock was that she didn't resist.

Her boss flicked a look at Logan before returning his attention to her. He watched her for a long moment as the silence expanded. "He doesn't normally work alone. He's got at least two men with him. And he'd be acting on his lieutenant's orders."

Taylor rubbed at her forehead. "God, I don't know what to think right now."

Logan rubbed a hand up and down her upper arm, wishing there was something more he could do for her other than give her a shoulder to lean on. From what he'd seen, she sucked at leaning.

"We'll find out all the details soon enough. For now, your safety is our number one concern. You'll have to use extreme caution until we have Wainright in custody. I'm working on finding you a safe location right now. Just waiting on a call back from the Deputy Administrator."

"Okay. Thank you."

Her boss tipped his head a little. "Is there anything else I can do? Someone I could call, or…"

"No, but thanks."

"As soon as I hear back, I'll let you know." He turned and headed back toward the kitchen.

Taylor leaned into Logan and rested her head on his shoulder. "I just can't believe this."

Yeah, it sucked. He kissed the top of her head and squeezed her shoulder. He hated that she had no family to turn to at a time like this. His family wasn't as close as a lot of others were, but they were there for each other when needed.

He wasn't sure how long they stayed that way, him lending silent comfort and support while she wrestled with everything that was going on. Footsteps approached from the kitchen and they both looked up as her boss came back in.

"Just got off the phone with the Deputy Administrator. We've got a secure place for you to stay for the duration of this case. Agents are heading there now to set everything up, and I can have someone pack a suitcase for you at your place if you tell me what you need."

"Sure." Taylor pulled from Logan's embrace and got up to grab a pen and paper from the kitchen counter. She wrote down a list and handed it to her boss. "Suitcases are in the hall closet. I'll need the biggest one, plus my briefcase and laptop."

He made a call and relayed the information. "I can take you over to the new location now, if you're ready." He glanced at Logan. "Unless you want to take her?"

"Yeah, I do."

"You don't have to—" Taylor began.

"I want to." He wanted to be there for her as much as he could, and he already knew that would push her out of her comfort zone.

The grateful smile she gave him made his heart squeeze. "Okay then."

Her boss gave him the address and Logan followed her to the door. The boss stopped him, pulled him out of earshot and gave Logan the stare down. "You'll take care of her?"

"Yes." Nice to see he cared enough to double check.

He seemed satisfied by that. "She's under a lot of strain, and she already works too hard at the best of times. I'm worried about her burning out or having a breakdown if this goes on much longer. I wish I could take some stress off her."

"Me too."

"Maybe see if you can get her to take a few hours off tomorrow. Somehow. I would order her to, but I don't want to take away her control right now."

"Okay, will do."

The man gave him a half-smile. "Good luck."

On their way out, Taylor hugged Charlie and Jamie and promised to call them when she got settled. Logan reached for her hand as they headed for the elevator, trying not to limp.

She flashed him a questioning look but didn't protest or pull her hand away. He considered that real progress.

"You're not supposed to be walking on it already, are you?" she asked in a dry voice.

"Not really."

She sighed and shook her head. "I don't want to be responsible for setting your recovery back."

She was seriously worrying about his knee now too, on top of everything else? "You won't be. And it's already way better than it was a few days ago."

In the lobby, he led her out the back entrance. "I switched vehicles with a teammate, just in case anyone got my license plate yesterday." He led her to Zaid's dark gray truck and handed her up into the cab.

The building of the unit the agency had reserved for her was a fifteen-minute drive across town to an urban area full of apartment complexes mixed with commercial buildings, shops and restaurants. An agent was waiting for them by the main elevator when they arrived. Logan showed the man his agency ID, then took Taylor's hand again as they headed up to the ninth floor where another agent waited outside the apartment.

"Everything's clean and ready," the woman told Taylor with a quick smile. "Your suitcases are in the bedroom and the fridge has been stocked with the basics. The building's security has been briefed and there are two agents posted outside to keep watch. Here's my number." She handed Taylor a card. "I'll be accompanying you whenever you leave the building, until further notice."

"Thank you," Taylor murmured, sounding tired. Not at all surprising. It was almost two in the morning now, and with the emotional toll of all this, she had to be exhausted.

The female agent nodded. "Try to get some sleep." She handed Taylor the key and left.

Inside, Logan locked the door behind them while she took a look around. The place was small, only one-bedroom, and from the size and cheap furnishings it looked like it catered to the student crowd who populated this area of town since it was close to campus.

Taylor wandered toward the bedroom where her

suitcase was visible through the open doorway.

"You hungry?" he asked, walking over to open the fridge.

Eggs, butter, milk, bread, a jar of jam and peanut butter, along with some apples and bananas. Enough to get her through a day or two. He'd grab more stuff for her tomorrow unless someone else beat him to it.

"No, just tired."

Shutting the fridge, he walked through to the bedroom and stood in the doorway, watching her. She'd put her suitcase on the bed and was in the process of unpacking it. "Need a hand?"

"No, I'm good." She didn't look at him as she bustled back and forth to the closet, hanging up her skirt suits. "I'm a freak about unpacking right away and getting everything in its place."

He slid his hands into his pockets and leaned one shoulder against the doorjamb. "That's probably why you're so good at your job. Making sure all the numbers line up in the right column and add up to what they're supposed to. Tracking down things that don't make sense, finding out where all the money's hidden."

She flashed a grin at him over her shoulder, and he was glad to see some of the strain lifting from her. "Exactly."

He stood there while she finished unpacking, admiring her strength in the face of a scare like this. Wherever Wainright was at that moment, his time was running out.

Logan wanted him to pay for what he'd done, for what he'd tried to do to her. It scared the hell out of him to think about what could have happened had she not noticed the batteries missing from the carbon monoxide detector.

If it hadn't woken her, she might not have woken up at all, and then this complex, smart and startlingly sensual woman would have been gone forever. Taken from him before he'd ever got the chance to explore what was happening between them.

It was too horrible to contemplate. He wanted Wainwright or whoever the hell was behind this taken down.

Taylor zipped up the empty suitcase, dragged it off the bed and tucked it away at the bottom of the closet. As she started to slide the folding door closed, Logan stepped up behind her and settled his hands on her hips.

She stilled.

He hadn't wanted anything from her when he'd first met her. He'd been totally satisfied with the way his life was, seeing different woman on a casual basis when it suited him and his schedule.

Taylor had changed all that in the space of a few weeks. He was too invested in her now, and couldn't walk away. Wouldn't even if she asked him to. He wanted to help her, be the one she turned to. Show her she could count on him.

Not wanting to examine his motives any more closely than that, he pushed all that aside and focused on the most important thing at the moment—her. Gripping her hips gently, he bent his head and nuzzled the side of her neck.

Taylor sucked in a sharp breath and shifted against him, then let her head tip back slightly. He took immediate advantage of the invitation and rubbed his lips against her smooth, soft skin, sucking gently at the pulse point that pounded beneath the surface. So fragile and delicate, in spite of the inner strength she projected that drew him so strongly. She shivered.

I'm here. I'm right here and you're not alone.

He conveyed the words with slow, seductive kisses meant to make her mind go blank, make her forget everything but him and this moment.

She gasped and came up on her toes when his tongue slid over a particularly sensitive spot, and he paused to rub his beard over it, enjoying her little hum of pleasure and the way she squirmed in his hold. He shifted his hands, splaying one across her abdomen while he skimmed the other up her ribs to rest a few inches below her right breast.

Taylor's breathing faltered. He could feel her heart pounding beneath his hand on her ribs.

She spun around and put her hands on either side of his face, staring up at him in the dimness. Her eyes searched his for a long, breathless moment, then dropped to his mouth before her lids fluttered down and she rose onto her toes to meet his kiss.

Logan plunged one hand into the back of her hair and wrapped his free arm around her hips to pull her close as their mouths met. He caressed her tongue with his, sucked at it gently, absorbing the shudder that rippled through her body.

She settled back onto her heels, her cheeks flushed, eyes glowing. "You did that to distract me, didn't you?"

He grinned. "You're giving me way too much credit there, because my reasons weren't nearly that selfless." The humor faded and he took her chin in his hand. "I was watching you put everything away, thinking about how things could have gone way differently tonight, and I had to touch you again to make sure you're really here."

Her expression softened as she gazed up at him, dark shadows of fatigue beneath her eyes. He really should let her sleep if she could. "I'm really here."

He nodded, his entire body pulsing with the need to claim her. But it was too soon. With her he had to go slow. Much slower than he wanted to.

She would be more than worth the wait though. She was worth holding on to.

"Want me to crash on the couch tonight?" He didn't want to leave her, even if the agency had people guarding the building.

"There's no way you could stretch out on that thing, and I know your knee's still bugging you." She softened the rejection with a little smile. "But you're sweet to offer. And, you know what?"

"What?" he murmured, hating to go but willing to give her space if she needed it. For now.

She lowered her voice to a whisper. "I'm really glad you came here with me. It…really means a lot to know you've got my back."

"I'll always have your back." She would learn to trust him, because he wasn't going anywhere. Whatever it took, he was going to win this woman over.

****

Dillon cursed when he slowly drove past the condo building on the other side of town. The DEA had moved fast, whisking Taylor here from her house.

He'd followed her at a careful distance, tracking the dark blue SUV they'd rushed her into, tailed by another one. He'd lost sight of them partway here, but managed to glimpse them pulling into the underground garage beneath the building as he turned the corner.

He hadn't stopped and waited out front for fear of someone noticing him hanging around.

Dammit. He still didn't know how this had happened. His plan should have worked.

How had she woken up and found out about the carbon monoxide, anyway? He'd disabled the detector personally before she'd gotten home from work.

He'd been in total shock when she'd walked out her front door in the pouring rain a few hours ago and headed straight to the agent watching her house. If Dillon had been in a better position, he could have shot her too. But the angle had been bad and he hadn't wanted to risk taking a shot and missing, wounding her and alerting her to his presence. Carbon monoxide poisoning had seemed so much easier. So peaceful for her. Painless. Actually having to put a bullet in her head…

Dillon kept going, driving two more blocks before turning right and doing a big loop back around to make sure no one was following him. When he came back around the front of the building, the dark blue SUV that had brought her here was leaving.

It had only been here for a minute, long enough for Dillon to circle around. Tugging the brim of the ball cap lower over his face, he drove past the building again and kept going. They'd have agents watching the building now, and maybe cops too. The hard knot of anxiety beneath his ribs expanded. Everyone would be on high alert tonight, so making a move would be stupid and likely get him killed.

The window of time Carlos had given him was closing fast. If Dillon didn't fix this within the next twenty-four hours, his boss would send someone else after Taylor, and…

No. Bad enough she had to die. He wouldn't let them torture and rape her on top of it.

Time was running out for her either way, but it was also running out for him. If he failed to find and kill her by the deadline, it was only a matter of time before he wound up on the hit list as well.

He glanced at the clock in the dashboard. As of right now he had under twenty-four hours to end this so he could get out of the country and back to the protection offered by the cartel. Failure wasn't an option. Not unless he wanted to become another one of its countless victims.

Either he finished this, or he risked it all and enacted his emergency exit plan.

Chapter Fourteen

ould this day be over yet?

Taylor paused to stretch her neck muscles in an attempt to ease the kinks in her neck and shoulders, then reached for yet another file stacked on the coffee table in the apartment. Home sweet home for the foreseeable future, at least until Dillon was taken into custody.

But she wasn't convinced that even that would end the threat against her.

The DEA was now using her as an expert witness to help them build a case around Dillon's involvement with the cartel. Her boss and other investigators had interviewed her for hours today already, going over timelines and everything she knew about Dillon.

Logically it made no sense, but a tiny part of her was still conflicted about turning on him, wrestling with her conscience while she tried to reconcile the memory of the teenage boy she'd known and worshipped with the man who'd tried to kill her last night.

That was impossible though. She'd been working

since seven that morning, stopping only to force down some toast with peanut butter and some fruit for lunch. It was after dinnertime now and she was starving, not to mention exhausted.

She felt more alone here than she had at home, and even Nimbus wouldn't come out to keep her company. He was molting in the corner of the bathroom right now, next to his litter box and food dish. He hated change and disruption as much as she did.

Her phone chimed. She picked it up, warmth and relief filling her when she saw Logan's message. He'd told her he would stop by after his doctor's appointment. *I'm on my way up. You hungry?*

He was here already? *Starved. If you brought food, you're my hero.*

That's me. Lumberjack hero. Hang tight.

She had just enough time to tidy up the coffee table before he knocked. She pulled open the door, her heart doing a little swooning thing that she was becoming more and more used to. "Oh, wow, look at you."

"Wore this just for you," he said proudly, carrying the bags inside, his limp still noticeable.

He looked exactly like the lumberjack she'd imagined him as the first time she'd met him. The red and black checked flannel shirt was unbuttoned over a white T-shirt beneath, and he'd rolled the sleeves up to expose his roped forearms. She wanted to run her hands over those arms in the worst way.

"Left my axe in the back of Zaid's truck, but I can go get it if you want. You know, if that would really do it for you."

He really did it for her, axe or no axe, even though they were opposites in so many ways and she kept telling herself there was no long-term future for them. Not when she was so emotionally closed off and afraid of the intimacy she craved with him. Real intimacy, the kind that a committed relationship required, meant trusting a partner enough to open herself up and share every part of her, even the dark or ugly parts. The prospect was still too terrifying.

She couldn't tell Logan. She wasn't sure she would *ever* be able to tell him. Both men she'd trusted in the past had hurt her, in different ways. The shame she still carried from that terrible night long ago when she'd been taken away from her home prevented her from laying herself bare to someone. She couldn't give her whole heart to Logan if she wasn't honest with him. And holding back meant certain disaster for their budding relationship.

Taylor forced a bright smile to hide her gloomy thoughts. "Nah, it's okay. I've got a good imagination. I'll just picture you with it."

And without clothes, since she'd done that countless times over the past few weeks anyway.

"Okay. Let me know if you change your mind." He waggled his eyebrows at her, and actually the idea of role playing with him seemed like it could be fun instead of ridiculous. And it might even be hot. Not that she had any experience with that sort of thing. "I brought Thai food. Hope that's okay."

"It's great. I was so hungry and not looking forward to the scrambled eggs I was going to make. This was really nice of you."

"Well I still want to actually take you out somewhere, but since that's not an option right now, dinner had to come to you. And I also brought this." He reached into the other bag and produced two pints of ice cream. "No pistachio."

It made her smile. "You remembered."

"Of course." He walked over to the kitchen and put the bags on the counter before popping the ice cream into the freezer.

"How's your knee?" With his jeans on she couldn't

tell if it was swollen or not, but his limp seemed a little less pronounced today.

"Better."

Uh-huh. She aimed a pointed look at him. "You're still supposed to be using your crutches, aren't you?"

He looked up with a grin that made her breath catch. God, he was sexy, and she'd been fantasizing about what his beard would feel like all over her naked breasts and between her thighs. "Don't tell my physical therapist. She's a real ball buster."

"Maybe you should listen to her then."

"What she doesn't know won't hurt me." His grin widened as he stared at her. "It drives you nuts that I'm not following the rules, doesn't it?"

"Yeah, but mostly because you're just delaying your recovery by being a pig-headed alpha male."

"Ouch."

Closing the distance between them, she took him by the shoulders and pushed, trying to propel him back toward the living room. It was like trying to move a brick wall. "How about you go sit down and I'll serve this up? You should be resting."

He didn't budge, and reached around behind him to snag her forearm. With one tug, he had her in front of him, both those powerful arms wrapped around her waist. Every one of her nerve endings lit up, anticipation curling inside her. "How about you kiss me first, then we'll both serve this up."

Well she couldn't turn down that offer.

Hands braced on his solid shoulders, she lifted onto her toes as his lips came down on hers. A burst of heat sizzled through her, energizing her entire body. His lips were warm and seductive, his short beard tickling her skin, and the way he slid one hand into her hair to cradle the back of her head caused her lower belly to somersault.

His tongue stroked hers, caressing and teasing,

making her nipples tighten and her core throb. Then one of those amazing hands slipped down her throat to graze the outer curve of her breast.

She pushed into his hand, seeking more, and he obliged, cupping her, gliding his thumb across the straining center. Making her crave more of his touch. His mouth. All of him, whether that was smart or not. They were too different in so many ways. If they tried a relationship he'd wind up bored within a few weeks and end it. She wasn't looking forward to having her heart broken, but she wanted him anyway.

Her pulse was thudding double time when he suddenly lifted his head a moment later and stared down at her, desire burning bright in his blue-green eyes. "Let's save that for dessert."

A delicious shiver spiraled through her. She wanted to strip those shirts off him and lick him all over, yet she loved that he wasn't trying to rush her into bed as pretty much every other guy she'd been involved with would have. He definitely knew how to fan the flame of her pilot light.

"I'll get the plates," she said, a little breathless.

They filled their plates with fragrant rice and coconut curry prawns with pineapple, and chicken cooked in a lemongrass/coconut sauce, and sprinkled toasted cashews over the top.

"Oh my God, it smells amazing." Taylor breathed in the mouthwatering scent on the way to the couch. Her stomach growled and her mouth watered.

She'd devoured half of it by the time she realized Logan was watching her with a bemused expression. She flushed. "I was starving. Literally starving. Been too busy to eat all day." She gestured to the stacked files on the table in front of them.

"No, it's all good. Big difference from last time we ate together, that's all. Including the cake you brought to

Jamie and Charlie's."

Because that time she'd barely eaten anything. The agency had sent her to dinner with him so Logan could keep an eye on Baker while Charlie and Jamie had eaten with the guy. Taylor had been so damn nervous, completely out of her element and wishing she was back at the hotel pouring over her spreadsheets.

She'd been such an idiot. "Yeah, no kidding," she said, embarrassed at how awkward she must have seemed then.

He'd placed a bag on the coffee table when he sat down, and reached for it. "Picked you up something else, too."

Glancing at him in surprise, Taylor took the bag, opened it and gasped. "Sudoku!" She'd been so busy getting settled and working on her files, she hadn't thought to ask someone to bring her books over.

He grinned. "Yep. Saw them sitting in a rack when I was in the grocery store picking up this."

The thoughtful gesture touched her so much it put a lump in her throat and for a moment she couldn't speak. Barely anyone in her life had ever made her feel like she mattered, let alone enough for them to take notice of the things that made her happy. And last night, the one good person from her past had tried to kill her.

She swallowed hard. "Thank you. How did you know I liked these?"

"Saw them on your coffee table the other night."

She bit the inside of her lip and looked away. Was he for real? A guy wouldn't go to all this trouble just to get her into bed, would he? She placed the books gently on the table. Try as she might, she couldn't figure him out.

Turning her attention back to him, she watched as he polished off his dinner. "Can I ask you something? It's personal."

His eyes swung toward her. "Sure, ask away."

There was no delicate way to put it. "I'm trying to figure out why she left you. Your ex."

His eyebrows shot up and one side of his mouth twitched. "So basically you're wondering exactly what's wrong with me."

She gave him a guilty grin. "Sort of, yeah."

"Wow, okay. Didn't see that one coming. But fair enough." She opened her mouth to mutter an apology but he waved it off. "No, it's fine. Like I said before, we were just too different. And we both had different expectations. I expected her to be more secure and independent after we were married, and she expected me to suddenly settle down and live the whole white picket fence lifestyle. So we were doomed right from the get-go."

Taylor nodded, considering all of that. "Unrealistic expectations."

"And then some. My undercover work made it extra tough. Put an additional strain on an already crumbling relationship. I wasn't ever going to be the kind of guy to work a desk job nine-to-five. She decided she wanted that more than she wanted me. We fought a lot. And don't get me wrong, it's not like I think I was perfect. But once all the messy stuff was behind us, we could both see that we'd made a mistake in getting married."

"What did you love so much about undercover work?" It was so dangerous. Not that his current job was any safer.

His eyes lit up. "The challenge. The rush of it. Working as a team with the best of the best. Knowing I was taking risks for the greater good."

"Is that why you wanted to join FAST?"

He nodded, that hot gleam still in his eyes. "Pretty much. I knew I wanted out of undercover work after a bust that took down someone I'd gotten close to. FAST had always been my goal, so as soon as I was able to leave undercover I applied to the program and started training."

"Did you make it in the first time?"

"No. Second. And the only reason I even made Bravo this year was because they lost a member to permanent disability a few months back. Poor bastard landed wrong during a jump and fractured three vertebrae in his lower back."

Taylor winced. "Oww."

He nodded. "Gave me my shot, though."

She propped one elbow on the arm of the couch and rested her head in her hand. "And do you love it as much as you thought you would?"

His answering smile was pure, sexy alpha male. God, he was so delicious. "Oh yeah. Love it so hard."

Taylor laughed and shook her head at him. "And I'm over here loving my spreadsheets and paperwork. I must seem so boring to you."

"Boring? No, not even a little. You're a complex puzzle I'm still trying to figure out. Like an impossible Sudoku."

She shot him a disbelieving look. "Me?"

"Mmhmm." Even the way he murmured that was sexy.

It was ludicrous. Her, a Sudoku puzzle he couldn't figure out? She was nowhere near that complicated, but maybe a little hard to get to know. She was choosy about who she let into her inner circle. Logan definitely tempted her to let him in.

She straightened and turned to face him more. He'd opened up to her, and since they were...kind of seeing each other, she supposed it was only fair that she open up to him a little too. "All right, then. What do you want to know?"

Logan hid his surprise at her offer. He hadn't expected this. Taylor was so guarded, even if she had become much more open with him, it surprised him that she was willing to do this. "You sure?"

"Yes. Fire away."

Where to start? There were so many things he wanted to know about her. And the way she'd just hugged the Sudoku books to her chest, like they were the most precious gift anyone had ever given her, had made his heart clench. "How did you wind up in foster care? I've been wondering about it since you told me."

She made a face. "It's kind of a long story. My parents were both addicts, but functioning ones. They were able to hide the worst of it, so no one really knew how bad it was, and they'd cut contact with their families years before. It wasn't until I was in fourth grade that the teachers started to notice little signs. Me joining the breakfast program and other children sharing their lunches with me.

"My clothes didn't fit right and my grooming and hygiene were substandard. Some days I'd miss school completely. My teacher called in a social worker, who came to the house to investigate. The police came and took my dad away for a few days. Things improved for a while, but then my mom died of a heroin overdose when I was ten."

She drew in a deep breath and picked at an invisible piece of lint on her pants. "After that, it got really bad. My dad couldn't handle it, let alone suddenly being a single parent. After an incident one night at our apartment, the neighbors intervened. The police took me away and I was put into foster care."

"What do you mean, 'incident'?"

"Abuse," she said without elaborating.

He could read between the lines well enough. "God, that's so shitty. I'm sorry."

She nodded, was quiet a moment before continuing. "It was hard. I was placed in two different homes within that first six months."

"Is that when you met Dillon?"

"Yes. He'd been placed into that home about a year before me. Our foster father's wife had died just after Dillon had come there. It was like history repeated itself. Frank started drinking more and more. We learned to stay out of his sight when he was drunk, because he got mean."

Logan didn't like where this was going, but he had to know. It would drive him crazy, wondering. "Was he abusive?"

"Very. Dillon always got the worst of it, because he used to put himself in Frank's path to shield me. A few times he took a beating for something I'd done." She glanced at him. "So he wasn't a bad guy back then. He protected me as much as he could."

So many pieces of the puzzle fit together now. He understood why she was so conflicted about the situation with Dillon. And it suddenly made sense why she was so rigid and orderly about everything in her life. She'd had zero control over anything in her life as a child, and now clung to every last measure of it she could get because it made her feel safe. Damn, he had even more respect for her now, and he hadn't thought that was possible.

"Why didn't your social worker get involved, and get you both out of that house?" he asked.

"One did, eventually. Janet. She's the one we both kept in touch with over the years. Dillon had already left, but I got her in touch with him." She paused a beat. "She gave Dillon my number and address last week, not realizing she might be putting me at risk."

He decided to leave that one alone for now. "Did Frank go to jail?"

"No. Because he was a cop, and the judge felt that his service to the community outweighed everything else. Things were different back then."

He shook his head in disgust. "That's fucked up."

"Yep. I lived with Janet for a while until I got a

housing subsidy from the government. I was old enough to look after myself. I worked part time after school, saved up my money to help ends meet, and took out a student loan to go to college."

He shook his head at her in wonder, even more amazed at the person she'd become. Given her background, the odds said she should be an addict or a drunk. "You're an inspirational success story. Most people who go through something like that would crumble."

And now he understood why his size might trigger her. She'd been abused by her father, then a cop of all people when she was just a kid. It made him livid.

"I was tempted to, plenty of times. I guess in the end, I'm just too stubborn to give in. I didn't want to end up like my parents, or Frank. It's also why I joined the DEA. Drugs took so much from me, and I want to help stop it from happening to anyone else. Even if it's only by crunching numbers," she added with an ironic grin.

He lifted a hand and brushed a lock of hair back from her temple. "Sometimes crunching numbers is what it takes to convict the bad guys."

"Yes. True."

Logan hated that she'd gone through so much trauma in her childhood, and wished he could take her mind off everything and get her out of here for a little while. A change of scenery might be just what she needed. She wasn't under protective custody, so as long as the agency knew where she was and that he'd take precautions with her, it shouldn't be a problem. And her boss had told him he wanted her to take time off, so...

"What are you doing tomorrow?" he asked.

She gave him a frown, as though the answer was obvious. "Work." She gestured to the files stacked on the table. "I'm slowly but surely making my way through all the banking info, figuring out who's who with the cartel investors."

"Can you take a few hours off? You must have others helping you with the workload."

Her eyebrows drew together. "Why do you ask?"

"I want to take you out for the day." To get out of the city and do something fun that she'd never done before. To spend time alone with her and see where this thing between them would go.

"Out? I can't go out."

"Sure you could, if I was with you and we took some precautions. We'll take a rental car, and you'll wear a disguise."

He could see her turning the idea over in her mind as she watched him. She had to be feeling trapped here. "Just for the day," he promised. "I'll call your boss and clear it with him personally, and have you back by dinnertime." Chris would sign off on it.

A little smile tugged at her mouth. "I'd love to get away for a few hours," she said, her expression wistful.

He'd move heaven and earth to make her happy. He kissed her slow and tender. "Then I'll make it happen." His phone buzzed in his pocket, the alert to remind him of his physio appointment across town. "Damn, I have to go already."

She nodded, but going by the disappointment in her eyes she wanted him to stay, and that made him so freaking happy. He was impatient to take things to the next level with her, but something warned him not to move too fast. No way he was screwing this thing up with her. "Okay. What about tomorrow?"

He dropped a final kiss on her upturned lips and pushed to his feet. "Be ready to roll by eight. I'll take care of everything."

****

Shit, someone was coming out of her apartment. The one he'd finally figured out was hers after almost blowing his cover once already. Coming up here again so soon was plain stupid, but desperation was one hell of a motivator. He was acutely aware of each minute that slipped past without him achieving his objective. Of the deadline placed upon him by the cartel, hurtling toward him at what felt like warp speed.

Halfway down the hall from her apartment, Dillon did an abrupt about-face as Taylor's door opened, and kept his head lowered as he pretended to check his phone while casting subtle glances out of the corner of his eye. When he saw the big dude who'd been at her place the other night, a spurt of alarm shot through him and he immediately headed for the stairwell he'd just come from. His maintenance worker uniform and ball cap would help disguise him, but only if the guy didn't get a good look at him.

Dillon didn't dare look back until the stairwell door had shut behind him. Through the small rectangular window, he risked a glance down the hallway.

"Fuck me," he whispered, his heart sinking.

One of the security agents had entered the hallway and was talking to the big guy. Dillon edged back so they couldn't see him, aligning his body so he could see what was going on. The agent laughed at something the guy said, then knocked on Taylor's door and went in.

Shit, that had been close.

Dillon set his jaw and hurried down the stairs, his pistol rubbing against his lower back with each step. Even with a silencer, attacking now was too risky. Other agents were already prowling the building and grounds, their movements too unpredictable to form a pattern.

Fucking hell. All he'd needed was a solid ten-minute window of time to get into the apartment, put a bullet through Taylor's skull without her ever knowing what had hit her, and then use the rest of the time to make a clean getaway.

Wasn't happening now. His disguise was useless because of the security cameras positioned throughout the building. With the guards constantly rotating, it made finding a window of opportunity impossible.

He'd have to find a new disguise before coming back here. And instead of killing just Taylor, it looked like he might have to take out a few DEA agents along with her...

Then pray he could make it out of the building alive.

Chapter Fifteen

———◇◇◇◇———

"**J**amie lent you his truck?" Taylor said in surprise as Logan walked with her into the underground parking garage the next morning.

"He did. Because he trusts me like a brother." That's the way things were in a unit like theirs. Even if he was the new guy. Logan opened the passenger door for her.

She tugged the brim of her ball cap lower over her forehead before climbing into the cab, her hair tucked up into the hat. "He must. According to Charlie, this truck is his baby."

"I'll take good care of it." He'd take good care of *her*. "An agent is going to tail us just past the city limits to make sure no one's following us." Neither of them were carrying anything that could track them, and he and Jamie had swept the truck just to be cautious.

"Good."

He slid in behind the wheel and cranked the engine. Strains of *Back in Black* blasted out of the stereo where he'd left his phone connected and he shot out a hand to turn it down.

"AC/DC?" she asked, raising one eyebrow.

"Yep. You like them?"

"They're okay."

"Just okay?" He shot her a horrified look. "They're the best band *ever*."

Her lips twitched. "If you say so."

"I do say so. But if you hate it, I'll turn on something else. What do you like?"

"No, leave it, it's fine. I like rock music."

"Yeah? Huh. Guess we've got something in common after all."

A little smile tugged at the corners of her mouth as she faced forward. "So where are we going, anyway?"

"It's a surprise." When he'd asked Charlie about this last night, it had surprised him that she'd never invited Taylor home for a visit, given that they were so close. But Charlie had been all for his idea.

"Am I dressed okay? You were kind of vague about what I should wear."

He eyed her snug black yoga pants and form-fitting athletic jacket. "It's perfect." And it didn't hurt that the outfit showed off the shape of her sexy body perfectly. "I'm looking forward to this." It had been a long time since he'd had something to look forward to.

"That grin looks a little evil to me. What exactly do you have planned?" she asked, sounding a little worried.

"You'll just have to wait and see." He turned onto the street, immediately spotting the plain-clothes DEA agent who would follow them, parked at the curb across the street from the front entrance. Logan nodded at him and the dark sedan pulled out behind them to follow. He didn't notice anyone else behind it. "We've got a long drive until we get there, so kick back and make yourself comfy."

"Okay." Her lips tipped up at the corners, her eyes hidden by her sunglasses. The sky was a clear, bright blue, dotted with fluffy white clouds. "I feel like such a rebel right now, skipping work like this."

"You deserve a break."

Since she'd gotten the most pressing work done yesterday and because Logan had assured her boss that he'd keep a watchful eye out for Taylor's safety, Chris had been more than happy to give her the day off. And they were going far enough out of the city that any threats from Dillon and the cartel were minimal. Logan would still be vigilant though. His job for today was making sure Taylor was safe, happy and relaxed.

He headed for the highway, relieved that no one else besides the agent seemed to be following them. At the edge of the city the agent called him to announce their tail was clear, and that he was going back to watch the building. "Roger," Logan said. "Appreciate it."

"So tell me about your family," Taylor said, sinking back in her seat. "I've been curious."

"About what?"

She shrugged. "Your parents, siblings. What they do, what they're like, whether you're close or not."

Wow, she sure knew how to hit on all his sore spots. "My mom and dad are still married. They met in college and now they run a residential construction business."

"Does your dad do any of the building?"

"He used to, along with me and my brother when we were younger."

She aimed a thoughtful smile at him. "You used to swing a hammer?"

"I did, on my summer vacations while I was in high school and throughout college." He shot her a smug look. "It's why I'm so good with my hands."

She laughed softly at his not-so-subtle innuendo. "I'll just bet you are. So you have a brother. Are you guys close?"

"Not as close as some brothers are. I'm four years older, and we're just really different. We butted heads a lot growing up, and then I went into undercover work and that didn't exactly bring me any closer to my family. I'm tightest with my mom. Try to call her every couple weeks or so, and I make a point of going home for big holidays if I can. My line of work doesn't make that easy though. They've learned to live their lives without me, for the most part."

"Oh."

"I'm not proud of that," he admitted. But after learning what Taylor had gone through, he appreciated his family a whole hell of a lot more. "I'm going to make an effort to keep in touch more often from now on, though."

"I'm glad."

That was it. No pity, no recriminations or admonishments. Just one more thing he liked about her, and the list was adding up fast. His parents would like her, maybe his brother too. If things progressed between them, maybe he'd ask her to go home to Maine with him for a quick visit. His mom would love that.

He and Taylor chatted for a bit longer, then fell into a comfortable silence as he cleared the city limits and headed west toward the mountains. Logan let himself relax, but remained watchful. "Ever been to the Shenandoah Valley?" he asked her a few minutes later.

"No. Is that where we're going?"

He nodded. "It's gorgeous. You'll love it." The spot he had in mind was quiet, tranquil, and would give them the perfect opportunity to relax and unwind together. He was looking forward to spending time with her, even if the circumstances sucked.

Two hours later they reached the sign welcoming them to Sugar Hollow. He turned onto Main Street, a quaint road lined with old shade trees and Victorian-style shops and B&Bs.

"It's so cute," Taylor said, staring out her window.

"Yeah, it is." Like something from a postcard.

He followed Charlie's directions and headed west once he was through town. The area turned into farmland almost immediately, with the Blue Ridge Mountains forming a smoky backdrop in the distance. A few miles out of town, he reached the mailbox at the end of the long driveway that read Colebrook.

Taylor leaned forward in her seat, excitement in her voice. "Is this Charlie's farm?"

"Yes." And Easton's. Well, it actually belonged to their father, but all four Colebrook siblings still came home to visit whenever they could, to spend time with their dad.

She looked over at him, the sunglasses still hiding her eyes. "What are we doing here?"

"Just picking up a few things."

The pale yellow farmhouse stood at the end of the driveway on a slight rise amid a carpet of green lawn. Beyond it, horses grazed in the pastures behind the barn.

Before he'd even put the truck into park in front of the detached garage, the back door to the house opened and Colebrook Senior came out with his cane, and an old basset hound waddling along at his heels.

Logan got out and walked toward him. "Hi."

"You Granger?"

"Yessir. Logan." He held out a hand. "Good to meet you."

Colebrook Senior shook it, his sharp hazel eyes scrutinizing Logan. "So you're the FNG Easton and Jamie told me about." His speech was slightly slurred, another side-effect of the stroke he'd suffered.

Oh. "Uh, yes sir."

Senior slapped him on the side of the shoulder and cracked a crooked grin, one side of his face unmoving. "Just giving you a hard time, son." He waved toward the garage. "Go on and help yourself to whatever you need. I want to meet your lady."

She's not my lady. Yet. But he hoped to change that today.

Taylor was already out of the truck and heading for them.

"And you must be Taylor," Senior said, his entire demeanor softening as he shuffled toward her, the dog at his side.

Taylor smiled back and took off her sunglasses. "Yes. Hi, Mr. Colebrook." She shook his hand warmly. "Charlie's told me so much about you, I feel like I know you already."

"Gray. Call me Gray, sweetheart. And I feel like I already know you too. Charlie loves you to pieces, and that's all I need to know about you." The dog was sniffing at her legs and wagging its tail. "This lazy, fleabitten thing is Sarge."

"Fleabitten, my butt. Charlie told me how you spoil him." She knelt down and ruffled the dog's long, droopy ears. "Hi, Sarge. I've heard lots about you too, and your friend Grits." Taylor's eyes twinkled as she looked up at Charlie's old man. "But I think my favorite story of all is the one when you took Jamie into your office for a little 'chat' when they were here last, before they moved in together."

Senior let out a gruff chuckle. "Yeah, that was a good one. Been planning that for a long time, ever since she started dating."

Taylor pushed to her feet and grinned at him. "Did you really clean your rifle the whole time?"

Logan grinned. Ah, yeah. Classic. Jamie had told the entire team about it a couple weeks back, about how he'd had to face down his girlfriend's scary-as-fuck former Marine Corps gunny sergeant father, and break the news that he and Charlie were planning to shack up together.

"I did," Senior said, his voice full of pleasure.

She laughed, and it sounded so carefree it made Logan

smile. "It's just too awesome."

Senior's hard mouth quirked and his eyes glinted with pride. "It's a father's job to look out for his little girl, and I take that seriously. Jamie still treating her right?"

"Oh, yes. He loves her to death, treats her like a princess. Well, not a princess exactly, since Charlie would hate that, but you know what I mean."

"Good. You let me know if that ever changes, hmm?"

"I will. But you don't have to worry. If he ever hurt her, Charlie would be the first one to kick his ass."

Senior barked out a laugh. "Isn't that the truth. Means I raised her right, I guess."

Logan watched the interaction with amazement. Taylor was more relaxed than Logan had ever seen her, and with a man she'd just met.

The twinge of jealousy caught him off guard, but it was there nonetheless. He wanted Taylor to be that at ease with *him*. He turned around and headed for the garage to grab the equipment, listening to the rest of their conversation going on behind him.

"And what about Logan there? He treating you right?"

"Oh. He is, but we're just friends."

More than friends. But not as much as he wanted them to be.

Taylor looked over at him as he carried the tandem sea kayak out of the garage. Her eyes widened. "Wait. We're going kayaking?"

"Yeah. This thing's built for two. You'll love it, trust me. And this way you won't have to work as hard because I'll do most of the paddling. Plus it's wider than a regular kayak, so you don't have to worry about us tipping over."

She relaxed visibly at that. "Okay. Good. And heck yeah, you'll be doing most of the paddling."

"Ready to go?"

"I guess." She didn't sound too sure.

They both said their goodbyes to Senior, who stood

there at the top of the drive, waving as they climbed into the truck and drove away.

"He's exactly as I pictured him," Taylor said, a thoughtful smile on her face. "Charlie's told me so much about her family, about all the ways her brothers and dad used to drive her nuts. But she doesn't realize how lucky she is to have them."

Logan heard the wistfulness in her voice and reached across the console for her hand. Lacing their fingers together, he squeezed. "Probably not."

Fifteen minutes later he found the spot Charlie had recommended, a quiet curve in the Shenandoah River, and parked. "This is our stop." He figured they'd spend a couple hours tops paddling on the river, then drop the kayak back at the Colebrook's and head into town for lunch before he drove her back to the city.

Taylor put her life jacket on and stood watching uncertainly as he readied the two-man kayak.

Holding the bow steady, he looked up at her, hiding a grin. "You ready to do this?"

"Yeah, I guess so." She came toward him, her expression dubious.

Logan made sure she was settled in front before handing her a paddle and climbing in behind her. "This is gonna be fun and *relaxing*, I promise."

She didn't answer, just stared straight ahead as he pushed them away from shore. The current pulled them toward the middle of the river. He guided her through the paddling technique.

She caught on fast, and within minutes he could tell she was enjoying herself. They talked a little, but mostly she was quiet, taking in the sights and sounds. There wasn't a soul around, the only sound the dip and splash of their paddles and the sounds of the birds singing along the banks.

"It's so peaceful out here," she said a few minutes

later, tipping her head back and taking a deep breath.

Logan could practically feel her unwinding, letting all the stress that had been smothering her melt away, even if it was just temporary.

"It really is." He sped up his paddling, taking them around a bend in the river. "Hey, I think I see some rapids up ahead. Wanna give 'em a whirl?"

"What? No!"

He chuckled, enjoying the hell out of teasing her. She turned at the waist to nail him with a mock glare and flicked the tip of her paddle at him, splashing him with cold water.

Grinning, he wiped a hand over his face and beard. "Sure you wanna go there? Because two can play at that game, and I'm a lot bigger than you."

"Don't you dare," she warned, but she was smiling as she turned back around again.

The sun was still high overhead when he turned them around and headed back to where he'd left the truck. "You're gonna have to work a lot harder now, because we're going against the current," he told her, holding his paddle across his lap and watching her struggle to move them forward. "Come on, harder."

She grunted in frustration and paddled faster. "I'm doing it as hard as I can. My arms are about to fall off."

Smothering a chuckle, he finally dipped his paddle in the water and helped her. By the time they reached shore where the truck was parked she was breathing hard and a fine sheen of sweat covered her face. "Whew, made it!" she said triumphantly.

"Yeah, look at that." He jumped out and dragged the kayak onto the shore, then gripped the side of it and leaned over her to take her sunglasses off.

She peered up at him with those big hazel eyes, and blinked. "You can't seriously be thinking about kissing me right now. I'm all sweaty and gross."

God, she was so adorable. And clueless about how guys thought. "Sweetheart, you're the furthest thing from gross, trust me," he murmured.

Her expression softened, and he couldn't help but lean down to cover her lips with his. One of her hands crept up to wrap around the back of his neck and she opened for him.

No, she melted for him.

Let her body sink into his as their tongues danced, her muscles pliant and a hum of pleasure coming from her throat. Her hands slid over his shoulders and chest, and the way she explored him sent all the blood rushing to his groin.

He went hard as a rock in his shorts, every nerve ending pulsing with the need to take, to claim. The throaty moan she gave when he cupped her breast in his hand and rubbed his thumb across the hard point of her nipple pressing against her shirt damn near made him shudder. He was dying to peel those form-fitting clothes off her so he could touch and taste every inch of her. Make her his in the most elemental way possible.

But not out here in the open. When he finally got her naked, it would be somewhere private where she could relax, so he could take his time learning every part of her, what she enjoyed the most before he slid inside her and gave her all the pleasure he could. God, she tested his control so effortlessly.

With difficulty, he pulled away, still cradling her head in his hands. Her eyes were half-closed, her expression dreamy and hungry at the same time.

"Thank you for bringing me here," she murmured, stroking her fingers over his nape in a way that made pleasurable shivers race across his skin. God, he wanted her.

"You're welcome." Planting one last lingering kiss on her soft lips because he couldn't help himself, he pushed to his feet, wincing as his sore knee protested.

"Are we going back now?" she asked, holding his hand as she stepped out of the kayak. She didn't sound excited about it, and he couldn't blame her. But they still had time to keep reality at bay a little longer.

"Not yet." After they dropped the kayak off, they had one more stop to make in town before heading back to the city.

Chapter Sixteen

"I would never have believed it considering everything that's happened over the past few days, but this was the best day I've had in forever," Taylor said as they neared the building she was staying at in D.C. She rubbed her thumb over his knuckles, their joined hands resting on the center console.

The closer they'd gotten to the city, the more the anxiety had begun to swirl in her stomach. She didn't want to come back and face everything waiting for her here, but she had no choice and the reprieve Logan had organized today was more than she could have hoped for.

None of what was happening between them made sense to her. The man had worked a minor miracle by getting under her skin in a matter of days. How could she feel this relaxed and safe with him, yet so jittery and aroused at the same time? He continually threw her off-balance, and she found she kind of liked it.

He shot her a sexy grin that set off a burst of heat low in her abdomen. The man had to know how insanely hot he was, but he didn't act like it. She liked that. "I'm glad.

I had a lot of fun too."

"I never thought I'd like kayaking." She never thought she'd like someone like him, either, but she was already in deep and sinking fast.

"What was your favorite part?"

"Spending time with you."

This time he looked over at her with a soft smile that made her heart flip-flop. "I'm glad."

"I didn't realize how much I needed to get away, even for a little while. Thank you for doing all this."

"You're welcome, but it was my pleasure."

Taylor let her mind drift back to a few hours ago, tucking the memories away in her heart. After dropping the kayak off at the Colebrook's, Logan had driven her into Sugar Hollow and stopped at an ice cream parlor Charlie had recommended.

That, more than anything else he'd planned today, had touched her the most. He'd insisted she order something extravagant, so she'd ordered a ridiculous sundae with four kinds of ice cream scooped over a homemade brownie, topped with three different sauces, all smothered in whipped cream and sprinkled with toasted almond slivers.

They'd sat in a corner booth and eaten it together, and even her self-consciousness at smelling sweaty and not looking her best couldn't spoil the experience. He'd insisted on paying, no matter how much she argued, and she'd quickly given up. She couldn't believe all the effort he'd put into planning the day for her and making all the arrangements. No one had ever done anything like that for her before.

On the drive home, they held hands the entire time and she loved the sense of belonging it gave her. Their chemistry was something she'd never experienced before either. Every time he rubbed his thumb over the back of her hand it sent a jolt of sensation up her arm, and when he lifted their joined hands to his mouth to press a lingering kiss to each of her fingers, she'd melted a little more.

The question was what she wanted out of this relationship. She already liked and cared about him more than she'd expected to, and she'd never wanted anyone this much physically. If she wasn't careful, she could easily fall head over heels for him.

Part of her was still hesitant to take that plunge, no matter how much he tempted her to risk her heart. Could they ever make a relationship work? They were so different, in almost every way two people could be different. Opposites attracted at first, yes, but a lot of the time they ended up driving each other away later on too. And yet...he was bringing out a new side of her that was fun and exciting.

Her body didn't much care how opposite they were at this point, however. Just being near him set her heart pounding and her blood racing.

The closer they got to her building, the more intense the physical craving for him became. And so did the nerves. They hadn't talked about a relationship or expectations of any kind. She needed to know what he wanted out of this if they continued seeing each other. Casual sex didn't interest her.

A few blocks from the building where she was staying, she couldn't take it anymore. "I'm just going to put this out there," she announced when he stopped at a red light.

He glanced over at her in surprise. "Okay..."

She exhaled, steeling herself for an answer she wouldn't like. "What are we doing here, exactly? Are we...seeing each other? Dating? Just so I know what's going on." And what to expect moving forward.

"What do *you* want?" he countered. "Because I know what I want."

"So what *do* you want? You were the one who started

this, so spell it out for me. Is it…do you want a casual fling? Because I can't imagine you going to all this effort just to try and get me into bed." She laughed, but it sounded forced and weak even to her.

He grinned, still looking ahead at the road, and he seemed to be enjoying teasing her. "Something tells me you don't do casual."

"I don't. But if that's what you want, then I need to know." So she could prepare herself for it to end, and not feel hurt when he moved on to someone else. Or so she could end it before it really started.

Logan released her hand and reached across the cab to grasp her jaw in his hand. Her gaze swung up to his and locked there, and the possessive gleam in his stole her breath. "The way I feel about you is anything but casual," he said, his voice deep and low as he stared into her eyes. "And make no mistake, I want to take you to bed so bad it keeps me up at night. But I want exclusive with you. Because to be honest, I can't stand the thought of another guy touching you."

Her heart knocked against her ribs at the possessiveness in his tone. A rush of desire shot through her, flowing through her veins like warm honey. She'd never expected a man like him to admit such a thing. The exclusivity part was a huge relief because she had no interest in seeing anyone else, and she didn't want him to go out with another woman while he was seeing her.

"But not until you're ready," he added.

"I'm down with the exclusive bit. I don't want anyone touching you either."

He shot her a slow, sensual smile that made her toes curl. She hadn't even noticed the traffic light change, too ensnared by the way he held her gaze to look away, but he let go of her and put his hand back on the steering wheel as he resumed driving. Taylor sat unmoving in her seat. All she could do was stare at that big, powerful hand

and imagine it stroking over her naked body.

She shivered and shifted against the leather as the heat inside her intensified, tightening her nipples and igniting a throb between her legs. It had been so long since she'd slept with anyone, and the thought of Logan taking her to bed today almost had her sliding into a puddle in the foot well.

Half a block later he turned right and pulled into the underground parking garage of her building. She felt a little lightheaded as they took the elevator to her floor, every sense heightened.

When he followed her into the apartment and locked the door behind them, the nerves hit hard. "I'm just gonna grab a quick shower," she blurted, and rushed for the bedroom to grab a change of clothes. If they did take things into the bedroom, she wanted to be clean and smell good all over, and she needed a few minutes to regroup.

The hot water did nothing to soothe the gnawing ache inside her, or settle her buzzing nerves. Logan was out there right now, and he wanted her. Wanted her exclusively.

Prior to their conversation in the truck she'd briefly considered the idea of agreeing to a fling if that's what he wanted, but now she realized she couldn't do that. She was already falling for him and there was no way for her to shut her feelings off at this point. Not after how protective and thoughtful he'd been.

Pushing it all aside for now, she washed her hair, shaved her legs, blew her hair dry and brushed her teeth before getting dressed and putting on mascara, eyeliner and lipstick.

Wearing a pair of snug jeans and a feminine black-and-white polka dot top with cap sleeves, she exited the bathroom to find him on the couch with his left leg propped up, watching TV.

He looked over his shoulder at her and smiled a little,

his hot gaze raking over the length of her body in a way that made her feel naked. Her bare toes curled into the carpet.

"My turn," he said as he got up.

"Your turn?" she mumbled, her mind going blank as all six-foot-plus of sexy alpha male prowled toward her.

He stopped a half-step away from her, a sensual smile tugging at the corners of his mouth. "For a shower," he murmured, then kissed her softly.

"Oh." Her eyelids fluttered as a delicious languor pervaded her body. Then he raised his head, gave her another of those knee-weakening smiles, and disappeared into the bathroom.

Taylor stared at the closed door, her skin tingling all over and her pulse thudding in her ears as the hiss of water started up in the shower. She wanted him. Why was she still standing here?

You are worthy.

Refusing to get lost in her head and ruin the moment by overthinking it, she walked over and grasped the doorknob. It turned easily under her hand, releasing a cloud of steam as she eased the door open.

At the sight before her, her lower belly did a slow, delicious somersault.

Logan stood under the spray facing away from her, the broad expanse of his muscled back and shoulders on display above the tiled half wall of the shower. His head was tipped back, the muscles in his arms and back flexing as he ran his hands through his wet hair.

Oh my God...

Her mouth went dry as she devoured the sight of him with her eyes.

He stilled, as though he sensed he was no longer alone. Lowering his hands, he half-turned to look at her. Taylor couldn't breathe, couldn't look away as their gazes connected and locked. He stood absolutely motionless while the water cascaded over his naked skin, watching her.

Waiting to see what she'd do.

She didn't care that she'd just spent all that time getting her hair dry and putting on makeup. She wanted this too badly to put it off for another second.

Her fingers shook a little as she reached for the top button on her shirt. Logan's eyes dropped to her hands, taking in every single motion as she undid the row one by one. With each one she released, her confidence grew, bolstered by the rapt hunger on his face.

As she undid the last button the two halves of her top parted, revealing the pink lace bra she wore underneath.

Logan turned fully around to face her, his gaze riveted to her breasts, his powerful chest and shoulders on display for her.

Emboldened, she slipped off the shirt and slowly reached for the button on her jeans. His eyes dipped down to follow her fingers, stayed there when she undid the button and eased the denim over her hips and down her thighs, leaving her in only her bra and panties.

Slowly he dragged his gaze up to hers, and the sheer desire written there made her heart pound.

Loving the sense of power it gave her to know that she was turning this sexy man on, she slipped off the bra and panties and stood there before him completely naked. Letting him look his fill.

With his features set in hungry lines, Logan placed a palm on the shower door and pushed it open. Then he held his hand out to her. "Come here." His voice was low, gravelly, and the raw desire in it sent sparks of heat radiating along her limbs.

She started toward him without conscious thought, drawn to him by some invisible force. And it wasn't scary at all. Well, it was, but in an I-just-stepped-off-the-edge-of-a-tall-building kind of way, making her stomach drop while a delicious tingle spread throughout her body.

The moment she placed her hand in his, his long fingers contracted around hers and pulled her up against that muscular, slick body. A shockwave of heat rushed through her as she stared up into his face.

His russet lashes were spiky with drops of water, his wet hair and beard a few shades darker than normal. And his eyes... That blue-green gaze was hot enough to melt her bones as he stared down at her, his hands sliding into her hair.

She tilted her head back into his hold and settled her palms on his wide shoulders, thrilling at the way the muscles bunched beneath her fingers. "I want you," she whispered, beyond caring what the consequences of her actions would be. Exclusive fling or not, she wasn't passing this up. All she knew was she'd never wanted anyone this way, and she needed to experience this with him.

Logan let out a low growl that made goose bumps rise all over her body, and covered her lips with his. She gasped and pressed into him, desperate for more, and relief from the ache he created within her. A moan of anticipation and desire spilled out of her at the feel of his hot, hard erection trapped against her lower belly. His tongue pushed into her mouth, stroking, exploring, increasing the throb in her breasts and between her thighs.

She rubbed against him, hungry for more, for everything he could give her. Logan set one hand on her hip and abruptly turned them, his scorching kiss muffling her excited gasp. He handled her like she weighed nothing at all, and that intense vulnerability made her hyper aware of her femininity. Instead of making her afraid, she reveled in it.

He pinned her up against the shower wall with his body and kissed her until she couldn't breathe, until she was rocking her pelvis against him in a desperate attempt for relief. Those strong hands threaded into her hair once more, his fingers curving around the back of her skull as he tipped her head to the side so he could rake his open mouth over the sensitive skin on her neck.

Her broken moan echoed in the tiled enclosure, quickly drowned by the rush of the cascading water. The prickle of his beard contrasted with the heat of his mouth and the soft, hot glide of his tongue as he laved her skin. "God, you're so soft," he rasped out.

She was already panting by the time he let go of her head and slid his slick hands down to cup her breasts. Her eyes slid closed and she leaned her head back against the shower wall, clinging to his shoulders to keep her upright.

He cupped her in his palms, teased her painfully tight nipples with his thumbs and fingers before lowering his head to one. "Lean back," he said in a low voice.

Taylor bit her lip and obeyed, glad for the shower wall holding her up since her legs were already weak. She opened her eyes just in time to see his lashes lower as his tongue darted out to lick at one straining peak. Her knees wobbled. She dug her fingers into his shoulders and arched her back, whispering his name.

He made a hungry sound deep in his chest and took one nipple into his mouth to suck at it. Taylor quivered in his grasp. Hot, wet suction surrounded the sensitive nub, sending streaks of pleasure radiating to the aching flesh between her thighs. She moved restlessly, little whimpers tearing from her throat.

But he wouldn't be rushed. He took his time, alternating between one breast, then the other, until the burn became too much and she buried her face in his wet hair, shuddering. "Touch me. *Touch* me." She couldn't stand the empty ache any longer.

Without releasing her nipple from the heat of his mouth, he slid one hand down the center of her body. Slowly, so torturously slowly that she trembled and fought for air. It blazed a path over her belly to her right hip, down the length of her thigh before slowly gliding back up the inside, his touch so light it raised goose bumps.

Taylor held her breath, waiting. Dying for him to touch where she needed him so badly.

His tongue swirled around her nipple at the same time his palm finally settled between her legs and cupped her swollen sex. A strangled sound came out of her. "Feel good?" he murmured.

"*Yes*. Don't stop."

Logan groaned and kept sucking as he gently rubbed her sensitive folds. God, she was so wet, so needy.

He glided his fingertips through her folds, spreading the wetness up to the pulsing knot of nerves at the top of her sex. She whimpered as he circled the fragile spot, the muscles in her belly pulling taut.

Pleasure streaked through her like fire, burning her from the inside out. More, she needed more.

"Want to feel you come for me," he muttered against her breast, and slid two fingers into her slick heat. "Been thinking about it for so long."

Taylor cried out and grabbed hold of his head, her hips rocking against his hand. The orgasm was already building deep inside her, rushing at her with every deft caress of his hand.

With a low, rough sound of approval, he began sliding his fingers in and out of her in a slow, relentless rhythm while his thumb caressed her swollen clit. Over and over he repeated the intimate caresses, never varying his speed as he continued to suck first on one nipple, then the other. She tightened around his fingers as the pleasure rose higher and higher, her heart pounding frantically against her ribs.

"Oh, God," she groaned, trembling all over. *Don't stop. Don't ever stop.*

He didn't.

She threw her head back and cried out over and over as the pleasure exploded in a black velvet wave. Pulse after pulse rocked her, every muscle in her body quivering. She curled around him, pressing her face into the curve of his neck and shoulder, nipping his slick skin while the orgasm faded.

His hand was still buried between her thighs. He released her nipple and straightened, and she caught the wince he tried to hide.

"Oh, your knee," she whispered, putting a hand to the side of his face.

His laugh was low, strained. "That's not what's hurting at the moment," he whispered, and claimed her mouth with his.

Taylor hummed and sucked at his tongue, sliding one hand between them to reach down and grasp his straining erection. Logan growled into her mouth and pushed into her grip, and his clear desperation filled her with longing. She slid her free hand into the back of his hair and kissed him with all the tenderness and passion he'd unleashed in her as she stroked the thick, hot length of his cock.

His entire body twitched and his breathing changed, growing choppy and labored. Raw, rough sounds came out of him as he pumped into her slippery fist, lost in their voracious kiss.

Sensing that he was getting close to the edge, Taylor slowed her strokes and reached her other hand down to grasp his butt. She squeezed once, then trailed her fingertips down and between his legs to caress the sensitive skin of his scrotum. Logan groaned, the sound almost pleading, and shuddered.

It was so freaking hot. "I want to watch your face when you come," she whispered against his mouth. She wanted to sink to her knees and take him in her mouth, too, but right now she needed to see his expression as she brought him to release.

His eyes flew open and focused on hers, glazed and desperate. His nostrils were flared, his face taut with strain, just inches from her own as she squeezed and stroked his thick, swollen cock.

He was the sexiest thing she'd ever seen as he stood motionless before her, holding her gaze while he let her take him closer to the edge with each slick pump of her hand. "God, I want to be inside you right now," he ground out.

Heat rippled through her abdomen. Staring into his gorgeous eyes, she felt the intimacy of their connection lock into place. In that single moment, she'd never felt more vulnerable. And because it was Logan, that didn't scare her one bit.

An instant later his breathing hitched and his eyes squeezed shut. His jaw clenched and his head tipped back as he neared his release.

She kept her rhythm steady, watched his face greedily as he spurted in her grip and groaned while the orgasm wracked his body. He grabbed hold of her hand to stop her, squeezing tight, then sagged against her, their bodies plastered together from chest to thigh.

And then he wrapped his arms around her and simply held her there under the warm spray while the water ran over them in their private little cocoon.

Chapter Seventeen

———◇◇◇◇———

*D*illon had once looked forward to Friday nights
during the school year. Not anymore.

*His team was down six points with less than a
minute to go in their second playoff game, and the other
team still had possession. If they lost, they were done and
wouldn't make the finals for the first time in six years.*

*At first, he'd loved the outlet playing on the varsity
football team gave him. The freedom it gave him and the
respect it had garnered from his classmates. Even a little
bit from Frank, who would show up to watch once in a
while if he wasn't working night shift.*

*Or too wasted to drag himself off the couch. Not that
he gave a fuck what Frank thought.*

*Despite the loss, Dillon had played well, throwing four
touchdown passes and only being sacked once. From the
sidelines, he watched helplessly as the clock dwindled
down in the final seconds while the visiting team's fans
went nuts in the stands.*

*Disappointment settled heavy in his stomach. The
season was over.*

He grabbed his helmet, stood, and accepted the back slaps and consolations from his coaches and teammates. Good game, man. The defense screwed you over. Get 'em next time.

On his way off the field he glanced up once into the stands, looking for Taylor. She was still sitting in her spot like she always did, waiting for him with a blanket wrapped around her and a knit cap on her head. Frank was still nowhere to be seen.

Taylor gave him a sunny smile and a thumbs-up to say she was proud of him. And damned if it didn't make something inside him glow. His whole life he'd never had anyone who meant enough to him to want to make them proud. But he did Taylor.

He showered and changed before meeting her outside the locker room. "You played really well," she said, wrapping an arm around his waist and leaning into him for a hug that he returned. "Too bad the score didn't match that."

"It's okay. Next year."

"Yeah." The parking lot was pretty much empty as they left the school and headed up the sidewalk through the residential neighborhood.

A few blocks up, the area changed to small shops and restaurants. Most of the football team was already at the diner with the cheerleaders and girlfriends. Dillon's stomach growled as they drew near, and he couldn't help a twinge of envy at the sight of his teammates wolfing down burgers, fries and milkshakes inside the warm building.

Next to him, Taylor shook out the blanket she'd folded up and wrapped it around her shoulders. Her coat was too thin and didn't zip up properly. She had to use safety pins to keep it closed. "That wind is killer," she muttered.

It was cold enough to sting his cheeks as it whipped past them, kicking up dry leaves that lay curled up on the sidewalk. He took his hands out of his jacket pockets and stuffed them into his jeans. Two dollar bills met his fingers. Enough for a hot drink, but nothing else. "Feel like a hot chocolate?"

"Nah, it's okay. Thanks, though."

She never let him spend what little money he had on her. Not even when she was freezing after sitting in the cold for three hours watching him play football. A sport she didn't even care about. She went solely to support him, when he knew she'd much rather be at home with a book or one of those math puzzles she liked.

Soon he'd have a lot more money and neither of them would have to worry about going hungry again. He'd have enough to buy them dinner every night of the damn week if that's what they wanted.

They passed by the diner, and he noted how Taylor kept her gaze straight ahead, not looking at the others inside. A few of his teammates had guessed things were tight financially for them, and had offered multiple times to buy them something after the game. Dillon always refused, out of pride. He didn't want anyone's pity or charity. He was going to make it on his own.

He was going to make it big.

They didn't talk much as they walked the remaining two miles to their house. He breathed a sigh of relief when he saw Frank's car missing. Maybe he'd taken another night shift or something. That would allow Dillon to relax the rest of the night.

The temperature inside the house wasn't much warmer than outside, but at least the wind wasn't cutting at them anymore. Taylor kept her knit cap and jacket on as she hurried to the kitchen and started warming up a couple cans of soup for them.

He was digging a box of stale crackers out of the cupboard next to the sink when he heard it. The rumbling of Frank's car engine came from the driveway.

At the stove Taylor froze and looked toward the front door. *God dammit*, he hated seeing that pinched, worried expression on her face. After what had happened to her to bring her to this place, he never wanted her to be afraid again. "Go to your room, Tay."

She didn't move, stubbornly staying where she was.

The front door banged open. Frank stomped in, wearing a heavy jacket over his uniform. One look at him and Dillon knew he was wasted.

Frank slammed the door shut with enough force to rattle it on its frame. "You had the lead into the fourth quarter, and you still lost," he spat, contempt spewing from every word.

He'd seen the game. Dillon's stomach balled up into a hard knot. He was in for it now.

"First time in six years the Warriors haven't made the finals, and first time you're the starting quarterback. Not a fucking coincidence."

Dillon clenched his jaw and moved to block the doorway to protect Taylor. When Frank was drunk and in a mood like this, neither of them ever knew what he would do.

Frank stalked toward him, his boots thudding on the scuffed wood floor. "Nothing to say for yourself?"

He knew better than to open his mouth, except to be polite. "No, sir."

"You could have clinched it with one more good pass, but you were too busy prancing around out there in the pocket like a fucking fairy."

Had he been in the stands somewhere? Dillon hadn't seen him.

He bit back a grunt as Frank shoved his shoulders, knocking him back into the wall with a thud. Immediately he shoved away from it and faced the man, hands balled into fists.

Frank's lips curled back over his teeth in a feral smile.

"You wanna hit me, boy?" His eyes narrowed to slits. "Go ahead and try."

Dillon was angry enough to do it, but he wasn't stupid. He would have run away over two years ago if it hadn't meant leaving Taylor here alone. The day would come for him to leave, however. And when it did, Dillon would punch Frank straight in his ugly fucking face, bust his nose and a few teeth before walking out over his unconscious body and never looking back.

As long as he'd made sure Taylor would be looked after first.

A meaty hand flashed out and cuffed Dillon on the side of the head. "Do it. Let's see what you've got, hotshot quarterback."

Dillon's knuckles ached from squeezing so hard.

The gleam in Frank's eyes made Dillon's throat go dry. This was going to be bad. Every muscle in his body tightened in anticipation of the pain coming his way.

"Huh?" Frank slapped the side of Dillon's face hard enough to crank his head around and make his eye water. "Let's go, tough guy."

Fuck this. He shifted his weight, brought his right hand back.

"Stop!"

Before Dillon could take a swing, Taylor darted in between them, smacking one hand flat in the middle of Frank's chest. Her face was livid as she glared up at the man. "Leave him alone."

Frank's gaze shifted to her and a wave of fear rushed through Dillon. "Taylor, no." He grabbed her shoulders, tried to push her out from between them, but she wouldn't budge, fighting to hold her place in front of him.

"Don't you touch him," she snapped at Frank, her voice shaking. Afraid but so damn brave as she faced off with their foster father. "You're drunk, and you're mean when you're drunk. He already feels bad enough that they

lost the game, but it wasn't his fault. If you'd showed up sooner, you would have seen all the touchdown passes he threw."

"Get the fuck outta my way," Frank snarled at her, his face mottled.

"No. You leave him alone," she cried, her voice breaking.

Taylor never cried. Would never give anyone the satisfaction of seeing her weak. The sight of her tears seemed to trigger something in Frank.

That angry gaze moved from her to Dillon and back, and it was as though a switch had flipped. He shoved her hand off his chest and swung away, muttering obscenities as he stalked through the kitchen. "Both of you just stay the fuck away from me."

His bedroom door slammed shut a few moments later. Dillon sagged against the wall and closed his eyes. Two thin arms wound around his waist, and the scent of her shampoo drifted to him as she laid her head on his chest.

Afraid she'd see the tears in his eyes, he hugged her in silence. "You shouldn't have done that."

"Someone has to stand up for you," she answered. "If I don't, who will?"

Who will?

No one.

Dillon opened his eyes and stared up at the darkened ceiling of the cheap motel room he'd rented last night. Taylor had always stuck her neck out for him, even when she'd suspected he was up to bad shit toward the end of their time together.

He had no one and nothing until he killed her and the heat was on. The local authorities and several agencies had a BOLO out on him.

After two days of doing everything in his power to finish this, Taylor was still alive. Now his window of opportunity was gone and he was running on borrowed time.

Carlos would have sent others after her by now. Possibly after him, too. The only way to save his skin was to kill her and send proof to the cartel before one of the *sicarios* caught up with him.

Rolling to his side, he reached for the prepaid phone he'd picked up at a gas station last night, and dialed Janet. The DEA was probably monitoring her phone now, but he was desperate to find out where Taylor was and had to risk it.

All he needed was to get within rifle range of her and set up a shot. One bullet to the head, and this nightmare would be over.

****

Taylor turned over in bed without opening her eyes, something tugging at the edges of her consciousness.

Logan.

He was no longer wrapped around her like a living blanket as he had been most of the night. Her eyes popped open, but his side of the bed was empty and the room was still dim. He hadn't been inside her yet, because neither of them had any protection with them, but after that much needed, mind-blowing release in the shower it had been heaven to snuggle up naked against.that hot, powerful body.

She'd never felt so safe and relaxed in her life as she had last night. Where had he gone?

She rolled to her side and half sat up, looking around the room. The apartment was silent. He'd left? Without saying goodbye?

Out of nowhere, a strange hollowness opened up in her chest. As if he'd taken a chunk of her heart with him.

The realization stopped her cold. God, was it too late? She had feelings for him. Big feelings. Just how far had she fallen for him?

Reaching for her glasses, she spotted the note beside them on the bedside table. *Gone to grab us something tastier than eggs and toast for breakfast. Back soon. Logan.*

The hollowness vanished instantly, replaced by excitement and anticipation. Was this what infatuation felt like?

She jumped out of bed and rushed to the bathroom to get showered, brush her teeth and get dressed. It was Sunday, and she'd planned to get more work done, but if Logan wanted to spend the day with her here then she'd catch up on everything later.

The realization that she was willing to put work aside for a man was so startling that she stopped in the act of brushing her hair to stare at her reflection in the mirror. "Who *are* you?"

The new, improved version of Taylor Kennedy. A wide grin spread across her face. "Because I am worthy." She liked this new her.

A lot.

While she waited for Logan to return she took some files back to bed with her. By the soft light of the bedside lamp she studied the columns of numbers and the reports the offshore banks had sent her.

For the first time in recent memory, she couldn't concentrate. On the pages before her, the rows and tables of data held no appeal whatsoever. The driving need to figure out the puzzle before her was absent, and the idea of sifting through the material for a key bit of information left her bored and unsatisfied.

Wow, two firsts in one day. Just a few days with Logan and he was already playing hell on her focus and work ethic.

Sighing, she took off her glasses and set them aside with the files, then rolled to her side and closed her eyes to rest them. She pictured Logan, smiling at her yesterday as he'd hauled the kayak out of the water. He'd been so wonderful to her, making her feel like a desirable and interesting woman rather than a dull and socially awkward numbers geek.

She must have drifted off, because the next thing she knew, her T-shirt was sliding up her back and the scent of coffee teased her nose. *Mmm, breakfast in bed?* She'd never done that before.

"You're back," she murmured sleepily.

"Yeah. Missed you while I was gone, too." Warm lips began trailing kisses up the length of her spine.

Smiling, all sleepy and warm, she kept her eyes closed and allowed herself to drift, enjoying his attention. The bedside lamp clicked off a moment later and the bed shifted. Logan's warm hands began peeling off her clothes, the touch of his fingertips leaving streaks of fire in their wake. She was wet already, her entire body soft and aching for him.

So when he tugged her hips backward to bring her onto her knees, she sighed and followed his cues. Her skin buzzed at the feel of his beard and lips moving up the inside of her thigh. She held her breath, belatedly realized she'd curled her fingers into the sheets and stopped thinking altogether when his tongue delved between her legs to stroke over her tender center.

"Ohh," she moaned, unable to form a more coherent response than that.

It felt like she was dissolving from the inside out, each tender lap of his tongue against her swollen clit increasing the aching need. She opened wider for him, resting her weight on her forearms, the muscles in her legs trembling slightly. The whole time he kept one solid palm pressed to the base of her spine and the other curled around her hip, anchoring her in place while his mouth took her toward heaven.

Soon she was gasping and panting, twisting against his mouth. She needed more. Needed him to push into her, fill her.

Logan sucked at her gently, making her back arch before he eased away. She let out a mewl of frustration and started to turn around but he stayed her with a solid grip on her hip. "Stay still."

She did, allowing her head to rest back on her pillow while the whisper of him stripping came from behind her, followed by a quiet tearing sound.

"Picked us up something else while I was out, too," he whispered, moving in behind her.

A wall of heat and strength surrounded her as his chest touched her back, his hips pressed tight to her rear. Her body responded to the feel of all that strength wrapping around her, not to hurt or control, but to cherish and protect. To pleasure.

There was no fear, and no self-consciousness. She trusted him completely. A light shudder rippled through her body, her heart swelling.

With tiny caresses, he slid the hard, thick ridge of his erection against her folds. She gasped and pushed backward, hungry for more, desperately glad he'd thought to buy condoms.

He obliged, slipping one hand around to cradle her sex, his middle finger rubbing her clit while he pushed inside her, inch by inch. Taylor groaned and pressed back as pleasure sizzled across her nerve endings. He was huge inside her, filling her completely with his heat and it felt so damn good combined with the way he was stroking her.

Nuzzling the crook of her neck and shoulder, he buried his cock inside her, one hand on her hip to keep her steady.

"Ah, hell, you feel so good," he breathed against her neck, his warm breath and the tickle of his beard making her shiver.

"You too," she gasped out. She was dizzy. Breathless.

There were no more words, only sensation, and she wanted more. She let her body take over, following Logan's slow rhythm, angling her hips so he hit just the right spot. Her whimper of surrender sounded loud to her own ears but he made a soothing sound and nibbled at the side of her neck as he rode her, stroking all the best places at once.

Ecstasy hovered at the edge of her consciousness. She let her body float toward it, guided along by Logan's sure movements. The muscles of her belly and thighs pulled taut. Her breath caught in her throat as the pleasure crested and burst, wringing cry after cry of ecstasy from her throat.

Logan wrapped his free arm around her and locked her tight to him, his teeth scraping at the side of her neck as he drove in harder. Faster. She was still coming down from her high when he buried his face against her skin and groaned in pure pleasure, his big body shuddering with the force of his own orgasm.

Taylor lay sprawled with her upper body flat on the mattress, too weak to move. It was like he'd melted all her bones and liquefied her muscles.

Oh my God. So. *Good.* So good with him.

After a minute, he gently eased out of her and kissed her shoulder. The mattress dipped again and she heard his soft footfalls on the carpet. She rolled to her side and drew the covers over her, too blissed out to find out where he was going.

The water ran in the bathroom sink a moment later, then he came back and slipped in behind her. He drew her back into the curve of his body, those powerful arms contracting around her. She groaned in utter contentment and forced herself to roll over so she could snuggle up against his chest, the scattering of hairs there tickling her nose.

"I actually did bring us breakfast," he whispered against her hair, stroking the fingers of one hand through it. "Not just condoms."

She had to be careful she didn't start drooling at the thought of eating in bed with him and then having another round of fabulous sex. "That was nice of you."

"You hungry?"

"Mmm, later. Don't wanna move."

"Well then, my work here is done," he said on a proud chuckle.

They lay quietly for a long time while she soaked up his heat and the thud of his heartbeat beneath her cheek as he held her. "You working today?" he finally asked.

"I should." But she still didn't want to, and that wasn't like her at all. And she really needed to get back to the investigation because she'd already taken most of yesterday off. She should feel more guilty about that, but apparently being targeted for death then having crazy hot sex with Logan had changed the way she looked at everything. "Might have a meeting later on, Chris said he'd call and let me know. You working?"

"Physio in an hour, then I'm meeting some of the guys for some light training and we'll grab something to eat after." He stroked her back with his blunt fingertips, making her want to purr. "Call me when you're done for the day? I don't want to hang around here and distract you if you've got stuff to get done."

"Good call." Because he was the biggest distraction she'd ever come across. Even in full workaholic mode with this time-sensitive investigation going on, she would never have the strength to resist him if he stayed here.

"Can I ask you something?"

She opened her eyes but didn't look up at him, something inside her stilling at his tone. She didn't want this peaceful interlude to end, but she knew it had to eventually. "Sure."

"I've been thinking about it a lot and wanted to ask you, but it never seemed to be the right time."

She was fully awake now, some of the sensual bliss fading away at his words. "Okay."

His hand never ceased its slow, gentle stroking up and down her back. Soothing. Caring. The man had amazing hands. "How did you wind up in foster care?"

Of all the things he could have asked, she hadn't seen that one coming. Maybe she should have. It was natural for him to be curious about her, since they'd been intimate and were still getting to know each other. Because she felt safe with him, she was willing to tell him. It was time. But she couldn't look at him when she did. There was still too much humiliation for her surrounding the incident.

"You sure you want to know?"

"Yes. But only if you want to tell me. If you don't, I understand."

She drew a deep breath. "I told you my parents were both addicts."

"Yes."

She hesitated only a moment before continuing. "They weren't bad people. They just made poor choices and then their addictions took over."

His fingers stroked lazily up the length of her spine. "Were you close to them when you were little?"

"I think so. My mom especially. I remember her making birthday cakes for me and turning off all the lights before she lit the candles and carried them to the kitchen table while she sang happy birthday. And the three of us liked going to movies together. Dad and I would always share some popcorn. On Saturdays, he and I would get up early in the morning and watch cartoons so my mom could sleep in longer." The thought brought a bittersweet smile to her face. It had been so long since she'd thought about them, or those times.

"I'm glad you've got some good memories of them."

"Me too. I missed them for a long time, but I think rather than mourning the loss of my parents, I mourned the loss of what could have been if they hadn't been addicts. You know?"

"Yeah, I understand."

A few beats passed while he waited for her to continue. Taylor hesitated about whether to keep talking. The next admission was hard for her. Other than Dillon and a few other people who'd worked on her case, no one knew what had led to her being taken into foster care. She'd made sure of it.

In all these years, she'd never told a soul about what had happened to her, not even Charlie. That inability—or unwillingness—to open up to anyone about it was part of the reason she'd never thought she could have a relationship with a man. At least, not a healthy one, due to her trust issues.

Logan had changed all that. She wanted him enough to exorcise her demons once and for all and lay herself completely bare to him. Even though it scared her to death.

"If you don't want to talk about it, it's fine," he murmured.

"No, I...want to." And that said it all, didn't it? She trusted Logan. And she had carried this burden for far too long as it was. This shameful, dirty secret that had stained her soul and all but obliterated her self-worth.

She swallowed before continuing, feeling exposed and vulnerable. "After my mom died of an overdose, my dad started using more and more. He went into a sharp downward spiral. At some point it got so bad that he stopped going into work. He would stay in bed with his door locked and I barely saw him. Eventually he ran out of money. Sometimes I went a full day or two without anything to eat."

Logan made a gruff sound and wrapped both arms

around her, strong and secure. "How old were you?"

"Eleven." She cleared her throat, the protectiveness of his embrace giving her the strength to keep going. Now that she'd started telling him, she wanted to get the rest of it out. "He started bringing people home with him. They'd shoot up together in the living room or kitchen. He'd make me go to my room first, so I wouldn't see it, but I snuck out a few times and saw him. Sometimes various dealers would show up at our place."

The shame started to close in on her again, thick and suffocating. She shook it off. *I am worthy.*

Her past did not define her. She'd been a child. She wasn't to blame for what had happened. And she trusted Logan. Trusted that he cared about her and wouldn't judge her.

"Then one night, my father couldn't pay for his next hit. He was desperate. He'd sold nearly everything we had that could be pawned to support his habit. The dealer came that time, and there was nothing. Nothing except me."

Logan sucked in a harsh breath, his entire body going rigid.

She squeezed her eyes shut, kept her cheek against his chest and just said it, wanting to just say it and get it over with. "The dealer asked if he could have half an hour alone with me in my room in exchange for the heroin. My father said yes." Drawing in a bolstering breath, she ran her fingertips over the center of Logan's wide chest.

"So while he was getting his next fix, the dealer came into my room. At first, I didn't realize what was going on. But the way he looked at me was wrong. He came over to the bed and grabbed me." The memories bombarded her like a string of flashbulbs bursting in her mind. Vivid. Terrifying. "I started screaming and fought him. He pinned me down but I bit and scratched and kicked. I knocked over my dresser. It hit the wall and my lamp broke on the floor. Thank God the walls in that building were thin, because my elderly neighbor who happened to be the superintendent heard me. He came over and broke the door down, dragged the guy off me and carried me out of there."

Logan didn't say anything, but the tension in his muscles told her exactly how upset he was.

She was silent a moment, letting the horror of the memory fade under the comforting warmth of Logan's embrace. "The police came with a social worker to take me away. The last time I saw my father, he was in cuffs being loaded into the back of a patrol car. He looked right at me, but he was so high I don't think he recognized me or realized what he'd done. I heard he died in jail a few months later. Got his hands on some potent heroin inside, and OD'd."

A resounding silence filled the room as she finished, pressing in on her. She couldn't look Logan in the face, not wanting to see the pity or the anger that had to be written on his face.

But he didn't say anything. He just rolled to his back and took her with him so that she was lying flush against his body, and wrapped his arms snug around her. Then he pressed his face into her hair and held her that way in the quiet.

A lump formed in her throat and her eyes stung. The sheer relief of his acceptance and support after what she'd just told him meant the world to her. She felt lighter inside now that she'd finally opened up to someone about her past.

"You sorry you asked?" she said quietly a minute later.

"No. But it kills me to think of you going through that. You were just a kid."

She nodded. "It sucked. I wouldn't go back and live through that again for all the money in the world."

"No kidding."

She was quiet a moment, collecting her thoughts. "For a long time I felt like they'd both abandoned me. That they must not have really wanted or loved me if the heroin was more important to them. It made me believe I was unlovable."

"That's BS. You're totally loveable, and they loved you as much as they were able to until the addiction finally took over."

Yes. "Guess that's why I'm so anal-retentive about everything now—I like to control my environment."

"Well, you're not anal-retentive about *everything*."

She tipped her head to look up at him in surprise. "No?"

"You're not like that in bed. Actually, I'd say you're the opposite and kind of like giving up control to me."

Her cheeks heated even as a thrill raced through her. She loved the way he took over in bed, it was the hottest thing she'd ever experienced. Yet another surprise discovery about herself. "With you, yeah."

But no one else. Maybe that's why it had never worked out with another guy. She hadn't trusted him enough to let go, let alone confess her darkest secrets.

A wide, satisfied smile spread across his face. "So I'm special, huh?"

"Yeah, I guess you are," she teased.

His eyes widened in mock outrage. "You guess? You *guess*?" He rolled her back beneath him, pinning her with his weight, and gripped her head to hold her still while he buried his face in the curve of her neck.

She gasped at the sensation and giggled as he rubbed his beard over her sensitive skin. "That tickles!" It kind of burned a little, too.

"I know. Too bad you're gonna have to endure more of it, huh?"

Squirming and wriggling, she laughed as he proceeded to give her a whisker rub all over her naked body. And soon the giggles and struggles turned to moans and arching into him.

Thankfully he got the message, quit teasing her, and put his mouth to much better use.

Chapter Eighteen

Damn, it was good to be back. Well, sort of back, but Logan would take reduced duty over nothing any day. His physiotherapist figured his knee was at around sixty percent and improving a little more each day. As long as he took it easy—including using his crutches when he was on his feet, something he didn't intend to do unless absolutely necessary—and didn't overdo it over the next few weeks, he should be fully operational in another month or so.

Besides, being here helped keep his mind off how badly he wished he was still back in that apartment with Taylor, curled up in the bed he'd crawled out of only a few hours ago.

Get it together, man.

Today's light training was already taking its toll on him though. He bit back a wince as he shifted his weight and waited behind Zaid as the team stacked up in a line beside the newly installed door of the shoot house. They'd already blown two off their hinges practicing various breaches, rotating through positions to give everyone a turn. He was due up next.

None of them spoke as they waited in position for Hamilton to give the command to enter. Nobody knew what scenario Commander Taggart and his helpers had set up inside the plywood maze of rooms and hallways.

A hand squeezed Logan's right shoulder, indicating that Kai and the five other guys behind him were ready to rock. Logan gripped Zaid's shoulder, who in turn pumped Freeman's.

Freeman didn't move, didn't give any indication that Zaid had alerted him, his entire focus aimed on the exterior doorway. "Execute," Hamilton said quietly through their comms.

Zaid hauled back the battering ram and slammed it into the lock on the door, the clang of metal-on-metal loud in the quiet building. He had to ram it four times before the lock finally gave way, and he was able to haul it back.

Freeman immediately rushed through the doorway— the fatal funnel—with Zaid right on his heels. Logan swept in next, doing a buttonhook maneuver that placed him up against the near-side wall, and sent a flare of pain shooting through his knee. He winced, stumbled.

His jaw clamped tight. *Goddamn it.*

"Stop, stop. What the hell was that, guys? My ninety-two-year-old grandmother could have set up and shot the first two of you through the door with that kind of delay," Commander Taggart called out from overhead where he was observing from the catwalk that ran the length of the shoot house. "Do it again. Night optics this time. Zaid, you're still the breacher."

Zaid let out a frustrated breath but didn't say anything as he trudged back from the hallway and passed Logan on the way out the door. They were all perfectionists, and in this line of work mistakes could cost lives. No one said anything to Zaid; they were all their own worst critics.

Everyone lined up at the door and waited while he and

Zaid put on a fresh door and the helpers inside moved into different positions. The moment the lights went out, Logan lowered his night vision goggles into place and switched them on. In the green glow of the display he watched as Freeman took point again. When Zaid was ready with the ram, Freeman gave the signal.

Zaid laid into the lock on the door with one ruthless blow and the lock cracked, along with some of the wood. He reared back and drove the sole of his boot into the weak spot, and the door flew open.

Freeman rushed in, Zaid right behind him, then Logan. "Clear," Freeman said.

Logan swept past his two teammates toward the corner of two intersecting walls that marked the start of the hallway. Movement caught his peripheral vision.

He swung the barrel of his rifle toward it and fired at the man trying to sneak out of a doorway a dozen yards away. Logan kept moving, footsteps behind him marking his other teammates' advance.

More movement, up ahead to the left.

Logan angled his body to neutralize the threat, fired at the same time one of his other teammates did. His adrenaline was pumping at full strength now but he didn't let it cloud his brain or reflexes, all his concentration focused on the remaining doorways in the hall.

The first door on the right was partially open when he reached it. With a teammate standing directly behind him, Logan peered through the gap in the door.

The far side of the room was empty. He shifted to the left to lean closer to the door while whoever was behind him got ready to kick the door in.

Logan nodded.

The door flew open and a shooter stood in the hidden corner with a rifle. He fired at the same time Logan did. A siminution round hit Logan dead center in the chest.

Shit.

But at least the other shooter was down now.

"Clear," Logan muttered, pissed off at himself.

"You can't say that, because in real life you'd be bleeding out at the moment from my armor-piercing round," a dry voice said from across the darkened room.

Logan recognized it instantly. "Taggart?" He'd thought their commander was still up on the catwalk.

"All clear—building's secure," Easton called out from somewhere down the far end of the hall.

The lights came back on. Logan shut his eyes to protect his retinas and shoved his NVGs back up on the helmet mount. In the corner stood the team commander, a big yellow splatter mark on the left side of his chest. "Not bad," he remarked. "You got me." Then a smug grin curved his mouth. "But I got you too."

Logan grunted and limped out of the room. His knee was not happy about being put through its paces so soon. The rest of the team was coming toward him.

Taggart fell in step with him. "How's the knee?"

"Good." It hurt like a fucking mother right now. But his pride hurt more. And getting shot in the chest even with a simunition round was a sobering reminder that he always had to get the first shot.

Hamilton walked up to him and clapped him on the shoulder. "Come on, hopalong. Time for a shower and a beer. First round's on me."

"Oh, I...can't."

Those steel-gray eyes swung his way. "No? Got a hot date or something?"

"Nah, it's—"

"Hell yeah, he does."

Logan sighed at the sound of Zaid's New Jersey accent coming from behind him.

"Really? So hot you can't even come for one beer?" Hamilton asked.

"Yeah, I'll come for one round. Maybe two." And then

he was getting his ass over to Taylor's as fast as he could. It had been less than seven hours since he'd last seen her, but he missed her already and wanted to make sure she was okay. Among other more pleasurable things he planned to do that made him hard just thinking about.

She was dealing with a hell of a lot of personal stress on top of the pressure her boss was putting on her to track down all the financial threads that might help them crack the case against the *Venenos* wide open. If she and her team could help find bank account information and verify the identities behind them, the agency would pounce.

After showering and pulling on fresh clothes, he went to his locker in the loadout room, careful not to limp even though his knee was throbbing again, and pulled out his phone to text her.

Hey. Just heading out to grab a drink with the guys. Can I head over after that? I'll bring dinner. He knew she wouldn't have eaten yet. The woman was as hyper-focused with her spreadsheets and graphs as he or any of his teammates were during an op.

Just got called into emergency meetings at work. They're coming to pick me up now. Not sure how long it will take. Text you when I'm done? I want to see you.

The last part made his heart swell. Taylor was opening up to him more and more every day, and he was damn thankful that she trusted him that much.

Sure. It was only four o'clock now, so he could grab them something to eat and have it waiting at the apartment for when she got back. *I can come pick you up at the office if you want.*

I'll let you know, thanks. Gotta go.

See you soon. He was smiling as he put his phone back into his pocket.

"What's with that look on your face?"

He looked over at Kai, who was staring at him from a couple lockers over. "What do you mean?"

"You know exactly what I mean." Kai snickered softly as he reached for a clean shirt and tugged it over his head. "Dude, you're toast."

On either side of him, Easton and Jamie both grinned and finished changing into their civvies.

Logan ignored the comment and reached for his leather jacket. Maybe he was toast, but he didn't care. He couldn't wait to see Taylor again. And tonight, he was going to make sure she knew he wanted way more from her than temporary or casual.

****

Dillon's hands shook as he reached for the vial of pills on the battered bathroom counter. He couldn't escape the crushing fatigue that threatened to pull him under, but somehow he had to if he wanted to stay alive.

Even the amphetamines weren't working anymore. It was like his adrenal glands had been maxed out and were now as exhausted as the rest of him.

He took two more anyway and tossed them back with the remnants of his energy drink, the sickeningly sweet taste making him gag. The irony didn't escape him.

He'd been involved with drug dealing and trafficking since the age of sixteen, and never once had he taken anything stronger than cold medicine. But he couldn't function without help now.

For the past three days he'd gone without more than a few hours' sleep combined, taking it in little snatches when he could. The rest of the time he'd spent on the move, looking over his shoulder and doing everything in his power to avoid the people hunting him. Including the two men he'd brought to D.C. with him.

Without a doubt, by now Carlos had tasked them with killing him and Taylor, because he was too high-risk for the cartel at this point. *El Escorpion* would have been made aware of the situation and would be watching it closely. He would either have made the decision to replace or demote Dillon. He'd brought too much heat upon himself and the organization as a whole.

Dillon also had another problem to worry about.

The men he'd trusted to guard his back for the past three years were the closest available *sicarios*, and they knew his habits. There would be others hunting him as well. Which was why he'd had to be so careful about being the opposite of predictable the past few days.

His plan had changed slightly. Salvaging his reputation and status within the cartel was paramount to him, even more so than saving his neck. His lifestyle and everything he'd risked to this point hinged on it.

He'd decided to allow himself one more shot at getting Taylor, then flee the country. Once he was free and clear he'd lie low until the fallout had settled and he could better read the situation within the cartel. If things had cooled off and he still held *El Escorpion's* favor, he'd return to Mexico. If not, he'd live out the rest of his days on a tropical beach in South Asia somewhere.

The drug hit his bloodstream in a powerful rush, bringing with it a wave of renewed energy. He was almost certain that Taylor was still being housed in the building she'd been taken to the other night. At high risk to himself, that same night he'd posed as a local telephone company employee and installed tiny surveillance cameras on all the telephone poles across from the various entrances and exits of the building.

From the safety of his hideout he'd remotely captured a brief glimpse of her as she'd returned late this afternoon in an unmarked SUV, with someone else driving her. He hadn't seen her leave again via any of the doors or in another vehicle, so presumably she was still there. As soon as it was full dark out he would take his rental car there and stake out the building.

He needed Taylor, one way or the other. Dead, or even alive would serve his purposes too, at least to begin with. Then he could use her for collateral and a human shield to buy himself enough time to escape the forces that would come after him once he attacked.

Chapter Nineteen

━━━◇◇◇◇◇━━━

"**Y**ou ready to roll?" Chris asked her from near the apartment door.

"Yes, one second." Taylor hurriedly pulled her hair into a ponytail at the back of her head and slicked on some pink lip-gloss to give her face some color. She hadn't been sleeping well lately, true, but today she was tired for a different reason.

A gorgeous, bearded, six-foot-two reason who'd tired her out before going to sleep last night, then again this morning.

Not that she was complaining. She planned to come back here and have a long afternoon nap once she was done with these meetings at the agency. Logan was coming over again tonight and she wanted to be ready for him when he got here, not on the verge of falling asleep.

She grabbed her laptop and briefcase holding all her files, and headed out of the bedroom. "Okay. Ready."

Chris opened the door and stepped out into the hallway. "Driver's waiting for us downstairs in the garage."

"Sure." A different car than yesterday. For precaution's sake, the agency made sure she never came and went from the building in the same vehicle twice.

In the underground garage a silver SUV was waiting for them when they stepped out of the elevator. Taylor hopped in the back while Chris rode up front with the driver.

"Looking forward to getting warrants and affidavits against these assholes," Chris said as he shuffled through the printouts she'd given him. So far she'd managed to match four people to the offshore accounts recovered from the files Charlie had sent from that flash drive at Baker's estate.

And one of them was Dillon.

She tried to push him from her mind and think about happier things—like Logan—but he weighed heavy on her mind. The agency wanted him arrested, and it was only a matter of finding him and taking him into custody.

Agency lawyers had already compiled a list of evidence covering his various crimes. When he was convicted, he'd serve his sentence in a federal prison. And it would likely be for the rest of his life.

The guilt beat at her but she shoved it aside. He'd brought all this on himself, and if it wasn't her helping uncover his crimes, it would be someone else at the agency. And he'd also tried to kill her, so by comparison, sending him to jail seemed a fair deal to her.

"This is great work, Taylor," Chris went on as the driver pulled through the raised mechanical gate protecting the garage and out onto the street.

The sky was heavy with clouds, a dull, leaden gray that matched her mood. All she wanted at this point was to get this wrapped up and know that Dillon was in custody. Then she could try to put all this behind her and move on. With Logan.

He'd slipped past her defenses with alarming speed

and ease, but there'd been no stopping it. She hadn't *wanted* to stop it. And now that he'd stolen her heart, she couldn't imagine having to let him go. When he came over tonight she wanted to make sure he wanted a real relationship with her going forward.

"Rest of the team is catching up on the latest intel you provided right now. They'll be ready for us when we get there," Chris added.

"Sounds good. I—" She stopped talking when a man dressed in a dark hoodie suddenly stepped out onto the road in front of them and raised his arm, pointing something at them.

"Jesus!" Chris didn't even have time to reach for his weapon before the driver veered hard to the left, but it was too late.

Three bullets slammed through the windshield in rapid succession.

Chris grunted and swore, and the driver slumped over in his seat, blood spilling down his face from the wound in the side of his head. His hands slid off the wheel as he lolled sideways in his seat, but his foot was still on the gas. The engine revved as the vehicle tore toward a row of parked cars on the far side of the street.

Chris made a grab for the steering wheel but it was too late. Taylor's seatbelt jerked taut across her chest and right shoulder, her head snapping forward with the impact as the crunch of metal on metal rang in her ears.

Ignoring the pain, pushing through the shock, she fumbled to undo her seatbelt and immediately crawled forward to shift the SUV to neutral and shut off the engine. The driver was obviously dead, and Chris was gravely wounded in the chest. He was slumped against his door, one bloodstained hand pressed to the wound, his breaths coming in wheezing gasps.

"Get...my weapon..." he managed, flailing his free hand out to hit the automatic door unlock button. They had to get out of the SUV and use it as cover.

Dillon. Dillon had found her and done this.

Taylor reached inside his sport coat for the pistol in the holster beneath his armpit, but the front passenger door yanked open. Chris let out a strangled yell as two gloved hands reached in and hauled him out.

Taylor shrank back and scrambled across the back bench seat to get out the other side, but one of those hands caught her ponytail and yanked her back hard enough to snap her head back on her shoulders.

She shot a hand out to grasp the wrist holding her hair to take away his leverage and half-twisted around to throw a punch at him. Her fist sliced past his face as he ducked away.

It wasn't Dillon.

A total stranger stared back at her. Olive skin, dark hair and eyes. And the utter lack of emotion in them chilled her to the core.

"You're coming with me," he muttered in a heavily accented voice, and shoved the muzzle of his pistol beneath her jaw.

Taylor froze and swallowed as she stared into those lifeless eyes, her heart lodged so far up her throat she was choking on it. There was nothing she could do as he unceremoniously hauled her out of the vehicle by her hair, dragging her backward across the seat.

Pain exploded across her scalp and through her neck.

She scrambled to get her feet under her as the man whirled her around. Chris was on his side as he spoke into his phone, pale face tinged with blue. He was trying to draw his weapon with his free hand despite the blood pouring from his chest wound.

The man yanked hard on her hair, jerking her head back, and fired a bullet into Chris's face. Taylor's scream was cut off by a hard, gloved hand slamming down over her mouth.

"Shut up or I'll put one into you too," he snarled under his breath, and dragged her upright. A car screeched to a halt beside them. The man holding her wrenched the back door open and threw her inside, climbing in after her.

Taylor swiveled to face the man as the driver sped away from the scene, and found her voice. "Did Dillon send you?" She was shaking all over, nausea rolling in the pit of her belly. Chris had just been killed point blank right in front of her.

The one who'd kidnapped her stared back at her, his expression eerily blank. "No."

Someone else from the cartel, then. "What do you want?"

"You'll find out soon enough."

Blood pounded in her ears as the car sped along the street and blew through a red light. She bit back a yelp and grabbed behind her for the door handle to steady herself as the driver whipped the car to the side to avoid oncoming traffic.

Her spine smashed into the door handle and the back of her head hit the glass with enough force to make her see stars.

****

Above the bar on the big flatscreen, the baseball game was in the top of the fifth inning. But for the first time in forever, Logan wasn't interested in watching. Didn't even care what the score was.

He took another swig of his beer straight from the bottle and resisted the urge to check his watch again. His knee was so damn sore he'd had to resort to using his crutches again. He'd have to find a way to be patient and let it heal more before he jumped back into training with the guys.

"Yo. Earth to Granger."

It took a second for him to realize Kai was speaking to him. And that both Easton and Jamie were staring at him too. "Sorry?" he asked Kai.

The big guy gave him an odd look before reaching for yet another wing on the enormous platter of appetizers he'd ordered for himself. And he hadn't offered to share with the rest of them. "You're totally spaced out, dude."

"That's because he's thinking with his little head instead of the big one," Zaid remarked dryly from between them, taking a pull from the bottle in his hand. The guy never drank alcohol, so Logan wasn't sure what he was drinking.

Kai cracked a grin at Logan. "Yeah? Well good for you, man. Is she hot?"

Retina-melting hot, especially when she was in the throes of release or when she gave him that sweet, unguarded smile she'd shown him a few times over the last couple of days. Both made his heart damn near explode. "I don't wanna talk about it."

Kai's eyebrows went up. "Oh, so you're all protective of her too? Well then it's gotta be pretty serious, huh?" He munched on a piece of celery without looking at it, his gaze leveled on Logan.

His neck and cheeks flushed, and not even his beard could hide all of it. He swallowed another mouthful of beer and answered without looking at him. "You could say that." He didn't know exactly what the future held in store for him and Taylor, but the idea of seeing anyone else wasn't the least bit appealing. Actually, it was repulsive.

And he sure as hell didn't want to think about Taylor seeing anyone else, either. Some guy putting his hands and…other parts all over her? No fucking way. It made his hackles rise. She was *his*. He wasn't perfect, and he'd made a lot of mistakes throughout his marriage, but he was also grateful for the lessons it had taught him. He was sure as hell not going to repeat those mistakes with Taylor.

Oblivious to his thoughts, Kai kept going. "Yeah? You gonna bring her here sometime, so we can meet her?"

Logan didn't know Kai all that well yet, but from what he'd seen and heard, the guy was a closet romantic and liked to know everyone's personal business. It would be annoying as shit if Logan and the others didn't like him so much.

"You already know her," Jamie said to Kai, his eyes on the ballgame.

Kai blinked. "I do?" He leaned his big upper body forward to peer around Jamie at Logan. "So who is it?"

Jamie darted a questioning glance at Logan, and Logan bit back a sigh and answered. "It's Agent Kennedy. Okay?"

Kai lowered the hand holding the celery stick to the bar, a wide smile forming on his face. "Well all right," he said, nodding in approval. "I dig her. Not in *that* way," he rushed on when Logan aimed a dark look at him, "but I can totally see why you'd be into her." He waved the celery stick at Logan and winked. "I like it."

"Well, glad I've got your blessing," Logan muttered, wishing someone would change the subject. Taylor was on his mind constantly. He wanted to do something nice for her tonight, something out of the ordinary. A heartfelt gesture to prove he wasn't just after sex. Although, yeah, he definitely wanted more sex, because the woman lit him up like a Christmas tree with a single touch.

He couldn't stop thinking about her, about how tough her life had been and how she'd overcome all the odds to make it to where she was. She amazed him.

There was a specialty ice cream place a few minutes from her building. Maybe he'd stop and pick up a carton of some gourmet flavor she couldn't find anywhere else. He could feed it to her spoonful by spoonful in bed while they were both naked.

And if he should happen to *accidentally* spill some on her in certain places, he would make sure he did a damn good job of cleaning her up. With his tongue. Until every sweet, sticky bit was gone and she was coming against his mouth.

Zaid coughed into his fist and failed to smother a grin. Then his expression sobered and he half-turned in his seat to look at something behind them.

Logan swiveled on his barstool and followed Zaid's gaze across the bar. The woman from the other day's briefing was walking toward them, and Hamilton was behind her. Agent Rabani, right?

"Hey," she said, aiming a smile at all eight of them, assembled along the length of the bar. Then she nodded at the stool beside Logan and tossed her long dark hair over one shoulder as she raised an eyebrow. "This one taken?" Her voice held the slightest trace of a British accent.

"No, please," he said, shifting a little and angling his body so she had room to climb up.

She hopped up onto the stool as Hamilton slid onto the one beside her.

"This one's on me," their team leader said to her, flagging down the bartender. "What'll you have?"

"Soda with lime, please," she said to the bartender.

"Beer," Hamilton said to him, then faced Agent Rabani. "Sure you don't want something stronger?"

"No, I'm not a drinker."

At that Zaid leaned forward and peered over at her. "Hey, me neither."

She offered him a polite smile. "What are you drinking, then?"

He held up the bottle and turned the label toward her. "Root beer."

The smile turned into a grin, showing the hint of a dimple in her cheek. "I like it. I'll have one too, instead of what I just ordered," she called to the bartender.

She and Zaid made polite small talk for a few minutes, until Logan started to get antsy. What time was it? Taylor's meeting must be underway by now. How long would it take? If he left now, he could grab them dinner and the ice cream and have everything ready when she got there.

Agent Rabani stopped in mid-sentence in her conversation with Zaid and Hamilton as ring tones went off. She reached into her pocket for her phone just as Hamilton did the same. She read whatever was on the screen while Hamilton hopped off his stool and walked away from the bar with a finger plugged into his other ear.

Rabani frowned and glanced back at Hamilton.

"Everything okay?" Zaid asked her.

"No," she answered, still looking at Hamilton.

Logan angled his stool to look at Hamilton. A cold shock rippled through him when he realized his team leader was staring right at him as he spoke to whoever was on the other end of the phone, his expression grave.

"What's going on?" Logan asked Rabani.

"There was an incident a few minutes ago, a shooting involving some of our local agents, in broad daylight out front of an apartment building they were guarding."

Logan shot out a hand and gripped her shoulder, urgency thrumming through him. "Where?"

She stilled for a heartbeat, then showed him her phone. "It doesn't say. Are you all right?"

No, he wasn't okay. Fuck. *Fuck.* Cold sweat broke out on his face as he fished his phone out of his pocket. He had to call Taylor. Just needed to hear her voice and know she was okay. What if Dillon had somehow figured out where she was and attacked?

"What about Taylor? Agent Kennedy?" he clarified, the desperation clear in his voice.

The words were barely out of his mouth when

Hamilton lowered his phone and strode back to the bar, his gaze trained on Logan before he glanced down the length of the bar at the others. "We've got a situation. Minutes ago, one shooter attacked an agency vehicle en route to a meeting at headquarters."

No!

"Two agents are dead and the gunman made off with a hostage in a getaway vehicle." When that steely gaze landed on Logan once more, his guts clamped tight. "It's Taylor. He took her."

Chapter Twenty

*D*on't let them know how scared you are.

Taylor kept repeating the command in her head while she fought to keep the panic at bay. They'd been on the move for the better part of forty minutes so far, best she could determine.

Her captors had stopped to change vehicles in a remote area before heading to the coast. One of them still rode in the back with her and had secured her hands behind her before putting her in this new vehicle. A van without any windows in back.

They hadn't bothered blindfolding her and neither man had spoken to her since right after capturing her. She didn't know where they were taking her, but they must have a specific purpose in mind for kidnapping her if they hadn't killed her outright. If Dillon hadn't sent them, who had?

She kept thinking about the scene of the shooting. It had been broad daylight. Chris had been on his phone, likely talking to headquarters.

Someone there must know what had happened and would be mounting some kind of rescue effort. She'd seen people standing on the sidewalk across from them, and other cars passing by. At least one of them would have seen them and called the cops. Right?

You can't depend on that. You've never been able to depend on anyone.

She had to get out of this on her own.

The van slowed and made a left turn. She couldn't see and didn't dare risk trying to peek toward the front out the windshield. But the way the van bounced, jostling them as it drove along, told her they'd turned off a main road onto either dirt or grass.

A minute later, gravel crunched beneath its tires. The driver made a half-circle then slowed.

Taylor's heart pounded harder. She sat up straighter, her entire body tensing as the van came to a stop. The man seated across from her pushed to his feet and aimed his weapon at her. "Get up."

Her legs felt numb but she did as he said, watching his gun hand. For one crazy instant she debated kicking out, taking him off guard and knocking the weapon from his grip.

But the driver was armed as well, and with her hands tied behind her she wouldn't be able to so much as escape the van before they shot her. For now, she had to go along with their demands. If an opening presented itself, she was taking it. Because the thought of enduring the kind of torture the *Veneno* cartel was notorious for made her stomach twist.

The driver's door opened and shut. His footsteps came along the left side of the van and stopped behind it. A second later the rear doors swung open, revealing the tool box in the driver's hand.

Taylor blinked at the sudden change in light and looked outside as a slight breeze brought with it the salty scent of the ocean. For the smell to be that distinct, they had to be right on the coast.

"Out," the man holding the weapon on her said.

With one careful step after another, she made her way to the open rear doors and hopped down. They were alone in some kind of grassy clearing bordered by woods, and she didn't know which way the water was. Were they going to take her somewhere by boat?

The urge to run was so strong it was almost overwhelming. But it would be suicide.

Without preamble, the dark-haired man from inside jumped down, roughly grabbed her bound wrists and began frog-marching her across the lot. She automatically resisted, pushing back against his iron hold, but he merely shoved her until she almost fell, and kept moving.

Through a gap in the trees ahead, she spotted a small building. A cabin or something. Icy cold fear sluiced through her. If they'd taken her to a boat, it would guarantee her living a while longer. But taking her to that shed...

Fear took over. She twisted and lashed a foot out at the man holding her. He sidestepped it easily and rammed his elbow into the side of her head.

She gasped as pain shot through her skull and neck, and dropped to her side in the grass. Before she could regain her wits, he'd wrenched her upward by her wrists.

"Ahhh!" She shot up onto her toes to try and relieve the awful pressure in her shoulders and elbows. Her captor didn't slow, and didn't ease up. A few more ounces of pressure and he'd either dislocate something or break her bones.

Up ahead, the shed loomed, coming ever nearer. The driver loped ahead to do a quick check and then opened the door. The man holding her shoved Taylor inside. She gasped at the sudden relief in her arms and pitched forward, landing hard on her knees on the rough concrete floor.

The sound of the door shutting sent another arrow of fear through her. She scrambled to her feet and backed away from the two men, noting the rusted metal cot in the corner, covered with a thin, filthy mattress. Still aiming the pistol at her, the dark-haired one motioned toward the cot.

There was no way she was going to give in and lie down on it.

Ignoring her, the driver knelt and set his toolkit down, then pulled something from it. A length of nylon rope.

Taylor swallowed and locked her knees to keep them from shaking.

"Lie down," the man with the gun said, the coldness of his voice sending a shiver through her.

"Fuck you," she spat, waves of nausea churning in her stomach. If they planned to rape her, she wasn't going to make it easy or enjoyable. She'd rip chunks out of their skin with her teeth, would never stop fighting.

One side of his mouth lifted in a smile as cold as his eyes. "We'll get to that eventually."

Taylor lunged toward the door. She made it only a step before he caught her and lifted her off her feet.

She shrieked and bucked in his hold, twisted around to try and sink her teeth into any part of him she could reach. Arm, chest, belly.

His fist slammed into her jaw. Her head snapped back, pain exploding through the side of her face. Dazed, she momentarily stopped fighting.

"We've got a live one here, Raul," he said on a laugh as he carried her to the cot. The other man responded in Spanish.

The man carrying her tossed her into the air. She twisted in mid-fall and bounced as she hit the mattress on her side, the impact on the hard surface knocking the air out of her lungs. As she jackknifed into a sitting position,

Raul snagged her feet.

She kicked and screamed but it was no use. Within moments he had her legs tied to the end of the cot. She remained in a seated position, arms bound behind her, quaking so hard her muscles hurt, and stared at her captors.

"They're coming for me. The DEA and the cops, probably the FBI." It had to be true. She couldn't bear the thought of going through whatever these two assholes had in store for her if there was no hope whatsoever of rescue. "You need to let me go."

The dark-haired one cocked his head to the side and studied her with an amused look on his face. "I don't think so, *chica*. You'll be dead long before anyone finds you."

Her chest constricted.

"But first, we're going to get all the information out of you that our boss needs." He stepped up next to the bed and his eyes were no longer flat. They gleamed with a cruel light that told her how excited he was about what they were going to do to her.

She arched up and flailed against his hands but he was too strong and she had no leverage. All she did was tire herself more, and the end result was being strapped to the headboard of the cot by a rope around her throat.

Raw terror clawed at her insides as the past and present collided. She was suddenly eleven years old at her father's apartment, trapped beneath the weight of the dealer he'd sold her to for his next fix.

Then something silver glinted beside the bed. She wrenched her head to the side to see Raul standing there with an electric drill in his hands.

She stared at it, horror closing her throat up. He grinned and pressed the power button. As the shrill whine of the drill filled the cabin, she screamed.

And screamed again.

The cabin door burst open beside her, slamming

against the wall with such force it bounced twice.

Raul whirled but two bullets slammed into his chest. He dropped, his eyes wide.

Behind him, the other man raised his weapon to return fire but whoever it was fired first. Two more bullets found their mark, punching into the man's chest. His pistol clattered to the floor as he fell to his knees, then onto his belly and lay there in a pool of his own blood, gurgling.

Taylor's heart threatened to burst as she lay there, bound and helpless, hope a painful pressure in her chest. Logan?

A tall shadow entered the cabin, weapon still pointed at the two dying men.

She stared, not daring to breathe, hardly believing what she was seeing. "Dillon!"

Dillon didn't dare look at her until he'd kicked away Diego's weapon and checked their carotid pulses. Diego was dead, and Raul would be within the next minute or so.

Lowering his weapon, her forced himself to look at Taylor. Anguish knifed through him.

She was trussed up on her back, the sounds of her ragged breathing loud in the cabin, but he didn't see any blood. He swallowed. When he'd heard those bloodcurdling screams a few moments ago, he'd feared he was too late. But no, he'd gotten here in time.

"Dillon," she whispered, her voice breaking. It cracked his heart in two.

"You okay?" he asked, sliding his weapon into the back of his waistband before crossing to the bed and starting on the knots.

"Y-yes."

Damn, they were tied too tightly for him to untie them. He left her to rifle through Diego's infamous toolbox and dug out his KA-BAR knife. "Don't move. This is razor sharp."

As he leaned over her, his stomach rolled at the way she stared up at him. Fear and hope. Dillon looked away and got busy. He wouldn't cut or torture her when the time came, but he would kill her all the same. He had to. Because when it came down to it, he wouldn't die for anyone.

A few quick slices and he freed her wrists and ankles from the rusted iron frame.

"Come on," he said quietly, looping one arm around her shoulders to pull her into a sitting position. She was shaking all over, from fear and shock.

"H-how did you f-find me?" she asked, allowing him to pull her to her feet. She swayed a moment, steadied herself with a hand on his shoulder. He couldn't stand her touch, the guilt was too raw, so he backed up a step to put some distance between them.

"I saw them take you out front of your building and followed." He'd lost them in traffic and missed the change in vehicle, but he'd had a gut feeling they would come here, to the place they were originally supposed to rendezvous at once Dillon had killed her. "We have to go." The cops and whoever the DEA had dispatched to find her wouldn't be far behind. He started for the door, urgency scraping along his nerve endings.

"W-where are we going?" She followed him outside, paused beside him as he surveyed the area to make sure they were still alone. He had minutes at most to make his getaway.

"Away from here." He grasped her arm and started walking at a fast clip through the trees behind the cabin. The marina was eighty yards east. He had a boat waiting there. If he could reach it before the cops got here, then he had a shot.

He mentally flinched at the word, thinking of what he had to do. He'd keep Taylor with him as long as he needed to use her as a human shield.

He'd let her think everything was fine, that he was saving her. When they were away from shore and cruising along the water, he could put a bullet in her head without her ever knowing she was in danger, and toss her body overboard.

It had to be done. There was no other way for him to survive this and maintain his position within the cartel. This was a test, and one he could not afford to fail.

A shrill beep emitted from his phone. The motion detector. And when he checked the camera on his phone, his worst fears were confirmed. Cops and unmarked SUVs entering the marina.

Cursing under his breath, he grabbed Taylor's hand and pulled her after him as he darted back through the trees. He'd set up a motion detector at the entrance to the marina earlier. It was the obvious choice for any law enforcement to begin the search of the area.

But Taylor dug in her heels. When he pulled harder, she wrenched her hand free and glared at him. "Dillon. What are you doing?"

"We need to get away. There's a boat waiting. We have to get to it."

She shook her head slowly and backed up a step. Panic spurted through him. He lunged for her and she jumped back, her eyes huge in her pale face.

"Just let me go," she whispered, her entire body still, poised to flee.

He couldn't let that happen. She was his only chance now.

"I can't." Or could he? It wasn't too late. If he decided to run and start over elsewhere, leave the cartel and his old life behind, he wouldn't have to kill her. He could let her go.

His pulse thudded in his throat as he stared at her.

"Yes, you can. You don't have to do this."

Maybe I don't. But he couldn't afford to let her know that.

Steeling himself, he pulled out his weapon and aimed it at her face. "Yes, I do."

Chapter Twenty-One

"You still got her?" Easton asked from behind the wheel of one of the SUVs the team was riding in.

"Yeah." The beacon on Logan's phone was holding steady at a location near a marina.

It was the only reason they even had a shot at finding Taylor—all because her boss, who was now dead, had activated a tracking device in her phone the day she'd told him about Dillon. Except it had stopped functioning suddenly about six minutes ago.

Logan prayed that she was still alive, and that the beacon had brought them to the right location. Every minute that ticked past increased the threat to her life, which was why FAST Bravo had acted so quickly. This wasn't their normal jurisdiction, but given the circumstances and the vicinity to the target, they'd been deployed for this mission.

While they'd been suiting up at headquarters, Taggart had personally called SSA Matt DeLuca, commander of the FBI's Hostage Rescue Teams. Both HRT squads were unavailable, and because of FAST Bravo's knowledge of and proximity to the target, they'd gotten the nod to respond.

"We're two minutes out." The cops were right behind them, and would set up a secure perimeter around the area once the team deployed. All in an effort to maintain surprise and hopefully catch the kidnappers off guard.

"Weapons check," Hamilton said over their comms from a different vehicle. "All teams report in from your location once you've swept the area. We'll rendezvous at point alpha."

There were four ways to access the marina by land. The kidnappers had been transporting her by vehicle, reportedly a dark van of some sort. With Taggart following the op from a mobile headquarters, the nine members of FAST Bravo's assault team would split into four different teams of two, with the exception of Logan, who was taking one route alone.

He fought the rush of adrenaline, mixing with the fear for Taylor. Both things he had to lock down. When Easton stopped the vehicle, Logan had to be one hundred percent locked in mentally. Calm. Methodical.

Emotion could not get in the way. But God dammit, thinking about what could happen to her—what already might have happened to her—filled him with rage and a sick helplessness.

Finally Logan's insertion point came into view. A narrow dirt road that wound through a grassy plain up to a wooded area bordering the marina. There was no one else around.

"See you soon," Easton said.

Logan nodded and got out of the vehicle, careful to land on his good leg. His knee throbbed but there was no way he could use crutches right now, and he didn't care if the damn thing imploded, he would take the pain and the consequences of it to get to Taylor.

He set the butt of his rifle to his shoulder, sweeping the area. Nothing moved except the tall grass waving in the breeze. Maintaining caution, he got up and started for the dirt road, staying parallel to it in the grass.

"Alpha squad in position," Zaid said through Logan's earpiece. "Searching area now."

Still no sign of anyone in this area, but the tire tracks on the dirt road looked fairly fresh. The back of his neck itched at moving out here, exposed and alone, but there was no help for it.

The other teams reported in, and Logan felt better knowing the guys were all fanning out and searching the vicinity. Once they cleared the area, they'd converge at the marina and continue the search. Taylor had to be nearby.

She had to be. When he thought of how she'd kissed him goodbye this morning, naked and sleepy in the apartment bed, a soft, happy smile on her lips as she'd looked up at him...

He mentally shook the image away and increased his pace, limping with each painful step as he angled to the northeast toward the thick stand of trees sixty yards away. Halfway to it, a glint of something metallic caught his eye.

He headed for it, his heart beating faster when he finally made out the rear bumper of a dark green van parked in amongst the trees. "Found a van." He recited the license plate.

"Copy," Hamilton answered. "I'll have the analysts check it. Be advised, HQ has reported that there's a small cabin hidden in the woods at your location."

"I copy."

"In the meantime, I'm sending Rodriguez and Khan to you."

"Roger." He'd be glad to have backup.

His pulse kicked up as he approached the van. It was

empty, the rear doors open. The trampled grass behind it led in a trail toward the trees and disappeared as the path turned to dirt. "Heading for the cabin now."

"Do not engage targets until backup arrives," Hamilton ordered.

Logan acknowledged the command but already knew he'd disobey it if Taylor's life hung in the balance.

A soft breeze rustled the leaves and branches of the trees as he reached the entrance to the thicket. He paused there, ignoring the pain in his knee, motionless as he listened and scanned for any movements or threats.

The path turned right and disappeared into the trees. He followed it, staying off the worn area and using the screen of trees to help conceal him.

Then he heard it.

Muffled voices. A scuffle.

He dropped to his good knee, all his senses training on the spot where the sound had come from. Then he crept forward, the pain in his knee barely registering beneath the rush of adrenaline in his veins.

"Contact thirty yards east of my position," he whispered, and gave his location. "No visual yet."

"We're five minutes away," Easton answered.

"Do not engage on your own," Hamilton warned.

Logan moved closer, picking up speed. The path narrowed again, and he saw the cabin. Just as he started toward it, someone burst out of the far side and started through the woods.

Taylor's voice, shaken but distinct. "Dillon. What are you doing?"

His heart seemed to stop beating for a moment, then shot into triple time. "It's her. Taylor. She's with Dillon." And that son of a bitch wasn't harming one hair on her head.

Logan's feet were already moving, his boots nearly soundless on the pathway. He didn't care about being exposed now. All he cared about was rescuing Taylor.

"Yes, you can. You don't have to do this."

Do what? He forced down the fear, fought the urge to let out a roar and charge toward them.

"Yes, I do." Wainright.

A sharp female scream rent the air.

Every hair on his body stood on end at the sound of his woman screaming in terror.

Logan exploded into motion.

His feet were a blur on the dirt path as he ran, each stride sending shards of agony through his kneecap. Then Taylor and Wainright burst into view, on the far side of the trees. The fucker had one arm locked around her neck and a gun jammed to her temple.

"Freeze!" Logan shouted, M4 up, finger itching to slide off the trigger guard.

Wainright froze and whipped around, sinking his head and upper body down to hide behind Taylor. Using her as a human fucking shield because he was a fucking pussy.

"Back off or I'll kill her right here," Wainright snarled. His eyes were wild, the whites showing all around the irises. Dude was on something, and it wasn't caffeine.

Logan held his ground and didn't move, ready to take a shot here and now. Except he didn't have the angle with Wainright hiding behind Taylor. "Drop your weapon and surrender now. You're surrounded."

Wainright kept backing away and dragging Taylor with him. Logan made the mistake of looking at her and his lungs seized. She had blood on her face, both hands locked around Dillon's restraining arm. Her face was slowly turning color from the pressure, the frozen look of fear on her face sent a wave of cold through him.

"I'll do it," Wainright yelled, everything about him agitated. Desperate and unhinged. "Back the fuck *off*."

"Drop your weapon!" he shouted, his entire body coiled like a snake ready to strike. He held his aim just over Taylor's left shoulder, waiting for Wainright to move a fraction of an inch too far.

But as of right now, Logan had no shot.

****

Logan.

Logan was right there. He would save her. But he either had orders to capture Dillon alive, or he didn't have a shot.

Taylor's feet scrambled to keep up with Dillon's jerky steps as he dragged her away from the trees. Clawing at his arm had done no good.

She fought to shove one of hers between his and her throat, managed to wedge part of her hand in and sucked in a greedy gulp of air. "Let me go," she choked out to Dillon, bucking once more in his hold.

His arm contracted around her throat like a steel cable, cutting off what little air she'd had. Her eyes bulged at the pressure, all the blood vessels in her neck and face expanding in a desperate attempt to bring oxygen to her brain.

A few more seconds and she'd be unconscious. A few more after that, she'd either be brain damaged or dead.

"Let her go," Logan commanded again, his voice sending an avalanche of emotions crashing through her. Hope. Grief. Regret.

She kept her gaze pinned on him, her heart ready to explode. He looked so strong standing there with his rifle pointed at them. Regret sliced through her, more painful than anything she'd withstood today.

She hadn't told him what he truly meant to her. This thing between them was so new, she hadn't been sure she could trust it. But she knew she could trust him. And that told her everything she needed to know.

"Not fucking happening," Dillon snapped.

Rage built, eclipsing the paralyzing fear. She was not dying here, right in front of Logan when her freedom was so close. Not without having the chance to experience the rest of what was between them.

As the black spots began to flicker before her eyes, something inside her broke. She twisted in Dillon's grip and went limp, knowing there was no way he could hold her steady under the force of her dead weight. He cursed and dropped with her, the coward, still using her as a shield.

The moment her knees hit the ground she whirled and attacked. She was more animal than human as she rolled and launched herself at Dillon.

He grunted in surprise and pain as she knocked him to the ground, her fingers like claws as she raked them down his face, his right arm. He yelled and threw a punch at her. His fist glanced off her cheekbone as they rolled. The gun slipped from his grasp and tumbled to the grass.

Somewhere nearby she could hear Logan yelling at her but she didn't stop. Couldn't.

Dillon had been like a brother to her. He'd betrayed her in the worst way possible, and tried to kill her. Would have killed her today as soon as he reached the boat he'd told her about.

Her back slammed into a rock. She cried out but didn't stop. She was possessed, even when Dillon's hands wrapped around her throat. She glared up at him, letting the fury take over as he stared down at her with eyes so dark they were nearly black.

The thud of running footsteps registered dimly in her ears. A blur of motion swept past her field of vision, then Dillon grunted as Logan slammed into him in a flying tackle.

Taylor gasped as she was knocked backward, landing hard on her side. She scrambled to her feet just as the men began rolling in the grass in a lethal wrestling match.

Their fists slammed into each other, too fast for Taylor to keep track of as they rolled and twisted over and over, Logan on top one moment, Dillon the next.

Pushing to her feet, she found her footing and frantically searched for Dillon's fallen pistol, her vision slightly blurry without her glasses.

She spotted Logan's rifle lying a few yards away. It must have been knocked loose when he'd tackled Dillon.

Taylor lunged for it, her legs stiff, almost wooden. Her body was on autopilot, her brain hazy as she grasped the weapon and whirled back toward the men.

Muscle memory took over. Stock snug against her shoulder, she sighted down the barrel, her finger resting on the trigger.

I don't want to kill you, Dillon. She wanted him to stop, so she wouldn't have to do this. Because she *would* do it if it meant saving Logan.

A glint of metal caught in the sunlight and her heart constricted when she saw Dillon had that wicked-looking blade in his hand. He swung it toward Logan in a deadly arc, and Logan barely wrenched to the side in time to stop it from plowing straight into his back. It tore across the back of his left arm instead, and blood streaked out of the wound.

Taylor fought to calm her breathing and widened her stance, watching for a tiny opening. Her target was blurry, her nearsightedness making it impossible to see clearly. She was shaking all over, terrified of hitting Logan if she fired, but more afraid of Dillon killing Logan before she could fire.

The two men twisted again in the grass, and this time Logan got the upper hand. His big body momentarily held Dillon beneath him, and Taylor saw all of Dillon's face.

Holding her breath, she fired.

Both men jerked and a spray of blood went up. Dillon lurched to his feet and took a running step away from her.

"*Logan*," she cried, horrified. She started to lower the weapon, but then jerked it back up to her shoulder. Taking aim at Dillon, she fired again just as Logan dove at him, taking him to the grass with a thud that shook the ground.

This time they both stilled.

Logan paused and came to his knees, straddling Dillon, one bloody fist raised to strike. Then he eased back enough for her to see the hole in the side of Dillon's throat.

He was choking, mouth opening and closing. Blood spilled out in a thin stream from his nose and mouth, flowed out of the wound in his neck. His dark eyes fixed on her, and the look on his face was one of pure accusation and betrayal.

Tears she hadn't even realized had formed spilled down her cheeks as she stared back at him, unable to look away. Suddenly the rifle felt like it weighed a hundred pounds. Her arms dropped and it tumbled from her numb fingers.

Sickened, she dropped to her knees and turned away from the sight, covering her face with her hands. Her legs gave out.

She slid to the ground and curled up on her side, overcome with horror by what she'd just done. What she'd been forced to do. And because right up until the end, part of her still hadn't wanted to pull the trigger.

"*Taylor*."

A tight, painful sob ripped free as Logan pulled her upright, his powerful arms contracting around her in a desperate grip as he crushed her to his chest. "Jesus, Taylor. Baby, are you all right?" His hand grasped her chin and forced her head up, making her meet his gaze.

Taylor looked at him through swimming eyes, another sob tearing loose. He was so dear to her, she'd had so little time with him and yet she'd almost lost him.

Logan cupped her face between his hands, his worried

eyes searching her face. "Sweetheart, are you hurt anywhere?" He let go of her to run his hands over her shoulders, her sides and over her back.

She shook her head, the motion jerky. Her teeth chattered. Everything was shaking. She couldn't stop it. Had no control over what was happening to her body. "N-no."

He expelled a relieved breath and grabbed the back of her head with one hand, tucking her face against his shoulder. She could smell blood.

"Y-you," she stammered. "You're h-hurt."

"I'm okay. Shhh, I'm okay. Just sit here with me for a minute and don't move, okay?" He drew a deep breath and released it slowly, burying his face in her hair.

She made herself nod again, then squeezed her eyes shut and shoved her nose against the base of his throat, breathing him in with every shaky inhalation. Her hands curled into the front of his uniform and clenched tight, holding on for dear life to the only thing anchoring her through the storm of shock and desolation inside her.

"I've got you," he murmured, his hold never lessening.

Dimly she heard the other men moving around them. Some of them spoke to Logan and he answered without easing the pressure of his arms around her. Gradually the numb fog began to lift. It was almost worse.

The moment of pulling the trigger was clear and sharp in her mind. Cruel in its vividness. And so was the picture of Dillon's face in her mind as he choked on his own blood, his eyes accusing. Devastated.

And afraid.

She swallowed hard as her stomach rolled. She swallowed again, gagged.

Shoving at Logan's shoulders, she wrenched to the side just in time to retch onto the grass beside them. She kept throwing up until her stomach was empty, until there was nothing, not even bile. Her throat burned. Her face was slick with sweat and she was clammy all over.

When Logan tried to pull her back to him she pushed away weakly. He ignored her and scooped her up in his arms, handing her back her glasses he must have found on the grass. "I've got you, sweetheart. Just lean on me."

Empty inside, she didn't bother fighting and curled into his hold, resting her head on his wide chest. She kept her eyes closed, terrified of seeing Dillon's body, those dark staring eyes.

Logan's gait was unsteady as he walked, his limp more pronounced now that he was carrying her. Or maybe because he'd injured it during the fight with Dillon.

Her face scrunched. Wishing she could vanish into Logan so no one else could see her, she pressed her face tight to his neck and let the tears fall.

Chapter Twenty-Two

Logan's heart was in his throat as he carried Taylor away from Wainright's body. He didn't want her to ever see that traitorous bastard again but his damn knee hurt so bad he wouldn't be able to carry her much farther.

"Zaid," he called out.

The team medic rushed over, already opening his pack. "Set her down." He pulled on some gloves as Logan eased her onto the grass and knelt behind her on his good knee, bolstering her with his body.

She shook her head and tried to turn back into him, and much as it killed Logan not to gather her to his chest right now, he needed to make sure she was truly okay.

"You're bleeding," Zaid said to him, nodding at his arm.

"Yeah. Not too deep though." Stung like a mother. The sleeve of his uniform was already soaked through, but the wound wasn't too serious. Wainright had gone for his throat and kidneys, so it would have been much worse if

Logan hadn't moved fast enough to block him.

He smoothed a hand over Taylor's rumpled hair. It broke his heart to see her like this, traumatized, completely vulnerable.

He hated that she'd had to be the one to take the shots, but damn, he was so fucking proud of her too. Couldn't believe her accuracy and resolve when she'd been facing down the man who'd been like a big brother to her for so long. God, he just wanted to hold her, take her away from all this and make it better somehow. But he couldn't make this better. No one could.

Zaid began assessing her, his touch gentle and matter-of-fact. She wasn't shaking anymore. He almost wished she would. Now she seemed to be too still. Like she was turning inward for comfort, locking herself away deep inside because she didn't know where else to turn.

He wanted her to turn to *him*.

"I'm going to cut off your shirt to check you for broken ribs and internal injuries, all right, Taylor?" Zaid said, his voice low, soothing. "You don't have to answer. I'm just telling you what's going on so you're not startled or anything."

Feeling helpless, Logan continued to brace her against him while Zaid cut away her shirt. Logan pushed her away from him gently, holding her by the shoulders while his teammate scanned her for injuries. She had multiple cuts and bruises on her face, one on her temple, a good-sized knot on the back of her skull, and a big bruise forming on her back.

"This hurt?" Zaid asked, gently probing the sore spot on her back.

She flinched and nodded slightly, but didn't say anything.

"Take a deep breath for me." Zaid had his stethoscope to her back now, and listened intently as she took several breaths for him. He took the buds out of his ears and draped the instrument around his neck. "Lungs are good. No internal injuries that I can tell. We'll have the paramedics take you to the hospital just to make sure though."

Approaching footsteps made Logan look to the right. Jamie was headed for them, a blanket in his hand. "Here," he said, hunkering down to wrap it around Taylor's upper body, covering her up so no one else could see her. "It's gonna be okay, Tay," he told her, gently squeezing her shoulder once before rising and looking at Logan. "Want me to take her?"

"No." It came out sharper than he'd intended, but he didn't want anyone else touching her but him.

Jamie nodded and stood. "You going to the hospital with her?"

Just fucking try to stop me. "Yes."

His teammate's amber eyes filled with empathy. "I'll let Charlie know. She'll come see you there, okay Taylor?"

Taylor didn't answer, just reached for Logan. His chest felt like it had been ripped wide open when she tucked her hands around his ribs and leaned into him. "Thanks," he murmured.

A vehicle approached. An ambulance. Lights flashing but no siren. "Ambulance is here," he told her softly. "Let's get you to the hospital."

"I'm not hurt," she mumbled, leaning her full weight against him now. As though she didn't have the strength left to hold herself up. And he was totally okay with that because it meant he could carry her for a little longer.

With Jamie's help he lifted her and somehow got to his feet, this time the white-hot agony in his knee sharp enough to have him hissing a breath between his teeth. He wasn't letting Taylor go. He'd carry her no matter how much it hurt.

Clenching his jaw, he started for the ambulance and

realized his eight teammates had gathered in a fanned-out line behind him, forming a human wall between Taylor and Wainright's body. Shielding her because she was one of their own, and because of what she meant to him.

Damn, he loved each and every one of those bastards.

Partway to the paramedics, Taylor let out a shaky moan. "I think he was going to let me go," she whispered. "After he got to the boat." She swallowed audibly. "And I killed him."

Logan stopped walking, a fierce ache stabbing through the center of his chest. "You did what had to be done. And I've never seen anything so brave in my entire life."

She raised her head and leaned back a bit to gaze up at him with heartbroken, drenched hazel eyes. So beautiful and precious to him, even in her misery. "Did I have to?"

Oh, honey. He nodded. "Yes. He wasn't going to be taken alive."

He watched the certainty of that hit home. Some of the guilt bled out of her expression. She lowered her eyes. "No. He wasn't."

No.

"I thought I'd hit you by accident," she said, her voice so quiet it barely carried to him. "That first time."

He'd been almost as surprised as Wainright when that first shot had gone off. "But you didn't."

She was quiet for a long moment. "That's the most terrified I've ever been in my life. I was more scared then than when he had the gun to my head," she said, sounding almost stunned by the revelation. "I was more afraid of losing you than dying." She lifted her head once more to gaze up at him, her heart in her eyes. "Because finally meeting someone as amazing as you after all this time spent protecting myself from every other man, losing you would be worse than dying."

Oh, Christ. His heart clenched, then turned over in his chest and it suddenly hurt to breathe. He had to swallow twice before he could get his voice to work, and started limping toward the ambulance again. "You're not gonna lose me."

And he'd felt the exact same way when he'd seen Wainright holding that gun to her head.

****

Taylor stood under the spray of Logan's shower for a long time, until the water began to cool. After spending hours at the hospital and getting the all clear from the doctor, they had finally discharged her.

Logan had needed seventeen stitches in the back of his left upper arm, along with a handful of bandages to close the shallow parts of the cut Dillon had given him, and was back to using his crutches. His knee was purple and blue all over, as bad as ever from the fight with Dillon.

Instead of being allowed to go back home or to Logan's place, they'd both had to go to headquarters to give statements, then sit through debriefings and talk to an agency shrink. Taylor had an appointment with her day after tomorrow. She sure had a lot to talk about.

Dillon was gone. Fingerprints confirmed that the two men who had kidnapped her were *Veneno sicarios*, both of whom had worked exclusively for him until sometime within the past few days. In typical, sick cartel logic, his own men had been sent to kill him once they'd killed her.

Taylor shivered. She'd scrubbed herself clean and the heat of the water had helped with some of the stiffness but everything still ached and her bruises were tender.

With a heavy sigh, she shut off the water, toweled off, then wrapped herself up in the robe Charlie had brought over for her earlier. After brushing her teeth and blowing her hair dry, she felt a little more human. For a moment she stared at her reflection in the bathroom mirror above the sink, the heavy weight of exhaustion pulling at her.

It showed. Her face was pale, her eyes bruised underneath. As tired as she was, however, she was glad Logan had asked her to come back here with him. She didn't want to be alone and it scared her how badly she wanted to be with him.

But she wasn't the only one who was traumatized by the past few days. Charlie had gone and picked up Nimbus at the apartment for her, and brought him here. He was curled up under a chair in the corner of the bathroom next to his litter box, food and water dishes, watching her with huge, unblinking green eyes. He would be too scared to leave the bathroom for another couple of days yet.

She got the impression that Logan wasn't exactly a cat lover from the past few days at the apartment, but he'd been insistent that Nimbus come here to be with her. He was stealing more of her heart with each passing hour it seemed, and after today she couldn't imagine life without him. A few weeks ago that would have scared her to death. Not now.

Crouching down in front of the chair, she reached out an arm to scratch her little fur baby under the chin but Nimbus didn't move or purr. "I know, buddy, you hate all this uncertainty and moving around as much as I do. But it's only for a little while. We'll be able to go home soon."

She hoped. She needed her own space back, the home she'd made, and the sense of independence and normalcy it gave her.

More than any of that, she needed Logan.

When she stepped out of the bathroom she smelled coffee brewing. She found Logan in the kitchen, his back to her as he fiddled with something on the counter while balanced on his crutches. He looked over his shoulder at her, his smile warming her from the inside out and making her bare toes curl against the laminate floor. The man turned her inside out with a single glance.

"You look better," he said, turning to face her with a

mug in one hand. "Feel better?"

"A bit." He looked fine, as though he'd never been stabbed a few hours ago. God, if Dillon had hit him in the lung or kidney...

"Here, it's decaf." He handed it to her.

"Thanks." Its warmth seeped through to her hands almost instantly. "How are you feeling?" The emergency staff had taped a long bandage over his stitches to help protect them.

"I'm good. Go sit down on the couch and make yourself comfortable. I've got a surprise for you."

That got a tiny smile out of her. And she wasn't going to refuse the offer to go veg on the couch for the rest of the night. "Okay."

She settled herself on his leather sofa and stretched her legs out, letting her entire body relax. Every so often pictures from today would appear in her head without warning, bringing with them that sickening avalanche of guilt and despair. She kept fighting them off, but wasn't sure how much longer she could keep the emotions at bay.

Logically she knew she'd done the right thing. Dillon had given her no choice, and there was no way of knowing whether he'd planned to let her go or not. The chances were low, though, and torturing herself about it now was pointless. As scared as she'd been to fire at him, she'd been more afraid of losing Logan.

"I was going to pick some of this up on my way to see you tonight, so I had Charlie grab it for me on the way over," Logan said, somehow crutching his way over with a bowl balanced in hand.

She took it with another smile. "More ice cream?"

"Not just any ice cream. This is dark chocolate with huge chunks of creamy peanut butter in it. All organic."

"Oh, so then it's good for us," she joked. It felt so freaking good to make a joke, even a dumb one.

He pointed his spoon at her. "Exactly." He sank down

next to her, held her gaze for a long moment and then held his spoon out toward her. "So, by the way. Thanks for hitting what you aimed at today."

Startled, she blinked at him. "I…"

He raised an eyebrow and waited.

"You're…welcome." She had no idea what else to say.

With a nod, he gestured with his spoon again and she tapped hers against it. "Cheers." Then he let out a soft laugh and shook his head. "You keep surprising me, Taylor. And damn, I gotta say you're the most badass accountant I've ever met."

His teasing was a relief, but she still blushed. "I was scared to death."

"And that makes what you did even braver."

She shook her head, the words pouring out of her now. "I haven't fired a rifle in probably three years. Charlie dragged me down to the range last time I had to qualify with my sidearm, for practice before my test. I've never been good with a rifle. I didn't have my glasses on and when I fired that first time I thought for sure I'd hit you instead of him." Thank God she'd been standing close enough that she couldn't miss even with her bad eyesight.

"Well, you were right on target when it counted, and that's all that matters."

The utter admiration and respect in his eyes touched the lonely, empty spot deep inside her, and filled it to overflowing.

She swallowed against the sudden tightness in her throat. Emotions roiled inside her, threatened to burst out of her mouth in a tumble of words she wasn't sure he was ready to hear yet. That he owned her heart. That she didn't want to be without him.

"Thanks for letting me stay here, and Nimbus too."

He made an offended sound and frowned at her. "I *want* you here, Taylor, I hope you know that."

She met his gaze again, and a pang shot through her,

hitting a hidden place she hadn't even known existed. It hurt, but it was a sweet, piercing pain that took her breath away.

He wanted her here. Wanted to be with her.

That word echoed in her head, tumbled around and seemed to click into place, aligning a column in her brain that had never balanced before.

Wanted.

No one had ever wanted her before. Not really, not unless it was for their own selfish purposes. But until that moment she'd never allowed herself to acknowledge how badly she'd needed to be wanted. All her life she'd wanted someone to want her, not for what they could get from her, but because of who she was.

Her throat closed up and to her horror, tears burned her eyes.

Logan's expression filled with alarm. "Hey," he protested, quickly setting his ice cream aside and taking her face between his hands. "What's wrong?"

How could she answer him? She reached up one hand and curled her fingers around his wrist. Strong. Solid. Just like him and his character.

"Sweetheart, what?"

His concern and tenderness undid her completely. Shoving her bowl onto the coffee table, she leaned forward and wrapped her arms around his neck. He locked his own around her and squeezed tight, his clean, masculine scent swirling around her.

"Thank you," she finally choked out. She didn't ever want to let go of him. Didn't want him to ever let go of her.

"For what?" he asked, sounding baffled.

"For wanting me as I am. Quirks and all." It was the greatest gift anyone had ever given her.

He didn't say anything, just kept hugging her, but she sensed his confusion. "Well then, you're welcome," he finally murmured after a long moment.

His baffled tone pulled a watery laugh from her. She felt lighter inside, as though a heavy weight that had been crushing her for years had suddenly vanished. "I promise not to overstay my welcome though." Things were so new between them, she didn't want to spoil it by being underfoot and spending so much time together that he either got bored or realized how neurotic she could be with her housekeeping.

Logan eased her away from him and met her gaze with a slight shake of his head. "That's not possible."

The tide of emotion rising inside her was terrifying, yet there was no denying how she felt about him. "We're really different," she said. "I mean *really* different."

"Yes we are," he agreed, his lips quirking in the hint of a smile.

"I'm a big homebody and you're not. I like quiet. I like my space, I like things tidy."

"And I don't," he finished with a grin, his eyes dancing with humor now.

"Well, at least you're honest." She smiled back at him, then sobered. "You think we could make this work? I mean, it's not like either of us is going to change. Not really. We're too set in our ways now."

"I think if we can each compromise a little here and there, yeah. We might even balance each other out real well."

"I'm afraid you're going to get bored with me. I mean, I'm not exciting like you. I'm not an adrenaline junkie."

He snorted softly and shook his head at her. "I won't get bored with you. Trust me. You're grounded. Settled. I need that in my life. I *want* that in my life."

The worry faded a little. She would try to relax her uptight tendencies a bit, because he was worth it. "So we're... You're looking at this as a possible long term relationship then?"

He gave her the most endearing smile and stroked the hair back from her cheek. "I've already made up my mind. And yeah, I want exclusive and long term. That scare you?"

"*Yes.*" It also thrilled her to her toes.

He huffed out a laugh. "Me too, a little. But I'm in too deep to let you go. My heart's already yours."

Aw, dammit, she was getting teary again.

She swallowed, dug down deep for the courage to say the words that scared her the most. She'd faced death twice today, and had overcome every other obstacle life had thrown at her. Telling Logan how she felt about him shouldn't be as scary as all that, but it was.

"Can I tell you something?"

"Sure, go ahead." He watched her intently, his big palm cupping the side of her face.

"I think I might be falling in love with you." She whispered it because she was afraid to say it any louder. Then she held her breath and stared into his eyes while her heart knocked against her ribs.

A smile lit his face, then he dragged her into his arms and crushed her to him. "I'm damn glad to hear that, because I'm right there with you. Plus I'm bigger and heavier than you, and that means I fall faster and harder."

It seemed surreal, almost impossible. Yet there it was. Logan Granger was falling in love with her.

"I'm all yours for the taking, sweetheart. And just so there's no misunderstanding, you should know that I don't plan on ever letting you go."

Before she could do something embarrassing like burst out crying, he tangled his fingers into her hair and tipped her head back to bring his mouth down on hers in a kiss that sent her body and heart soaring.

In that instant, it seemed like all the broken little pieces of herself knit back together. Logan wanted her, wanted a lasting and committed relationship with her. And she was

ready to take that leap with him, because…
I am worthy.

Epilogue

<hr/>

Oh my God. Why the hell had she agreed to this insanity?

Taylor's heart was stuck somewhere in the upper third of her esophagus as the large inflatable raft plunged down a swell in the river, headed straight for the churning rapids ahead. The biggest ones of all in this whole trip.

"I hate this!" she yelled over her shoulder at Logan, uncaring that there were seven other people in the boat, too terrified to take her eyes off the looming rapids or stop her frantic paddling for even a moment. What an asshole, for putting her in this predicament. "I hate *you!*" She was going to kill him once this was over.

If she lived through it.

His deep, slightly evil chuckle rankled her nerve endings. "Hey, the best part is yet to come!"

Best part? How was any of this even remotely fun? Her idea of fun was relaxing and unwinding. This was nuts.

It was the first weekend she'd had off since the whole Dillon incident, and instead of staying home curled up all nice and warm with Nimbus and Sudoku up in her loft, she'd let Logan talk her into white water rafting. He'd been so sweet to her over the past few weeks, taking her out on quiet dates, just the two of them, being patient as she recovered from the mental and emotional aftermath of what had happened with Dillon.

Over quiet dinners, movies or sometimes just a walk or a drive together, he'd revealed a tender and romantic side she never would have guessed someone as tough as him could have. She'd convinced herself it was time to move outside of her comfort zone because Logan so clearly loved doing outdoorsy stuff and she wanted to make an effort to share them with him.

She'd never regretted a dating decision more. Now, here she was, stuck in this rubber boat for at least the next hour, soaked to the skin by all the spray and the water sloshing over the sides of the boat and trying not to throw up or scream like a little girl as they hurtled down the raging river.

The bow of the boat dipped suddenly and another wall of water crashed over her head. She gasped and sputtered, arms flailing like mad as she sportingly tried to keep paddling.

Logan laughed again. "Lower your arms. You're paddling through nothing but air."

Her cheeks burned and she scowled as she realized what she was doing. She was tempted to turn around and whack him over the head with her fucking paddle but she was too afraid to stop so she dipped the end lower, hit water, and pulled in a hard stroke.

The muscles in her shoulders and arms were knotted, burning, screaming for a break, and there was none in sight. Up ahead the water looked like it was boiling where the rapids swirled in the center of the river. There was no escape, nowhere to go but through them.

"Hold on tight," he called out gleefully as they reached

the rushing mass of white water.

You asshole, you did this to me! "Fu—" The blistering curse word she'd meant to snarl at him ended on a terrified intake of breath as the boat lurched upward and shot sideways.

"Keep paddling!"

Oh, fuck, they were all going to die.

Her eyes were stretched wide as she paddled for her life like a frantic woman, sputtering each time the water hit her in the face. *Please don't let the boat flip over, please don't let the boat flip over.*

Logan howled with pure glee as they bucked up and down, back and forth, like they were caught in some kind of psychotic washing machine from which there was no escape. What was *wrong* with him?

She lost all sense of time or direction as they plunged further into the rapids, every sense focused on surviving this trial by fire. Then, finally, the water began to calm and smooth out.

Her arms were like lead, a rapid tremor streaking through her body. She was alive. Freezing and still dealing with the shock, but alive.

And strangely, a feeling of euphoria began to rise inside her. Probably because she'd just had another near-death experience and lived to tell about it.

A strong hand closed around her right shoulder and squeezed. She winced and moaned at the pleasure-pain of it, barely resisted the urge to throw it off.

"Good job. Put your paddle down and rest for a bit."

The paddle dropped into her lap like it was a lead weight. It took a good five minutes until her brain started functioning normally again.

After another twenty minutes of relatively smooth water they turned a bend in the river and the tour company vehicle came into sight on the left-hand shore.

She expelled a relieved sigh. Thank God, it was almost

over. And bless them, someone had even started a campfire for them. Anxious to get to shore, she even managed to paddle the rest of the way.

By the time they got to shore, she was feeling pretty damn pleased and proud of herself. Exhilarated almost. Now that she'd survived her first white water rafting experience, she could kind of see why Logan loved it so much. The thrill of conquering nature.

Not that she would ever tell him that.

Logan and the guide hopped out to pull the raft onto the bank and everyone else climbed out. Taylor's legs felt like over-boiled noodles.

Her waterlogged shoes squished with each step she took up the bank and she was pretty sure her hands would be numb forever. She was dying to get dry and warm again, then devour whatever supper the tour provided.

Halfway up the bank, a pair of muscular arms wound around her waist from behind. She stood rigid as Logan pressed up tight to the back of her, his beard lightly scratching the side of her temple as he nuzzled her.

"You did great," he murmured, his warm lips making her shiver. "Still mad?"

A growl emitted from her throat. She jabbed an elbow lightly into his stomach and he laughed softly.

"How mad? Scale of one to ten."

She folded her arms, scowling straight ahead at the fire that beckoned to her weary body. "Nine-point-six."

"Ouch. That's pretty mad."

"Yeah. Plus I'm freezing and wet and tired." Not to mention proud.

"Hmm." He lowered his head to nuzzle at the side of her neck. "Bet I can warm you up real quick."

What? "Don't you da—"

Too late. He was already swinging her up into his arms and striding up the sloping bank in spite of his still healing knee, making a spectacle. Taylor balked and tried to get down. He wasn't having any of it, just held her tighter as he headed to the fire.

"Put me down," she whispered, mortified. People were staring. They were all staring, and smiling at them.

"Nope. Not until you're warmed up."

She shoved at his shoulder. "I'm warm, okay? I'm warm."

He tightened his grip. "Not as warm as you're gonna be in a minute."

Her face was burning when they reached the fire. Someone handed Logan a blanket. He plopped down in one of the chairs around the fire and wrapped the blanket around her before tucking her securely into his lap.

She looked up at him in annoyance. A grin twitched his lips when she glared, and he smoothed a strand of wet hair away from her forehead. "I really love you, you know. Like, totally pathetic, head over heels, can't live without you love you. You're it for me."

Her glare melted away, replaced by shock. Neither of them had said the actual words yet, and it was a huge deal to her. She'd been waiting for the right time, had planned to tell him tonight when they were alone. "You're going to tell me that now? Here?" In *front* of everyone? "Really?"

"Guess so," he said, looking mighty pleased with himself. He cupped her jaw with one hand and pressed a kiss to her cold lips, his thumb resting in the dip beneath her lower one. "I love you to death. And I want us to move in together full time. Even though I annoy the crap out of you when I leave my wet towels on the bathroom counter and don't load the dishwasher properly."

Warmth flooded her and she melted, unable to hold onto her annoyance. He was ridiculous, and alpha, and yet sweet and thoughtful too. Not to mention protective and supportive. How could she not love him?

"I love you too," she whispered back, smiling as she

wound her arms around his neck and hugged him. "And yes, I want you to move into my place for good. Even though I'm still a little bit mad at you for today." She couldn't let him off the hook entirely.

Logan pumped one fist in the air in triumph. "She loves me," he announced to no one in particular, his tone full of male satisfaction.

The entire group cheered and Taylor buried her face against his neck, laughing. He was so unexpected, so opposite from her in most ways, pushing her little by little out of her shell until she hardly recognized herself anymore.

Though that wasn't necessarily a bad thing, for someone who'd been as isolated and rigid as her.

Logan had been right: in all the ways that mattered, they did complement each other pretty well. That would help them navigate the uncharted waters of this relationship. But the absolute *best* part was knowing that as they paddled through the rapids of life together, he would be there for her at every turn.

—The End—

Thank you for reading FAST KILL. I really hope you enjoyed it and that you'll consider leaving a review at one of your favorite online retailers. It's a great way to help other readers discover new books.

If you liked FAST KILL and would like to read more, turn the page for a list of my other books. And if you don't want to miss any future releases, please feel free to join my newsletter:

http://kayleacross.com/v2/newsletter/

Complete Booklist

ROMANTIC SUSPENSE

DEA FAST Series
Falling Fast
Fast Kill

Colebrook Siblings Trilogy
Brody's Vow
Wyatt's Stand
Easton's Claim

Hostage Rescue Team Series
Marked
Targeted
Hunted
Disavowed
Avenged
Exposed
Seized
Wanted
Betrayed
Reclaimed

Titanium Security Series
Ignited
Singed
Burned
Extinguished
Rekindled
Blindsided: A Titanium Christmas novella

Bagram Special Ops Series
Deadly Descent

Tactical Strike
Lethal Pursuit
Danger Close
Collateral Damage
Never Surrender (a MacKenzie Family novella)

Suspense Series
Out of Her League
Cover of Darkness
No Turning Back
Relentless
Absolution

PARANORMAL ROMANCE
Empowered Series
Darkest Caress

HISTORICAL ROMANCE
The Vacant Chair

EROTIC ROMANCE (writing as *Callie Croix*)
Deacon's Touch
Dillon's Claim
No Holds Barred
Touch Me
Let Me In
Covert Seduction

About the Author

NY Times and USA Today Bestselling author Kaylea Cross writes edge-of-your-seat military romantic suspense. Her work has won many awards and has been nominated for both the Daphne du Maurier and the National Readers' Choice Awards. A Registered Massage Therapist by trade, Kaylea is also an avid gardener, artist, Civil War buff, Special Ops aficionado, belly dance enthusiast and former nationally-carded softball pitcher. She lives in Vancouver, BC with her husband and family.

You can visit Kaylea at www.kayleacross.com. If you would like to be notified of future releases, please join her newsletter: http://kayleacross.com/v2/newsletter/

Made in the USA
Lexington, KY
05 May 2017